T0062385

THANKS FOR THE MEMORIES

James Kerlin

Order this book online at www.trafford.com
or email orders@trafford.com

Most Trafford titles are also available at major online book retailers.

© Copyright 2009 James Kerlin.
    Edited by Sandy Richardson.
All rights reserved. No part of this publication may be reproduced, stored in a retrieval system, or
transmitted, in any form or by any means, electronic, mechanical, photocopying, recording, or
otherwise, without the written prior permission of the author.

Printed in Victoria, BC, Canada.

ISBN: 978-1-4251-8298-4 (sc)
ISBN: 978-1-4269-2454-5 (dj)

*Our mission is to efficiently provide the world's finest, most comprehensive book publishing
service, enabling every author to experience success. To find out how to publish your book, your
way, and have it available worldwide, visit us online at www.trafford.com*

Trafford rev. 12/9/2009

www.trafford.com

North America & international
toll-free: 1 888 232 4444 (USA & Canada)
phone: 250 383 6864 ♦ fax: 812 355 4082

ACKNOWLEDGMENT

A special thank you to three old friends of more than 50 years, Joe and Marie Capela of Arroyo Grande, California and to Sarah Shearer of Dayton, Ohio, for their encouragement over the past ten years to finish this novel. It actually was more like harassment, but it did inspire me. Also, to my daughter, Becky who kept encouraging me to finish the novel. And a grateful thank you to my family for putting up with the hundreds of hours I spent in the computer and at the library doing research.

JIM KERLIN

CHAPTER 1.

IN THE FALL OF 1995, in widely separated cities of the
world, three distinctly different couples were getting on with
their lives without a clue as to how their lives would become
emotionally and violently entangled. The couples were as
different as the cities and countries in which they lived.

Two young medical students in Fayetteville, Arkansas,
had just left medical school, were newly married, and eagerly
looking ahead to new careers.

In Washington, D.C., a couple in their late thirties was
enjoying his new position with the Department of Commerce,
and her new challenge in operating the travel agency they had
just purchased.

In the Emirates capital city of Abu Dhabi, a young couple
in their early thirties, deeply, but very secretly, involved in
terrorism, was busy planning their future and the future of
civilization.

The lives of millions of people would depend on the outcome
of the involvement of the young medical research couple that
would be drawn involuntarily into the middle of a desperate
CIA attempt to save the Western world from a terrorist nuclear
bombing of major Western civilization cities.

Fate and Providence must be the agents that lead humanity down the seemingly predestined paths to glory, greatness, chaos, and the holocausts of the world. No individual human being can look down that path and see the fate that lies ahead. These three couples were no exceptions; they had no way of anticipating the terrifying experiences in their future.

It was a beautiful Sunday afternoon in Fayetteville, a small university town in the Ozark Mountains of northwest Arkansas, and Jessica and Rob West were relaxing in their apartment.

"Rob! Throw me a towel, I forgot to get one," Jessica yelled from the shower where she was enjoying the flow of water over her body.

"Be there in a minute, Hon. I'm watching the last play in the half, the Cowboys are about to score!" Rob said as he hunched forward in his chair. He looked as though he was trying to get inside the television for a better look at the play.

"Damn!" complained Rob, as he watched the Cowboys fumble on the three yard line, losing the ball to the Eagles.

Rob stood up fetched the towel for Jessica. He ambled into the bathroom and handed her the towel, giving her a peck on the cheek as he returned to the half-time show and scores.

On the way out of the bathroom Rob asked, "Did you all get much done on the shop today?"

"I helped Dad finish with the roofing, and then Mom and I started painting the inside walls," Jessica replied.

Rob nodded approval as he resumed watching the game. Jessica had been helping her parents put the finishing touches on her parents' new building, which was needed to handle the increasing volume of craft products they made.

Steve and Mavis, Jessica's parents, fully complemented each other. Mavis was outgoing and a doer, pragmatic with a pleasing personality. She was the type who could do anything and do it extremely well. It didn't matter if it was craftwork, building a house, sewing, cooking, raising a child, wife, lover, companion, or just being a friend. Everything was done well and everybody loved Mavis.

Steve, an outstanding rock mason, carpenter, and craftsman, had enlisted in the Marine Corps during the Vietnam conflict, served eighteen months in Vietnam, and achieved the rank of sergeant. His father had served in the infantry in World War II, and was very proud of Steve's accomplishments. He often bragged to his friends that Steve's rank of sergeant in the Marine Corps was equivalent to the rank of brigadier general in the Air Force.

Steve was intelligent, a bit of a dreamer, and loved to read and talk to people. With Mavis to keep him focused, they made a good team producing and selling their products at craft shows throughout the country. Jessica was their only child, and there was an exceptionally strong bond among the three of them.

Jessica and Rob had been married a little over three years, although they had lived together for two years during their final years at the University of Arkansas. They were very content with their careers, their apartment, her Camry, his Jeep, and life in general.

Jessica was born and raised in Fayetteville, and had attended school there through high school. She had then graduated with high honors from the University of Arkansas with a Bachelor of Science degree. She majored in biochemistry and, following graduation, was accepted into medical school at the University of Arkansas at Little Rock.

After two years, she earned a degree in medical technology, again graduating with highest honors. All six years of her university training was paid for by scholarships, grants, and working part-time in fast food restaurants. She also worked as a research assistant in various university laboratories. Jessica was very attractive, with light brown hair, brown eyes; 5'4" tall and 110 pounds of boundless energy, enthusiasm, and independence.

Rob was rather quiet and laid back in contrast to Jessica's energy. He was 5'10", 175 pounds, brown hair and eyes, athletic, a real sports fan, and golf addict. Rob and Jessica had met during their junior year of college, both having the goal of becoming medical doctors. Both had graduated with Bachelor of Science degrees with high honors and both applied for entrance into medical school in Little Rock.

It was a huge disappointment when Jessica was accepted, and Rob did not make it due to the large number of openings going to minority applicants. Rob worked in Little Rock during the period that Jessica attended medical school. They were a good team and very supportive of each other. However, when Jessica started her second year in medical school, they learned that again Rob had not been accepted. This was a bitter disappointment for both of them. Rob was discouraged and Jessica felt guilty in being allowed to pursue her career while Rob was in limbo. She was also getting burned out with the pressures of attending school and working part-time.

It was then that she decided to shorten her curriculum and settle for a medical technology degree that only required two years of medical school. After finishing the second year, Jessica graduated with top honors in her class, and she and Rob returned to Fayetteville to start job hunting.

Before embarking on the job-hunting circuit, they took a four-week driving tour through a great many of the states east of Arkansas. After a brief stop in Pennsylvania to do some genealogy work for Jessica's father, they continued on through the Carolinas, Virginia, Washington, D.C., Maryland, Delaware, New York, Massachusetts, and on back to Arkansas.

While visiting Williamsburg, Virginia, they had a chance encounter with a person who would play a major role in changing their lives forever. It was just about dusk with a light rain falling as Jessica and Rob approached the outskirts of Williamsburg. Jessica was driving when Rob spotted a car stopped on the shoulder of the road with a woman standing in the rain beside the car.

"Slow down, Honey, let's take a look to see if she's in trouble," said Rob, evaluating the situation as Jessica eased the car alongside the woman's vehicle.

Rob lowered his window. "Are you having trouble?" he asked, as he motioned her to get into their car.

The lady, a very attractive and well-dressed blonde in her early forties, shook her head yes as she looked at the young couple in obvious relief. She was rain-soaked and cold as she climbed into the backseat of their car.

"I knew I was low on gas, but I was in a hurry and thought I could make it into town where I'm meeting my husband this evening," she explained, as Rob handed her some paper towels to dry her face and hands.

The blonde-haired lady introduced herself as Cheryl Crockett, and related that she was on her way to meet her husband, Scott, for dinner at the Williamsburg Inn where they were staying.

Jessica said, "There's bound to be a gas station a few miles down the road, so we'll just take you there to get gas and then bring you back."

Cheryl protested that they didn't have to bring her all the way back as she could contact the auto club. Jessica and Rob wouldn't hear of that and insisted. As they chatted on the way to the gas station, Rob noticed how wet and cold Cheryl appeared and quietly mentioned it to Jessica.

Jessica looked in the rear view mirror and said, "Cheryl, let us take you to the Williamsburg Inn where you'll be warm and dry and can meet your husband. We'll get some gas and retrieve your car, providing that you trust us to bring your car back!"

Cheryl laughed and said that she was quite cold and very wet and would be happy to accept the offer on the condition that they would be her and Scott's guests for dinner.

Rob said, "That isn't necessary, Cheryl, but we'd enjoy having dinner with you. We'll gas up your car and return it to your motel with your luggage so you can change clothes. Then we'll go check into the Holiday Inn where we're staying and return to meet you for dinner at seven o'clock. Sounds like a good time!"

At a few minutes after seven, Jessica and Rob walked into the restaurant and were introduced to Scott Crockett. He was an impressive individual about six feet tall with dark hair, dark eyes and rugged suntanned features.

With a wide engaging smile he said, "Thank you so very much for taking such good care of my Cheryl. Watching the gas gauge is not one of her strong points. It's happened before! She was so lucky you two came along to rescue her."

Jessica and Rob immediately felt at ease with both Scott and Cheryl. Over drinks and dinner, they discussed their trips, families, and occupations. The Crocketts were sincerely interested in hearing about the young couple's experiences in getting through school, the jobs they held, their great disappointment in Rob not getting into med school. Scott was high in his praise of their positive attitude and their eagerness to get on with their careers.

Cheryl told the couple about her occupation as owner of a small travel agency. She explained that she had been lucky enough to find a very capable manager, Max Thorn, to run the agency so that she only worked there part time.

Scott's occupation was unusual and very interesting. He described his work as an international trade emissary for the Executive Branch of the government. He spent a great deal of his time in the Middle East, Asia, and Europe, as well as Washington, D.C. Owning the travel agency made it easier for Cheryl to meet Scott and spend time together on his overseas assignments.

Jessica and Rob marveled at all the places the Crocketts had visited. They also observed afterwards that even though Scott was friendly and at ease, there was something about him that would make you think twice before you crossed him. At the end of a very enjoyable dinner, they exchanged addresses and phone numbers. Cheryl insisted that the young couple promise to stop in Washington to visit them on their return trip. Tired but pleased with the events of the day, the couple headed back to their motel looking forward to the balance of their trip.

Four days later, Jessica and Rob pulled into a truck stop for coffee and a phone call. At a little after 4 p.m., they were less than forty miles from Washington. While Rob got gas and ordered the coffee, Jessica placed a call to Cheryl Crockett.

"Cheryl, this is Jessica. You asked us to call you when we came back through Washington. Right now we're at a truck stop on I-95; we just passed through Baltimore."

Cheryl replied, "I'm so glad you called, as we were just leaving. I have to take Scott to his office for a brief meeting, and then to Dulles Airport, as he is flying to Frankfurt tonight. Where are you staying, and can we spend some time together tomorrow?"

Jessica was nodding her head, "We would enjoy that very much. We're staying at the Marriott Suites in Bethesda."

Cheryl smiled. "That's perfect; you couldn't have picked a more convenient area. I have to stop by the travel agency in the morning, and your motel is less than a mile away. Why don't I pick you up at about nine, and then you can visit my agency. I'd love to show it to you. Then we'll have lunch, and tour around town in the afternoon."

Jessica was a little hesitant as she felt they might be imposing. "That sounds wonderful, but are you sure we're not taking too much of your time or disrupting any plans you may have had?"

"Not at all," replied Cheryl. "Scott and I were hoping you would call. He'll be disappointed that he missed you. I'll be at your motel about nine in the morning, and I'll be back home tonight around nine-thirty if you need to reach me."

The two friends said goodbye, and Jessica returned to the restaurant table to tell Rob of their plans.

It was a few minutes after nine when Cheryl pulled up in front of the motel lobby in her Lexus LS 400. It was white with a gray leather interior that seemed the perfect accessory for her. Rob helped Jessica into the front seat, and he rode in the back. They chatted and joked about Cheryl running out of gas and getting drenched in the rain. It seemed like only a few minutes until Cheryl pulled into a parking garage on Massachusetts Avenue.

They took the garage elevator up to the second floor, got out, and walked down the hall toward the front of the building. On a large, heavy, oak door, in brass letters, was TRAVEL - USA and beneath the name was SUITE 2-A. Cheryl pushed open the door and they walked in. On the left was an open area with three desks occupied by travel agents. A copier, two fax machines, and three computers were on the desks and another computer was on the literature counter beside some cabinets.

Cheryl's office was in the corner where she enjoyed a double set of windows. To the right, as you walked in the front door, was a paneled wall with one door in its center. Cheryl explained that area contained Max's private office, as well as a private office for Scott who spent quite a bit of time there.

The three employees were all on telephones, but smiled and waved. Cheryl motioned to Jessica and Rob to follow her into her office. She walked to the coffee maker on the credenza and raised a cup to the couple. Both shook their heads yes and indicated no cream or sugar. Jessica and Rob settled on the couch with Cheryl taking the easy chair facing them as she started to tell them a little bit about the agency.

She and Scott had founded the business about four years prior to give Cheryl something to do since Scott was gone so much. She had always been very interested in the travel business, and had put a great deal of time and effort in establishing the business during the first three years. Now, with a good and experienced staff and an excellent manager in Max Thorn, she found more time to join Scott in his travels throughout the world. Rob commented how nicely the office was organized and also how well equipped it was.

He asked, "When we turned into the parking garage, I noticed the three large satellite dishes on top of the building; are they all used for this office operation?"

"Yes," Cheryl replied. "We subscribe to three different network travel programs, two of which are overseas. These days we need quick worldwide communications to satisfy customer needs in the Washington area."

Just then there was conversation and mild laughter in the outer office, and an imposing figure appeared in the doorway of Cheryl's office.

Cheryl exclaimed, "Max! I didn't expect you back yet! I want you to meet two good friends."

The introductions were made and both Jessica and Rob were impressed with Max who appeared to be in his late thirties. He was 6'2" with a muscular athletic build, dark hair, and hazel eyes. With a ready smile and good sense of humor, he was very likeable. However, as both Jessica and Rob noticed, there was something about his eyes they found a little unsettling. It was the fact that even as he smiled, his gaze was very intent and penetrating, as though he could read your thoughts.

Max pulled up a chair to join the group, and found it amusing as Cheryl told the story of how she met the young couple. After a few minutes more of conversation, Max stood up to leave. He told the couple how much he enjoyed meeting them, and wished them a pleasant trip home. He then disappeared through his office door.

Rob expressed his surprise with Max's role as office manager. "It just seems he ought to be the quarterback for the Dallas Cowboys or some sort of leading man in Hollywood."

Cheryl smiled, "Yes, I agree with you. We were very fortunate to hire Max as he is very bright and has traveled extensively. He is single, so he spends a lot of time here working. He and Scott are very close friends, almost like brothers."

As she stood up and took a few steps toward the door of her office, Cheryl continued, "Let's go have lunch and then we'll tour the city."

"Lunch sounds great, Cheryl. But then we'd like to get on the road heading home. We checked out of our motel this morning before you picked us up," said Jessica, looking at Rob for agreement.

"I do wish you could stay longer, but I understand your desire to get home. We can go to Sfuzzi's for lunch. It's not too far from here on Manhattan Avenue; then I'll take you back to your car at the motel."

Lunch was pleasant with much talk about the future plans of Jessica and Rob and what kind of jobs they would be searching for. Cheryl held their interest as she related her college days, where she majored in political science and finance, and then her career in the State Department, where she met Scott.

After lunch, it was back to the motel parking lot with goodbyes, hugs, kisses, and promises to write and stay in touch. Cheryl said that Scott often had business at the Air Force bases in Little Rock and Oklahoma City, and she would find a way to accompany him, and then drive to Fayetteville to visit while he conducted his business. With that, they parted ways, and Jessica and Rob headed home for job interviews and new careers.

CHAPTER 2.

T HAT TRIP HAD BEEN THREE years ago and things had changed considerably for the young couple. Jessica was very fortunate to have been hired as assistant director in a small but prestigious research lab that was a joint venture between the University of Arkansas and the United States government. There had been quite a few highly qualified applicants for that job, but because of her academic credentials, and because she was known for her work as an undergraduate in various labs at the university, Jessica got the job.

Of course, the fact that Dr. Judy Clark, Director of Medical Research, University of Arkansas, had given her a strong endorsement didn't hurt her application. Dr. Clark had been good to Jessica during all her years at the university. Through all the counseling, motivating, and mentoring, Dr. Judy and Jessica had developed a mutual deep respect and close relationship. Now at age twenty-eight, the third youngest person employed at the lab, she had been appointed Director with several new grants and projects underway.

Rob had also been very fortunate in finding a job, but in a rather roundabout way. While searching for employment, he had taken a job on a temporary basis with the local plant of a large food processing company. The job entailed taking random samples of food products off production lines and running certain tests to assure the quality of the products. Rob had been on that job for about six months when he was promoted to foreman of the testing group.

He had been in that position for about two years when he encountered unexpected good fortune. His job required considerable contact with personnel from the corporate headquarters quality control group. He made friends with the corporate personnel director, Bill Keeler, with whom he played golf and watched sports on TV.

The phone rang on Rob's desk and he picked it up recognizing the voice of Bill Keeler. "Rob, I think you have a chance here to hit a long shot!"

Rob replied, "Since when did we start playing the horses?"

"We haven't," Bill said, "and we're not talking about basketball either. Our corporate manager of quality control is leaving abruptly for a position in California. Because of our recent expansions, we need to fill that job as quickly as possible. The top brass is insisting on a person with academic qualifications that fit yours exactly. The only question mark is your lack of experience and age. You are twenty-nine years old and have only two-and-a-half years experience in food processing.

"However, the experience you have in that particular plant is of importance. I took the liberty of arranging an interview for you with Frank Parenti, the Vice-President of Processing. You met him when he toured your plant several weeks ago. In fact, he recalls that you're the one who demonstrated the new testing routine for him. Sorry for the short notice, but be at his office here at Corporate Headquarters at four-thirty this afternoon."

Rob was stunned. "It sounds too good to be true, but it concerns me that I won't have time to change clothes or clean up much before then. What should I prepare for?"

"Rob, just be yourself and be confident that you can do the job. You have a good solid background and you learn fast. I'll be there to introduce you. Take care and good luck!" And with that Bill hung up.

Rob met Frank Parenti at four-thirty and finally finished the interview over two hours later.

At the end of the session, Frank looked at Rob with a smile, "Rob, you're a younger person than I wanted on that job, and you don't have much experience in food processing, but I'm going to give you a shot at the position. You have all the academic qualifications, and you relate well with people. Your supervisor gave you a fine recommendation, and I personally have the feeling that you can do the job.

"Suppose you start at $35,000 and in six months, if you're doing well, we'll jump you to $45,000. After the first year, you'll be considered for the management bonus program. Would you find that agreeable?"

Rob was astounded; he felt as though he had just won the lottery.

He jumped up and shook hands. "Thank you so very much, Mr. Parenti. I'll work hard to prove that your confidence in me is well-founded."

Frank Parenti said, "I know you will, Rob. Meet me here at seven-thirty on Monday morning. I'll arrange a conference with all department employees, so I can introduce you to them and explain your responsibilities. Now go tell your wife the good news!"

Both men left the office with good feelings. Frank Parenti knew he had hired a young man who was dedicated and would work his butt off for him. And, of course, Rob was ecstatic with his new job.

He called Jessica, "Honey, you won't believe what happened!"

Before he could say more, she cut him off, saying, "Where in the world are you? You always call if you're going to be late. I've been worried sick about you!"

"I am sorry, Jessica, but when you hear what happened you'll understand. I'll be home in fifteen minutes and then we're going out for dinner! No questions, just get ready and I'll be there shortly." And Rob was off and running.

He jumped into his Jeep and raced home. Jessica was ready and waiting for him at the door. They took off immediately for their favorite restaurant, the 36 Club. Dan Roberts owned the club and worked there most of the time. As they walked in the door, he welcomed them and showed them to their favorite table.

Dan smiled at them, "You two look like you've just been told you're going to have twins. What's up?"

Jessica smiled back at Dan, "No little ones yet, but I do hope Rob tells us what he is up to before we both explode."

Rob ordered drinks and motioned Dan to pull up a chair. Jessica and Dan listened with great interest as Rob related the events of the afternoon. Jessica was thrilled to hear of Rob's promotion and jumped up to give him a big kiss. Dan said securing such an important promotion in such a short time beat anything he ever heard of.

Dan told Rob, "You're very fortunate in more ways than one. Frank Parenti is a fine person and you'll enjoy working for him. He and I worked together on the Fine Arts Building fund raising program last year. Congratulations, you two! The drinks and dinner are on the house."

The following Monday Rob was off to his new job and Jessica headed out to the research lab. She walked into the lab and found Dr. Judy Clark sitting in her chair in her office.

Dr. Judy said, "Well it's about time you got here; I've already started thinking about lunch."

Jessica replied, "Come on, Dr. Judy, it's only seven-forty, and I'll bet you just finished breakfast. What brings you out here?"

"Well, I did just finish breakfast, but I couldn't wait to tell you the good news," Dr. Judy said with a big smile. "The university has received two new very large grants from the Federal Government that involve brain research in the areas of Alzheimer's disease and the aging process.

"And along with that, the Federal Government is helping the university fund a new super computer that will be tied into that special research and your laboratory. Rebecca Coles will be here Thursday morning from Washington to explain the grants, the details of the funding, and what is expected in terms of results. She will meet with you and your staff at nine. Then Rebecca, you, and I will have lunch together at the Post Office restaurant."

Jessica hugged Dr. Judy and thanked her for the tremendous opportunity to participate in the research programs and for the chance to take advantage of the super computer. It was Jessica's turn to excitedly call Rob and tell him of good fortune.

After work, Jessica and Rob stopped by the 36 Club to have a celebratory drink and tell their friend Dan of their continuing good news. He said he couldn't believe the run of good luck the two were having, and he hoped that some would rub off on him.

The meetings and luncheon with Dr. Judy Clark and Rebecca Coles went well. Jessica was excited with all aspects of the projects, which included full access to many confidential studies and government information gathered from around the world. She found it hard to sleep that night as her mind whirled with the possibilities of endless access to all kinds of knowledge and information.

As Jessica and Rob were eating breakfast the next morning, the phone rang. Jessica picked it up and was surprised to hear Cheryl's voice, "Did I wake you, I hope not."

"No, we're just finishing breakfast. It's so good to hear from you. I hope you called to say you're on the way out here!" Jessica replied.

Cheryl had visited them six times in the past three years, twice with Scott, and each visit was very enjoyable.

"You're right! That's the purpose of my call. Scott has business at Tinker Air Force Base next Friday morning, and we thought we would drive to Fayetteville Friday afternoon and spend the weekend with you. That is, if you don't have plans already. Scott would like to do some fishing with Rob and your father. They got him really interested with the fish stories they told on our last trip out there," Cheryl said, with a tone that inferred fishing was fine for the guys, but don't include her.

"That sounds great, and we'll be looking for you Friday afternoon. We've got lots to talk about," replied Jessica, as she happily smiled at Rob.

Everybody enjoyed the weekend. Dan Roberts and his wife Anita joined the two couples for dinner at his 36 Club on Friday evening. On Saturday, Jessica, Cheryl, Dr. Judy, and Heather Shelby, Dr. Judy's assistant, had lunch and toured Jessica's laboratory. Rob, Scott, Steve, and Rob's friend Bill Keeler went fishing at Beaver Lake where they caught plenty of crappie and several bass.

That evening, they all gathered at Steve and Mavis's home for a fish fry. Scott and Cheryl showed a lot of interest in the projects Jessica had going in her lab, as well as the use she was making of the super computer. On Sunday afternoon, Cheryl and Scott were on their way back to Washington.

CHAPTER 3.

A LONG WAY FROM FAYETTEVILLE, ARKANSAS, a man in
Abu Dhabi, the capital city of the United Arab Emirates,
was on the balcony of his apartment looking out across the
imposing skyline. He was thinking how this city had grown
and prospered in the past ten years and how he had grown and
prospered with it. He had been born in Algeria, orphaned at
age ten, and wandered around the Middle East until, at age
twenty-five; he had gotten employment with the Oman Oil
Transport Company.

It was a group that shipped crude oil, natural gas, propane,
and methane from the Oman Bay area to various parts of the
world. He had worked hard for his education, and, using his
street smarts and a clever mind, he progressed rapidly in the
company. At the age of thirty-two, he was promoted to Director
of Shipping, Traffic and Warehousing, and was in charge of all
shipments of crude oil, propane, and natural gas made by the
Oman Oil Transport Company throughout the world. Now,
at age thirty-eight, he was traveling through the Middle East,
Europe, Russia, the Far East, and the United States.

Amahl Jabel, a name he had taken as a youngster, had a
slender build and was a little less than six feet tall. He was
noticeably attractive, with jet-black hair, dark eyes, and a short

black beard. He had a quick smile and the type of personality that you warmed to immediately. He spoke five languages fluently and moved easily through all strata of society. He also had spent much of his young life as a member of an Algerian Islamic terrorist group.

Amahl was born in 1958, in the walled city of Sidi-bel-Abbe s in Algeria. Sidi-bel-Abbe s had been the headquarters for the French Foreign Legion for 120 years until the Algerian government had demanded its withdrawal in 1962. There was no love for the Legion by the Algerian people, and there was great rejoicing when they left. In 1960, when Amahl was two years old, two legionaries raped his mother. The rapists were apprehended and shipped out of the area, but the toll on Amahl's family was devastating.

His father could not accept what had happened and put much of the blame on his wife. In 1964, when Amahl was six years old, his mother died, leaving him heartbroken, and his father lonely and bitter toward Western society in general. Amahl was old enough to understand, and over the years he assumed his father's hatred of French and Western culture.

When Amahl was ten years old, his father died and the boy went to live with an uncle, Omar Habash, in Libya. He was raised and schooled in Islamic culture and hatred for Western civilization. During that period of his life, Amahl joined a small but active terrorist organization. When he was twenty-one, he attended the terrorist training camp in Sebha and then, through the influence of his uncle, went on to the exclusive terrorist training camp at Ran Hilal near Tokra. The camps were sponsored by Qaddafi to train terrorists from many countries throughout the world.

As Amahl matured and gained experience and stature in the group, he became their leader at the age of twenty-eight. The terrorist group headed by Amahl was resourceful, extremely radical, and with no apparent links to any particular country.

As individuals, they were bound together with their Islamic culture and hatred of Western civilization. To vent their hatred, the group had been working on a master plan to inflict horrible damage to major population areas in Europe and the United States.

Amahl's position with a legitimate petroleum shipping company gave him a perfect cover to move freely throughout the world without being suspected or challenged. Amahl was now thirty-eight years old and had carefully thought out his master plan for "Judgment Day". For five years, the group had been buying drugs, primarily through Kurdish connections in Turkey, and then selling the drugs in Europe and the United States to a ready and willing market. The profits were accumulated to finally make a major purchase from the Russian mafia.

Through his Uncle Omar Habash, Amahl had made contact with Petr Karshev, one of the leaders of the Russian mafia. In late 1995, Amahl met with Petr in St. Petersburg in a small cafe. The two men talked for several hours, finally reaching an understanding of the total package wanted by Amahl. They also reached agreement on the cost and timing of the scheme.

The mafia would steal eight one-megaton nuclear warheads from a missile base in Russia and deliver them to a warehouse in St. Petersburg. Petr said that he would need eight to twelve months to arrange and execute the theft. Amahl requested that it be as close to eight months as possible. Further, Amahl demanded that non-mafia individuals involved in the action be executed to cover all tracks. The price for the warheads was set at 20,000,000 U.S. dollars.

Amahl studied Petr for a few moments, and then posed a question: "Petr, why are you so confident that your group can obtain eight nuclear warheads? All the information I have indicates such a theft would be nearly impossible with all the security surrounding nuclear missile bases."

Petr looked at Amahl with surprise on his face. "Ah, you have not lived in our country during the past three years. Before that, there would have been no way to accomplish such a theft, but things have changed radically since the collapse of the Soviet Union in 1991. All facets of living have deteriorated badly for many, many of our people, especially the military.

"That is why large groups of us joined the mafia, to get money for our families to live decently. Our once proud and powerful armed forces are in disarray, vastly overmanned and greatly underpaid. Most soldiers and officers have been paid their salaries only once or twice during the past year.

"Over 400 officers have committed suicide in less than a year; the prime reason being that the government will pay death benefits immediately to a military person's family. Out of desperation, many choose suicide to benefit their family. My cousin Yuri, who lived right here in St. Petersburg, was one of those. He and his wife were both in the military and had three children to take care of with no income. One night Yuri put a gun in his mouth and killed himself. We can find many such individuals who will sell us their help if they can be convinced they are not acting against their own country. It will take time and money, but I have no doubt that it can be done."

Amahl and Petr shook hands, and the deal was made.

Amahl reviewed their deal. "Petr, to make sure we are both in agreement and understand each other, let me tell you what our deal is. Within one year, and preferably less, you and a small group of your most trusted men will obtain eight one-megaton nuclear warheads. Any Russian military personnel involved in the action will be killed to keep our identity confidential. The warheads will be delivered to our warehouse here in St. Petersburg.

"My men will meet the drivers of the truck on the outskirts of St. Petersburg and guide the truck to the warehouse. After the warheads are delivered to the warehouse, both of the drivers will be killed and the truck will be driven into the harbor."

Amahl continued, "I will convey to you five million U.S. dollars tomorrow, and fifteen million U.S. dollars after the warheads are in the warehouse in St. Petersburg. I have your word that if any of your men talk of this operation to anyone outside of your trusted group, you will dispatch them to their death immediately. Are we in agreement?"

Petr nodded. "That is what we have discussed. I have but one question. I don't like killing my men unnecessarily. If I send two trusted men as drivers of the truck to St. Petersburg, why must we kill them? They will not talk."

Amahl gazed at Petr with a stern look on his face. "Petr it must be that way; there is no choice. What we are doing is far more important than the lives of two such men! When we complete our deal, I want no trace at all to St. Petersburg. You haven't asked what my plan is, and I respect you for that. If you asked, I would not tell you, although I did tell you at the outset of our conversation that this operation is in no way directed at your country."

Petr looked upset, and with a touch of sarcasm said, "I will do as you request and will pick the drivers very carefully, making sure they have no families!"

Amahl looked at Petr and said, as though with a word of caution, "If any of your group thinks of crossing you and me in this operation, remind him that Omar Habash and Col. Qaddafi are behind me and would be unhappy with such actions."

Amahl knew that wasn't true, but he also knew that Petr didn't know it, and even the Russian mafia did not want any action from those two terrorists. Petr and Amahl shook hands, and the deal was made. The next morning the money was on its way to Petr's headquarters in Moscow, and Amahl was on his way back to Abu Dahbi.

During the following year, the Russian mafia used money, murder, and threats to arrange, through corrupt military officials, the theft of eight nuclear warheads. The warheads came from a storage complex that housed many of the nuclear weapons that were still armed but had been taken out of "ready" status because of the START I and START II Treaties between the United States and the USSR.

In 1982, President Ronald Reagan supported the Strategic Arms Reduction Treaty (START) that called for deep cuts in land-based missiles. Negotiations carried on for several years, and finally President Reagan and Soviet Leader Mikhail Gorbachev signed the Intermediate Range Nuclear Forces Treaty in December of 1982. Negotiations continued after George Bush was elected president in 1988, and in July 1991, President Bush and Mikhail Gorbachev signed the START I Treaty, by which it was agreed to reduce the number of nuclear warheads by twenty-five per cent. That treaty was not fully implemented until 1993, when the Ukrainian parliament ratified it.

The START II Treaty, signed by Bush and Russian President Boris Yeltsin in January 1993, called for the elimination of almost three-quarters of the nuclear warheads still held by the United States, Russia, Ukraine, Belarus, and Kazakhstan. As a result of those treaties, many of the Sega SS-11 and the Savage SS-13 Soviet ICBMs had been moved from the "ready" status and put into "active" storage. With the collapse of the USSR as an entity in 1991, there was a lapse in the control and security of the nuclear missiles and the military bases within which they were supposedly well secured.

The Russian mafia agents, working with bribes and murder, had recruited a group of eleven military guards and technicians who would take the one-megaton warheads from eight of the Sega SS-11 missiles at the ICBM base near the city of Kozelsk. The warheads were to be removed from the eight missiles and the nose cones carefully replaced, so that the theft would not be noticeable.

Promptly on December 19, at 3 p.m., the day agreed to in their plan, two missile maintenance trucks and a large enclosed military truck pulled up to the guard gate and presented the counterfeit maintenance orders. There were eleven uniformed military men in the trucks, five of whom were mafia members. The two guards at the security gate were a part of the plot and waved the three trucks into the missile storage compound where they pulled up to a loading platform at the rear of the third storage building.

The large military van backed up to the platform as the other technicians left their trucks and went inside the building. The one security guard on duty in the storage building was also one of the "recruits" and kept a sharp lookout as the group went to work on removing the warheads and loading them into the large truck at the dock. The nose cones were carefully replaced on the missiles. At 5 p.m., the three trucks pulled out of the compound and left the base.

The large truck carrying the warheads was driven by two mafia men and headed for St. Petersburg. The two smaller trucks each carried three military men and two mafia men. These two trucks were heading for Kozelsk where the six military men were to be paid by the mafia. The trucks pulled off the highway and went about two kilometers down a long lane to an abandoned farmhouse. There were three mafia members waiting by a crumbling barn.

They waved to the six military men as they climbed out of the trucks. As the six men walked toward the barn, there was a sudden burst of gunfire and all six men dropped. Petr Karchev walked among the bodies and put a bullet into each man's head. The bodies were hauled out into the pasture and dumped into a shallow grave.

The three guards at the missile base were off duty at 7 p.m., and rode together to meet the mafia group for their "payday". They proceeded to the prearranged meeting place along the main road where they met and transferred into the mafia car. They also went down the long lane to the abandoned farm and were murdered and dumped into the same grave as the others. The grave was covered and Ptre and his men headed for Moscow.

The next morning, the truck used to transport the warheads the 1050 kilometers to St. Petersburg, stopped at a prearranged meeting place just outside the city. Two of Amahl's men met the truck to serve as guides in directing the truck to the warehouse. After unloading the warheads, both of the truck drivers were murdered. Their bodies were lashed into the truck and it was driven into the deep murky water of the harbor five kilometers from the warehouse.

Within eighteen hours of the theft, the warheads had been safely stowed in the Oman Oil Company warehouse in St. Petersburg. The warehouse was staffed and closely controlled by associates loyal to Amahl. One of the ships controlled by Amahl had already been loaded with its regular cargo and as soon as the special "merchandise" was loaded, the ship sailed out of the harbor, carrying the warheads to a secured warehouse in Abu Dhabi. The warheads had been stolen and shipped out of the country in less than twenty-four hours!

Prior to the final shipment of the nuclear warheads to their respective destinations, each had to be installed inside its own carrier. That installation would take place in the secured warehouse in Abu Dhabi. For that installation, Amahl had ordered sixteen two hundred gallon cylinder-shaped propane storage tanks. They were each 30" in diameter and 7' long, gleaming white, strapped and stacked horizontally two high to a skid. The top tank of each group of two was a normal tank and would carry the normal load of propane or methane.

James Kerlin

The bottom tank in each two tank "pod" had false ends and would contain the warheads and arming mechanisms along with intricate timing devices. The false ends of those altered tanks were each 30" in diameter and 30" long. This left a center portion of the tank that was 30" in diameter and 24" in length and would hold forty-six gallons of propane that would be available if any customs officials desired to open the valve to check the tanks contents.

The final destination points, or targets, were Berlin, Paris, London, Rome, Brussels, New York City, Washington, D.C., and Los Angeles. Within three months after being armed and strategically placed, the terrible destruction would take place.

A smile crossed Amahl's face as he contemplated the terrible carnage that would be inflicted on western civilization. He walked back inside the apartment to sit down on the bed beside Lattah. She was slender and well-built, a little on the muscular side, but very attractive with her dark hair and dark eyes. She had a pretty smile, but it didn't come too readily, and she was more on the serious side in her facial appearance.

Lattah had no last name, an orphan known simply as Lattah. She had been raised in southeastern Turkey in a Kurdish settlement outside the city of Kars. Lattah knew she was in her early thirties, but she did not know where she had been born or anything about her parents' nationality. The Kurdish families with whom Lattah lived during her formative years were all members of the Kurdistan Workers Party, known by the initials PKK.

The PKK waged a twelve-year war to establish an autonomous Marxist state in the Kurdish area of Turkey. The PKK had never shied from violence and terrorism to achieve its goals. According to FBI and State Department records, the PKK committed more terrorist acts from 1991 through 1995 than any other such group in the world, attacking targets in Turkey and Western Europe. PKK terrorists would regularly plant bombs in crowded areas of Istanbul, killing and maiming foreign tourists as well as Turks. More than 21,000 people died in fighting since the PKK started its war in 1984.

To raise money to buy weapons, they turned to heroin. Eastern Turkey is known as the crossroads and processing center of Afghan heroin on its way to Europe and North America. The PKK demands protection money from the Afghan labs and operates some of them as well for an estimated annual income of $500,000,000. While more popular in Europe, heroin processed in PKK-controlled areas has made inroads into the United States, especially to those cities with large Middle Eastern populations, including New York, Detroit, Chicago, and Los Angeles.

While still in her teens, Lattah had been attacked in a rape attempt by the brother of one of the Kurd leaders. In the furious struggle, Lattah grabbed a knife and repeatedly stabbed the man until he dropped to his knees fatally wounded. Fearing reprisal, and although Lattah had many close friends among the Kurds, she fled the area, drifting through Iraq and Syria before ending up in Abu Dhabi.

In 1989, she met Amahl and became associated with his terrorist group. By 1991, she was living with Amahl and had proven her hatred of Western culture. With her leadership strengths and her intelligence, she quickly became recognized as the second in command of the group. In early 1991, Lattah had been the key to arranging the heroin deals that would be used to finance the activities of Amahl's terrorist group. She called and talked with the Kurdish family that she lived with prior to her flight after the murder of her assailant.

During the call, she learned that she had fled unnecessarily as the man she had killed was disliked and distrusted by the Kurdish leadership. Lattah requested that the family arrange a meeting for her with the leadership of that Kurdish faction so that she could arrange a deal for the purchase of a large quantity of heroin. The family assured Lattah that they would make the contact and that she would be given a return call.

The next morning at dawn the phone rang and Lattah answered, "Hello! Who is this?"

"I wish to speak to Lattah. My name is Abdullah. She requested to speak to me!"

Lattah responded, "This is Lattah, and I am interested in purchasing a large quantity of your merchandise. Can we meet to discuss purchase terms and delivery?"

Abdullah was abrupt. "First we meet to discuss availability and for me to meet your partners. I will be in Abu Dhabi in two days and will call you at this same time to make arrangements for our meeting." With that, Abdullah concluded the conversation and was gone.

Lattah related the conversation to Amahl and they made their plans for the meeting with Abdullah. Lattah said she recalled an Abdullah among the leaders of the PKK in that particular Kurdish area. He was a tough and aggressive individual and did most of the negotiating for the drug deals. In two days, at dawn, the phone rang and Abdullah gave Lattah directions to the meeting place.

He instructed her to be at one of the benches facing the waterway beside the site of the future Zayed City Sports Complex. She must be there in exactly three hours and carry two small books, one in each hand, so that Abdullah could identify her. She informed Abdullah that only she and Amahl would be involved in the meeting.

Precisely three hours later, Lattah and Amahl were seated on the center bench adjacent to the future sports complex and facing the waterway, with Lattah holding a small book in each hand. Several individuals walked by paying little attention to the couple seated on the bench. Finally, a stocky middle-aged man walked past them, then turned around and motioned to them to approach him.

They got up and walked toward the man. Lattah murmured to Amahl that this was not the Abdullah that she recalled. Amahl quickly glanced in both directions along the walkway, making sure the guards he had secretly posted were still in position, then Amahl and Lattah moved forward toward the man.

Lattah smiled and greeted him, "Are you Abdullah?"

"No, I am Abdullah!" came a voice from behind them. "That gentleman is my associate and his name is of no significance to you. Also, you may tell your guards that there is no need for concern as we have no intentions of doing anything beyond talking."

Amahl felt a surge of humiliation that his guards had been so easily detected. However, he kept a cool and collected appearance as he introduced Lattah and himself. Abdullah said he recalled Lattah from her days in the Kurdish village, saying one of such beauty could not easily be forgotten. Also, he related how he had asked many questions of people with whom Lattah had lived and associated with. His people had told him that Lattah could indeed be trusted. He suggested that they walk along the waterway as they discussed the merits and costs of dealing with each other.

Knowing that Abdullah was sympathetic to terrorist causes, Amahl explained that his group was working on a plan for a major strike against western culture and that they needed twenty million dollars to execute the plan.

He stated that he had no intentions of explaining the details of the strike, but that he needed Abdullah as a source from whom they could buy and resell the drugs to raise the twenty million dollars.

He told Abdullah how the vast shipping network that he directed could be used to distribute the drugs throughout the Western world, and how much he enjoyed the irony of Western civilization paying for the drugs and in effect providing the funds for the massive destruction that he planned.

Amahl further explained that he trusted Abdullah because he had carefully checked on him through his Uncle Omar Habash in Libya with whom Amahl had lived for many years. The uncle had worked up through the ranks of loyal Qaddafi supporters and was now one of the top ranking security chiefs. When Amahl had gotten the name of Abdullah from Lattah, along with a description of his activities and areas of operations, he immediately contacted Omar who subsequently ran an investigation and determined that Abdullah was a trusted operator.

For reasons of security and self-protection, Amahl let it be known to Abdullah that Qaddafi, through Omar Habash who was known and feared throughout the Mideast area, was providing the initial "seed money" for their deal. Abdullah would think twice before crossing Amahl and his organization.

That meeting and the subsequent relationship had happened five years ago. The arrangement had proven to be prosperous for both organizations. Now, in 1996, Amahl and his group had earned over $23,000,000 by selling drugs. They had purchased the eight nuclear warheads for $20,000,000 and were ready to move to the next phase of their plan which was the distribution and securing of the warheads in their hiding places throughout the Western world.

Lattah and Amahl were not only lovers, but she was his top confidante and right hand in everything he did. She was propped up on the bed going through a worldwide directory of warehouses and storage facilities used by the Oman Oil Company. Facilities that would be used to temporarily store each of the nuclear devices in its designated city until its final placement in a strategic location in that city just prior to the day of reckoning. Only Amahl and Lattah would know the exact locations of all eight bombs. Lattah started talking about the potential storage sites, but Amahl placed his hand over her mouth softly saying, "Tomorrow!" With that he quickly undressed and slid into the bed wrapping her in his arms.

CHAPTER 4.

E IGHT WEEKS AFTER THE THEFT of the nuclear warheads, a meeting was about to take place in the oval office of the White House. The President was somewhat mystified not only by the secrecy and urgency for the meeting as expressed by the Director of the CIA, but also by the participants, several of whom he had never met.

However, the President was very close to the Director and had a great deal of confidence in him. The Director had by-passed the President's personal secretary and the Chief of Staff to request the meeting, and left it to the President to explain the necessity of having to cancel the other meetings previously on his agenda.

President William Hartmann, fifty-four years old and a graduate of Ohio State University with Master's Degrees in Business and Finance, had served twelve years in the Navy reaching the rank of Commander. After he retired, he started his own business as a financial consultant. Along the way, he got heavily involved in Republican politics, finally serving two terms as the Governor of the State of Ohio. In 1992, he was elected President and then re-elected in 1996. President Hartmann had performed well and was held in high esteem by most Americans. He was honest, forthright, outspoken, and had shown good leadership.

In his mind, the President reviewed the individuals who would participate in the meeting. First, the Director of the CIA, Colm O'Hara, fifty-three years old, a graduate of Texas A&M University with a Bachelor of Science Degree who then attended graduate school at Harvard where he earned his law degree. Following graduation from Harvard, he enlisted as an officer in the Marine Corps for three years, serving two years in Vietnam as a helicopter pilot.

After Vietnam, he spent eleven years working with his father and two brothers in the family's oil exploration business, doing all the legal work for the corporation. Tiring of the corporate routine, Colm became interested in politics and at age thirty-eight, he was elected to the House of Representatives where he served for twelve years. At age fifty, he was elected to the Senate and in his third year in the Senate, President William Hartmann appointed him Director of the CIA.

Gordon Brown, Director of the FBI, fifty-eight years old, was a graduate of UCLA with a Bachelor's Degree in Science and a Master's Degree in Aeronautical Engineering. He had worked for Lockheed, Douglas and Boeing in the development of attack and defense aircraft for the Air Force. He had also done considerable consulting work for NASA in the design and development of space vehicles.

Along the way in his career, he had worked closely with both the Secretary of Defense and the Director of the FBI in the detection of spies within the air defense and aircraft industry. Gordon had become an expert on espionage and infiltration of spies. Because of his unique experience and qualifications, he was President Hartmann's choice to fill the job when the Director of the FBI resigned due to poor health. Also, President Hartmann was very aware of the friendship, respect, and good working relationship between Gordon and the Secretary of Defense, Jordan Henning.

Secretary of Defense Henning, sixty-two years old, was a graduate of the Air Force Academy and had served twenty years in the Air Force attaining the rank of Brigadier General. He retired at the age of forty-four, entered politics and successfully ran for congress serving twelve years in the house and six years in the senate. He served on both the Armed Services and Foreign Relations Committees. President William Hartmann appointed him to the position of Secretary of Defense.

Also in attendance, Secretary of State Glenna Quisenberry, sixty-five years old, a graduate of University of Kentucky with majors in Sociology and Economics. She received her Doctorate and Law Degree from the University of Michigan. She spent several years in a large law firm in Washington, D.C., but very quickly became interested in politics and government. During her twenty-eight year career in the State Department, she had served Ambassadorships in Japan, Egypt, England, and just prior to her appointment as Secretary of State, she had served as Ambassador to the United Nations. She was one of the President's closest advisors.

The President's National Security Advisor, Davis Benson, was sixty-four years old, of slight build, and a young-looking face with smooth skin and bright eyes that always appeared to be smiling and seemed to match his dry sense of humor. He was an intellect with advanced degrees from Cornell and Harvard in both Science and Political Science. He had made a career in serving on numerous study committees and think tanks studying problems throughout the world. He was recognized internationally as an expert in nuclear weapons and world terrorism, as well as a world-class tennis player.

Another requested participant in the meeting was Vice-President Frank Hughes, forty-six years old and the first black Vice-President. Frank was born and raised in California and graduated from USC with a law degree. He was a gifted athlete, All-American wide receiver, MVP in the Rose Bowl, and then played professional football for the San Francisco Forty-Niners for seven years.

After that, Frank started his own law firm in San Jose and became active in Republican politics. After two terms in the state legislature, he was elected Lt. Governor of the State of California. In 1992, William Hartmann chose Frank to be his running mate and now they were in their second term. They worked well as team. Frank was energetic and a good negotiator, and had proven to be an outstanding trouble-shooter in serving as the President's personal representative in many hot spots throughout the world. Frank and Scott Crockett had resolved many situations together and were well acquainted.

The last two participants were the ones that had surprised the President. One was Sergei Andropov, fifty-two years old and a personal representative of the Russian President, Nicolai Padrov. President Padrov had been recently elected President following the resignation of Boris Yeltsin who left due to illness. President Hartmann had only met with President Padrov one time, but the two had gotten along well and had made great progress in their talks on many issues.

Sergei had been a high-ranking official in the KGB prior to its dismantling following the collapse of the USSR in 1991. He now served as the Russian President's personal representative in overseeing matters of Russian national security. President Hartmann had known Sergei for many years and liked him as well as trusted him. However, he was rather curious as to why he hadn't been briefed prior to his meeting with a foreign dignitary.

The final participant was Scott Crockett. Publicly Scott was an employee of the Commerce Department, serving as an International Trade Representative reporting directly to the Secretary of Commerce. Secretly Scott was a case officer for the CIA Directorate of Operations reporting directly to the Deputy Director for Operations. He headed up the Office of Near Eastern and South Asian Analysis, but was often requested to serve in a special office that had worldwide responsibilities and focused on particular issues or kinds of analyzes. In his prime job, he specialized in espionage in the Middle East and monitored Russian activities in those countries.

Scott and Sergei had become good friends and shared a great deal of respect for each other. Each recognized and accepted the responsibilities of the other, meaning that regardless of their friendship, the line was drawn when it came to the security of their respective countries.

The President had heard of Scott Crockett, but had never met him and his personal attendance at the meeting further perplexed the President. There was nothing going on currently that he could think of that would involve an urgent gathering of these unique individuals. In another hour, he would wish that he had never heard of the diabolical situation that brought these men together.

It was 7 a.m., and the President was in his office having coffee when all the participants were ushered in by the President's somewhat bewildered secretary who had not expected this particular group and especially at this hour. The only participant who was not acquainted with the entire group was Scott Crockett who was introduced by Colm O'Hara to the President.

They exchanged greetings and the President motioned the group to help themselves to the coffee, juices, fruit, and pastries spread out on the side table. The President smiled and looked at the Director of Central Intelligence saying, "Colm, this better be important as I had to cancel two meetings with high ranking congressional committees at the last minute, and they sure as hell won't like it! On the other hand, this looks like a more interesting meeting, but don't quote me on that!"

The President noted that Colm wasn't smiling, and his usual quick wit and laugh were gone.

Colm responded, "Mr. President, I hate to lay this on you at this hour of the morning, and when you are obviously enjoying the day, but it is critical that we develop an immediate plan of action to deter the potential massive destruction of much of the Western world. I requested this meeting with only these individuals because I feel it is best to proceed on a 'need to know' basis only. Word of this problem must not be discussed beyond this room. If word of this situation gets out, there will be world wide chaos which could impede our solution of the problem."

"For God's sake, Colm!" the President said. "I've never seen you so serious and you're scaring the hell out of us! Please explain what you're talking about."

The looks on the faces of Davis Benson, Jordan Henning, and Frank Hughes reflected the same concerns.

Colm began, "Last night at about 9 p.m., Scott called my home and requested a meeting with him and Sergei as soon as possible. Because of the urgency in his voice, I invited them to meet at my home. They immediately came and related a situation that caused me to call you late last night requesting this meeting. Sergei, would you please tell the group the story you detailed to Scott and subsequently to me."

Sergei shared what had transpired in Russia during the past eight weeks. "Almost exactly six weeks ago, nine military men were reported absent, I believe you call it AWOL, from our ICBM base near Kozelsk. That base is about 250 or so kilometers southwest of Moscow. Having individuals go AWOL is not unusual, but having nine at one time is most unusual!

"There was a half-hearted search through the nearby towns thinking that they probably got drunk, went on a binge, and were afraid to return to their units. However, last week a boy playing with his dog in an abandoned farm pasture near Kozelsk, found a man's hand sticking up out of the ground. There had been heavy rains and the earth had washed away from the hand and arm. The boy reported it to authorities, and they not only found one body but all nine of the missing military men. Each had numerous gunshot wounds, but also each had been shot in the head to make sure he was dead."

Sergei continued, "First, we suspected that probably drugs were involved, but that theory was quickly proven wrong. Next, we considered a possible gambling problem, but it likewise was proven wrong. We finally considered what now appears to have been obvious; why would nine military men be murdered at an ICBM base? But of course, to steal nuclear weapons! All of the missiles were examined and we found that eight of the SS-11 missiles had the one megaton nuclear warheads removed and are missing; the nose cones had been carefully replaced.

"All of the individuals in Russia who know of this situation are sworn to absolute secrecy under penalty of death. The warheads have vanished, and we have no idea yet where they are. President Padrov ordered me to brief you personally by contacting you through Scott Crockett whom we knew could be trusted and would effectively arrange a meeting with as few individuals as possible. President Padrov also recognizes the danger of world chaos if word of the theft becomes known."

Sergei looked at the President and said, "President Padrov and I have discussed the need to share this situation with you and to seek your help by involving individuals like Davis Benson with his knowledge of nuclear armament and the terrorist groups throughout the world.

"Further, we suspect that the problem has its roots in the Middle East. We would like Scott's help, as he is an expert in knowing who is doing what in that area. Frank also can be of great help with his knowledge and contacts in the Middle Eastern and African nations. We must find those eight warheads as quickly as possible!"

The President thanked Sergei for the briefing and requested that he thank the Russian President for sharing the situation with the United States. He looked at the concerned faces around the room and urged Davis to assess the situation.

Davis was quietly thinking, and then after what seemed like an eternity, he began to speak, "First of all, each of you must understand what it means to have a one megaton nuclear warhead in the hands of a terrorist. At this point we have no idea as to who took the warheads. Nor do we know for what purpose they were stolen. We can be sure, however, that the organization that has the eight warheads plans to use them, and probably within several months or a year. It seems we all have become rather blasé about the horrible damage that can be inflicted on humanity by nuclear devices.

"We glibly talk of missiles and bombs, of radiation, blast and burn damage. But do we really understand what would happen if a terrorist exploded a one-megaton warhead in a major city? We're not talking about a World Trade Center or Oklahoma City type of bombing, as terrible as they were. These nuclear devices could kill and wound tens of millions of human beings! We must cooperate with the Russian officials to save our civilization from a terrible, terrible act of terrorism." His gaze covered each person in the room and his mood was intense.

Davis continued, "A one-megaton weapon would weigh at most a few hundred kilograms. There is a factor of one million between the energy released in an electromagnetic interaction and that of a nuclear interaction. It takes a billion kilograms of TNT interacting electromagnetically to match the energy released from a few hundred kilograms of nuclear matter interacting strongly.

"When a one-megaton weapon explodes, it releases energy equal to the amount released by exploding one million tons of TNT. That amount of TNT would fill a freight train 300 miles long. The fireball from the explosion of a one-megaton nuclear

James Kerlin

weapon grows to more than a mile in diameter in seconds and rises into the atmosphere, forming a mushroom cloud ten miles across and extending to an altitude of 70,000 feet."

As Davis paused, the Secretary of Defense interrupted with a question, "Davis, tell us...."

Davis held his hand up and insisted, "Jordan, let me finish my complete story on this, and then I'll answer any questions you may have."

He then continued his comments. "There is no way to adequately describe the aggregate effects of a modern thermonuclear weapon on a human population. Hiroshima and Nagasaki will not serve as precedents. The weapons used on those cities were much less powerful than the nuclear weapons of today. To try to imagine the effects of a single one-megaton weapon requires us to try and imagine eighty Hiroshima explosions at the same instant in one place.

"The causes of death and injury in a nuclear explosion are three forces: blast, heat, and radiation. The medical aspects of an attack by nuclear weapons can be understood by considering the nature and impact of each force separately, and then their combined effect, and the problems of survival."

Davis got up from his chair and walked to the service table to get a glass of orange juice and took two long sips.

There was dead silence as he walked back to his chair, sat down, and continued with his explanation. "To be specific, let us consider the detonation of a one-megaton weapon in the heart of a target city. Blast effects are produced by a huge shock wave created at the surface of the fireball in the first fraction of a second after the nuclear explosion. The shock wave travels as a sudden increase in air pressure followed by high winds. The primary blast effects would be the collapse of all buildings, bridges, and other structures, and the crushing of humans within, below, or near them.

"In the inner circle of destruction, that area within a 1.5 mile radius from the center of a one-megaton explosion, the static over pressures would exceed 220 pounds per square inch, sufficient to collapse and destroy even the strongest steel and reinforced concrete multi-story office buildings.

"The gale force winds that follow the shock wave are sufficient at 4.5 miles to hurl a standing human being against a wall with several times the force of gravity causing glass shards, stones, or metallic objects, anything shattered by the over pressure, to fly with velocities above 100 miles per hour.

"Within a five mile radius, few persons in the open or in ordinary buildings are likely to survive the overwhelming force of the blast. Trees will be uprooted and heavy vehicles overturned. Many people inside will be crushed as buildings collapse or will be wounded by the debris. Even farther away, those in the open will be struck and lacerated by flying debris."

Davis stood up and paced the floor as he told of the effects of radiation. "A one-megaton weapon exploded on the earth's surface will dig a crater about two hundred yards in radius and fifty to seventy yards deep in ordinary soil. Most of the excavated material will be ejected to a distance about twice the radius of the crater, but a substantial amount will be vaporized or pulverized and lifted into the upper atmosphere by the rising fireball and updraft winds.

"This material attaches to a radioactive nuclei of weapon debris and is the major source of the lethal radioactive fallout down wind from the ground burst. In general, an area of at least 1,400 square miles would have to be evacuated for between a month and a year depending on the saturation of the radiation.

"The initial radiation burst is composed of highly penetrating and dangerous gamma rays and neutrons, a radiation dose so intense as to be locally lethal but very limited in range. At one mile from a one-megaton explosion, all the population would be killed by the initial burst of radioactivity, even if shielded by twenty-four inches of concrete. A ground burst in Detroit with the wind from the northwest, could deposit lethal fallout on Cleveland and as far away as Pittsburgh.

"Now as to the heat or fire force, when a nuclear weapon explodes a great wave of heat, traveling at the speed of light, is emitted from the fireball. This enormous pulse of thermal radiation causes flash burns of exposed skin. Such flash burns accounted for nearly one-third of the fatalities at Hiroshima. In a one-megaton weapon explosion, one of every two unshielded victims will suffer second-degree burns at a distance of 9.5 miles from ground zero, and third degree burns from a distance of eight miles. At distances of up to five miles, shielding the skin itself is not necessarily protective; spontaneous ignition of clothing will cause flame burns with even more severe injury and a higher probability of death.

"The heat flash is so intense that paper, dry trees, leaves and grass, debris and wood outside of buildings will burst into flames as far as ten miles away from a one-megaton blast. Within buildings, there will be spontaneous ignition of clothing, upholstery, bedding, carpets, papers, and fabrics. All are likely to create self-sustaining and spreading fires in the wake of the gigantic thermal pulse that radiates from the explosion.

"To these innumerable fires must be added the blast induced fires created by exploding boilers, overturned furnaces and stoves, broken gas mains, and downed power lines. Fires will directly ignite or spread to gasoline stations, fuel storage depots, large natural gas storage tanks, and industrial and chemical flammable stockpiles.

"Any stores of liquefied natural gas would be an enormous additional hazard. Control or containment of such fires, hundreds of them per acre, would be virtually impossible. Water mains would be shattered and water pressure non-existent. Streets would be impassable. Fire fighting crews and equipment would be disabled or destroyed. In a one-megaton explosion, the 'lethal area', the circle within which the entire population is counted as fatalities, is usually drawn at the five psi over pressure line which is a radius of 4.3 miles from ground zero."

The group members shifted uneasily in their chairs as Davis was bringing his comments to an end. "Virtually all hospitals would be severely damaged or out of commission. Aside from the blast, heat, and fire damage, which would be substantial, almost the entire area would be without electric power. Generators and all the transistorized and electronic equipment within their walls, including computers, cardiac monitors and such, will have been destroyed by the electromagnetic pulse that follows the bomb's detonation.

"The ratio of surviving uninjured physicians to the number of seriously injured nuclear attack victims would be between 1:500 and 1:1500. The ruins of the buildings would be lying in what would be left of the streets. There would be no transportation, no emergency or rescue vehicles. There would be no telephone or other communication systems.

"There would be no emergency rooms, no operating rooms, no diagnostic or therapeutic equipment within reach. There would be no blood banks or drug stocks. Survivors huddled in any available shelter could not leave to rescue the wounded without risking dangerous or lethal radiation doses and the probability of contaminating their shelters when they returned.

"A one-megaton device exploded in Los Angeles with a population of just under nine million people, would kill over two million people and injure a like amount for total casualties of about four and a half million. There are eight such warheads in the hands of terrorists with the potential of killing or maiming over 28,000,000 human beings. We must commit all of our collective resources to find these warheads as quickly as possible."

Davis paused and then said to the group, "Too many people do not fully understand the horrors of nuclear warfare. I apologize for this detailed description of the hellish devastation that the present thermonuclear weapons can bring upon humanity, but I want you all to fully comprehend the magnitude of the problem we have with these one-megaton warheads in the hands of irresponsible terrorists.

"And as mentioned before, even though it will hinder our efforts to find the warheads, we must keep the theft of the warheads completely confidential. Such information, if released to the world, would cause chaos beyond comprehension and would serve no purpose in safeguarding humanity."

The President stood up and paced around the room. "Thank you, Davis, for putting this horrible situation in its proper perspective. Before we discuss how to approach this dilemma, I have a question for Sergei. Does your organization have any leads or suspicions?"

Sergei responded, "As I said before, we have ruled out drugs and gambling. We have carefully evaluated the involvement of Chechnya. Russian troops have been withdrawn from Chechnya, and Chechnya has postponed the demands for immediate independence. It was a consensus of all of our considerations that the Chechnya rebels would not jeopardize the current relationship by stealing warheads. The Russian mafia could be involved, but whom would they be dealing with?

"Most of the middle-eastern countries that would be apt to carry out such an operation are aligned with our country. However, that doesn't preclude them from using the weapons against the western nations. We have swept the Kozelsk area and have no leads as to the location of the warheads, nor of any foreign persons being in the area or on the base. However, the mafia has strong roots in that area and could readily operate there without attracting too much attention. In addition, people fear the mafia and would be afraid to provide any information."

Scott spoke up, "I think you're on the right track, Sergei, it's the most logical lead we have at this point. I would like to make a suggestion, Mr. President."

The President responded. "Feel free to go right ahead, Scott, we need all of our best thinking to solve this problem!"

Scott proceeded, "Let's assume it was the Russian mafia that stole the warheads and that they were acting on behalf of a middle-eastern country or active terrorist organization. It would seem imperative that Sergei return to Russia and really put the pressure on any connections to the Russian mafia, especially in the Kozelsk area. Also, I think that my fellow agent, Max Thorn, and I should work all our connections and sources in the Middle East to find information. Further, I would suggest that Frank, if he is agreeable, hit all his connections in the African/Middle-East area. Frank, Sergei, and I will stay in contact, and when we are ready, Frank can contact the President within seven to ten days to arrange our next meeting to evaluate the situation and plan future action."

The President nodded in agreement, "What do the rest of you think?"

Secretary of Defense Jordan expressed his agreement that it was a good starting point.

Secretary of State Glenna Quisenberry also agreed, but emphasized the need to keep the information confidential and involve the least number of people possible. She said that all the State Department's resources would be available to assist the investigating agencies.

Sergei said, "The plan makes sense to me, and we must move fast! I will return to Moscow immediately and relate our plans to my President. Not to be presumptive, Mr. President, but it might be advisable for you to call my President to confirm this mutual action. I am sure he will greatly appreciate this cooperation!"

The President responded, "I fully agree with you, Sergei. I will call him immediately."

Colm stood, "Since we are all in agreement, let's get moving. I will arrange transportation and notify the appropriate people of a visit by the various representatives of our Middle Eastern trade commission. Scott, let me know of any additional support you may need in terms of manpower, equipment, or special services, such as satellite surveillance."

"Very well," Scott said. "I will be meeting with Sergei and Frank, along with Max Thorn, before Sergei leaves, and then I'll get back to you."

Frank was in full agreement. "I think it is the best approach at this point. I have been requested to attend a two-day meeting in Algeria, so this will work in perfectly. Scott, in our meeting with Sergei before he leaves, let's be sure to cover all our arrangements for methods and times for communications. Also, plan our schedules so there's no overlap in our investigations."

Scott nodded.

Davis said, "I like this approach and think it's the best course right now. While these actions are being taken, I will get our computer section going with a thorough review of all classified information on activities of terrorist groups in the Middle East. Again, just a reminder to be very discreet and not divulge the theft of the warheads to anybody."

President Hartmann said, "Thanks again, Sergei, to you and your country, for alerting us and letting us help try and save humanity from these madmen. I thank all of you for your assistance in this crisis. God-speed and good luck to you Sergei, Frank, and Scott in your missions. Please keep me informed by direct line, and let me know when you want to meet again."

The President shook each man's hand as he filed out of the oval office, and then sat down in his chair with a long sigh, pondering his responsibilities to inform other cabinet and congressional members or agency directors of the situation. He decided that for the time being he would inform no one. He then reached for the phone to call his counterpart in Moscow.

President Hartmann gave President Padrov a detailed briefing on the meeting and the actions that were being taken. He explained that although Sergei was on his way back to Moscow, he would be in constant contact with Frank Hughes and Scott Crockett. Those three individuals would not only be the prime investigators, but would also direct the operations and provide communications between the two nations.

President Padrov advised President Hartmann of the progress of the investigation currently taking place in Russia by Sergei's special intelligence team. President Hartmann then questioned the need to alert certain members of NATO. President Padrov quickly objected on the basis of keeping the problem confidential.

President Hartmann responded, "We have no choice. If it were only your country and my country involved, we could do that. However, we don't know what countries are targets of the terrorists. There are eight warheads missing, and we don't know if the terrorists are targeting one country or eight countries."

"We must alert NATO nations that they are possibly in great danger. Further, they positively must know it is not a Russian act of aggression. I would propose that you and I agree on which nations to involve, and then we will arrange a conference in Europe with just one representative from each. Sergei, Frank and Scott will brief them, so they can return to their respective countries and determine what protective actions they must take.

"After each head of state has been briefed, you and I will arrange a meeting with those countries through a telephone conference call with all involved to determine that we are working in harmony to solve this terrible problem. Would you agree with that plan?"

There was a rather long pause before President Padrov answered. "I am very apprehensive about the involvement of so many people. I feel that common knowledge of this could cause great chaos throughout the world. However, I do agree with you that each country has the right to protect itself and should be informed of the potential danger this situation presents. Let us proceed as you have outlined. I will inform Sergei of this plan. Please keep me informed of any developments, and I will do the same. Thank you and your associates for your understanding and cooperation!"

President Hartmann said, "No, I thank you, Nicolai! You showed us trust and compassion. You could have kept the entire situation under wraps, and let us be sitting ducks for a horrendous tragedy, but you didn't do that. My countrymen and I thank you, and will do our best to help find the warheads."

With that, the two leaders exchanged goodbyes and hung up.

At this same time, there was activity at the Travel-USA agency. Scott, Sergei and Vice-President Frank Hughes were inside the special office of Max Thorn. Scott quickly reviewed the situation for Max's benefit.

Max shook his head. "This is a son-of-a-bitch! Sergei, do we have any leads at all? Somebody on that missile base had to see or hear something."

Sergei related to Max all the details he had told the group at the meeting in the Oval Office.

Max questioned Sergei. "Didn't your country have a similar situation at the missile base in Perm a couple years ago?"

Sergei responded, "Yes, we did, but it was quite a bit different. Chechnya rebels tried to openly attack the base and take whatever missiles they could. However, they were repelled and that was the end of it. All the rebels were killed and nothing in this situation points in that direction."

The four of them were seated at a small conference table discussing their plans for the next week. The room was full of electronic equipment and two very powerful computers. There was also an administrative secretary, Rozann Blackwell, and a code clerk who was busy taking a message from one of the satellite dishes on the roof of the agency. Rozann was the contact for all communications from Scott and Max that had to be dispersed to other Federal agencies or individuals.

It was agreed that Scott and Max would leave that night and work all their contacts in the appropriate Middle Eastern countries. Sergei would head back to Russia to intensify the Russian investigation. Frank Hughes would attend his scheduled meeting in Algiers and then he would pursue other contacts in Africa and the Mideast. It was agreed that all communications be handled through the CIA regional office in Frankfurt.

Agent Dayle Sutton would be the contact person in that office. Only he would know the daily locations of the four men. He and Sergei would work out a high security satellite feed for communications between the Frankfurt CIA office and Sergei's office in Moscow. He would also be in constant contact with Rozann Blackwell who in turn would keep the President and the others informed.

CHAPTER 5.

I N THE FULBRIGHT RESEARCH LABORATORY in Fayetteville, Jessica was deeply involved in the brain research being done in the areas of Alzheimer's disease, the aging process, and various other projects contracted by the university. She had been making maximum use of the time allocated to the laboratory for using the super computer, capable of one trillion calculations per second. The University of Arkansas and several federal agencies owned it jointly. Jessica had hired two computer specialists to handle the computer operations and two graduate students to assist in the laboratory work.

She had also hired Heather Shelby as her assistant. This was done, of course, with the blessing of Dr. Judy Clark who was willing to give up her capable assistant to help Jessica on this particular program. Much of Jessica's personal research was in the area of Alzheimer's disease and mapping the areas of the brain involved in the Alzheimer problems.

She was working very closely with Dr. Michael Laird, a distinguished neurosurgeon. Dr. Laird practiced at the Washington County Regional Medical Center in Fayetteville and was very actively involved in the University's medical research. Dr. Laird was the author of many medical papers and publications on brain surgery and was known internationally for the advances he pioneered in that practice. The University and the Washington County Regional Medical Center were extremely fortunate to have Dr. Laird on their respective staffs.

Jessica and Heather were making final preparations to conduct an experiment they had run many times before without success. However, they were very excited about their prospects for success in this particular experiment. They had made several critical changes in the procedure and felt good about what they had accomplished. The research involved two laboratory rats identified as A211 and A214. The rats had been very carefully trained to work their way through a maze to find their food. They had learned rather quickly, and finally were able to zip through the maze with few, if any, wrong turns.

After the maze training, the rat identified as A211 received additional attention. It was a special rat whose brain had been altered by molecular techniques that allowed specific genes of the rat's chromosome to be changed in a precise way to bring on Alzheimer's disease. The change created a rat model of Alzheimer's disease.

All vertebrates possess a brain composed of the same basic subdivisions found in the human brain: the hindbrain, midbrain, and forebrain. Everything learned through this research could possibly be applied in solving Alzheimer's problems. After the gene alteration, rat A211 quickly became confused in trying to make its way through the maze, and was showing a great deal of frustration and stress in not being able to reach the food.

The goal of this particular experiment was to achieve the transfer of memory. Jessica had been curious as to the possibility of connecting the brains of the two rats with electrodes, sensors, and cables, which would enable rat A211 to utilize the memory of rat A214 to help it find its way through the maze. The research team had very carefully rehearsed every aspect of the experiment.

The team used devices such as electroencephalography (EEG), Positron Emission Tomography (PET), and Magnetic Resonance Imaging (MRI) to carefully select the locations on the skull and positions in the brains for the insertion of the electrodes and sensors.

The electrodes were placed in the areas of the brain that had been identified with the memory and recall process such as the limbic system which includes the thalamus, hypothalamus, the hippocampal formation, amygdala, caudate nucleus, septum and mesencephalon, the frontal areas of the cerebral cortex, and the corpus callosum, that is a massive bundle of fibers that connects the two cerebral hemispheres and carries the communications between them.

A general anesthesia was not required, as the brain has no pain receptors. A local anesthesia was used for the small incisions in the scalp and skull. A light anesthesia was used on rat A214 in order to immobilize it and keep it still during the experiment. In addition, a small dose of nicotine was introduced into the bloodstream of each rat. Recent research had shown that nicotine strengthened the communications between neurons in the hippocampus, a structure in the brain involved in learning and memory.

The research team was excited with the anticipation of success as they made their final preparations. Rat A214 with the electrodes, sensors, and tiny cables all in place, had been lightly anesthetized to immobilize it, and was secured on a small platform directly over the maze.

Located below rat A214, and at the other end of the cables, rat A211 was being held at the entrance to the maze. It also had all the electrodes, sensors, and cables in place and was wearing a tiny harness device to keep the cables above the rat and out of the way to prevent the electrodes from being pulled from the brain. The rat was active and impatient to move around as it was being held prior to release. It had not been fed and was especially hungry.

Heather gave the rat a small bit of food to whet its appetite, and then released it to move into the maze. The rat stood still momentarily, shook itself as though trying to get rid of the harness, and then took off through the maze going directly to the food. Jessica and Heather both jumped up with squeals of glee, giving high fives to all the research team members. As the rat was busy eating its reward, Jessica gently picked it up and returned it to the entrance of the maze. Again the rat raced through the maze and returned to the food. However, the jubilation quickly turned to a rather somber silence as the small research team fully realized the great importance of their achievement and the potential impact on mankind.

Later that afternoon, all the instrumentation had been removed from the rats, and rat A211 was hungry again. Heather carefully placed rat A214 at the entrance to the maze, and it raced through the maze to the food. She then placed rat A211 in the maze, and it again displayed the frustration and stress of not knowing the route through the maze. Heather picked up A211 and placed it back in its cage and fed it. She softly stroked the rat as she thanked it for its contribution to science.

Heather and Jessica were very quiet as they wrote their detailed notes on the amazing experiment.

Two days later, Jessica, Dr. Laird, Dr. Judy Clark, and Heather Shelby were huddled in the laboratory conference room in a very intense discussion. Dr. Laird was a handsome man in his early forties. Over six feet tall, athletic build with broad shoulders and a small waist. An outstanding golfer and a good tennis player. He was greatly respected by his peers and loved by all the nurses on the hospital staff. Through his many accomplishments in the field of neurosurgery, and several published papers in medical journals, he had acquired an international reputation. He and Dr. Judy Clark played tennis regularly as doubles partners and were a tough combination to beat, having twice won the county mixed doubles championship.

He was looking intently at Jessica as he asked, "Tell us again what you and Heather recorded in your research notes on the experiments with the rats. I know what you said, but I find it so very fascinating that it's almost beyond belief! I want to hear it again."

Jessica repeated her report. "Two days ago we were continuing the Alzheimer's research with our rats. Two of our laboratory rats, A211 and A214, were trained to find their way through a certain maze to get the food at the end of the maze. The rats went through identical training, and both learned quickly how to take the correct route to the food.

"A gene in rat A211 was carefully altered to simulate Alzheimer's disease. As the change took over the brain in rat A211, the rat lost its recollection of how to find its way through the maze. All efforts to retrain it failed. The rat would become very frustrated by taking wrong turns and not finding the food."

She continued, "Then I became curious. I was thinking about whether or not it would be possible for rat A211 to borrow, or share, the memory of rat A214? Could rat A211 tap into the memory of rat A214 to find the route to the food?"

Heather commented, "At first I thought Jessica had lost her mind, but the more I thought about it, and the results of all of our experiments, the more I thought it might be feasible."

Jessica went on, "Our initial thinking focused on maybe trying to down-load the memory from A214 into a computer and then feed it into the brain of A211. But in what form would the download communication come through?"

"Would it be electric impulses from the neural network in some digitized mode, or would it be electro-chemical images? And then what type of receptor would we need to receive and interpret the communications from the brain so that it could be translated into the computer? With our computer, we've searched thoroughly the world of neuroscience, but the answers to our questions cannot be answered."

"In the future, we'll have the answers as to how to do these things, but not yet. Therefore, we concentrated on the transfer of memory using a rat brain to transmit the information, and a similar rat brain to receive and read, or translate, the communication."

Dr. Laird and Dr. Clark both asked the same question simultaneously, "Have you actually tried to transfer memory in the rats?"

Just then the telephone on the conference table rang, and Jessica picked up the phone. "Hello, yes Lisa. Oh, damn, I completely forgot! Please show her into my office."

Jessica looked over to her guests to explain. "My friend from Washington, Cheryl Crockett, arrived this morning to visit, and in my excitement to tell you of our experiment, I completely forgot she was coming. I have asked Lisa to show her the way to our conference. Does anyone object to her joining us?"

Dr. Laird said, "I have no objection if you can be quite certain that Mrs. Crockett will keep this information confidential. This research information could have worldwide ramifications, so it is vitally important to keep it confidential. What do you think, Judy?"

Dr. Judy Clark responded, "Michael, I concur 100 per cent with your comments. However, I know Cheryl and her background, and I feel that she is completely trustworthy."

Jessica got up and walked to the door to greet Lisa and Cheryl. Jessica and Cheryl gave each other a hug, and Jessica introduced Cheryl to Dr. Laird.

Lisa smiled at the group and said, "I'm one of those old fashioned secretaries who serves refreshments to our guests! Who wants coffee, tea, or a soft drink? The doughnuts are all gone!"

While the group exchanged pleasantries with Cheryl, Lisa served the group their drinks and departed with a smile. Jessica quickly briefed Cheryl on the content of their discussion. Cheryl expressed amazement with what they were discussing and indicated her appreciation for being allowed to listen. She also voluntarily stated that she would keep confidential anything that was discussed.

Dr. Laird exclaimed, "Jessica, please continue! I am dying to hear your answer as to whether or not you have actually tried the transfer of memory."

Jessica stated, "Yes, as a matter of fact, we have managed to successfully transfer memory from rat A214 to rat A211. Even more interesting, with the sensors between the two rats intact, and rat A214 immobilized, rat A211 used its memory and the memory of A214 to successfully work through the maze. We are so excited about what this may mean if the procedure can be reproduced successfully in human beings."

Dr. Laird said, "This is fantastically exciting news with all kinds of potential ramifications. You know that I will work with you in any capacity to continue the research. But, we know there is a long road ahead before it can be demonstrated and approved for use on human beings."

Jessica nodded her head in agreement, "Yes, we're well aware of all the work that lies ahead; in fact we're in the planning stage now for additional funding for continuation of our work."

Dr. Judy Clark was excited and proud; excited about the tremendous possibilities of the research, and extremely proud of her research team, Jessica and Heather.

Dr. Clark proclaimed that both she and Dr. Laird would back the project and that funding should not be a problem. Dr. Laird said he fully agreed with Dr. Clark and again stated his willingness to participate whenever the research team requested his help.

Cheryl commented, "I have never been so flabbergasted in my life. I arrive here to spend a leisurely few days with Jessica and her family, and I'm immediately allowed to listen to the most dramatic discussion I have ever heard. I am astounded that you all can remain calm and collected as though this happens every day. I am anxious to hear about future plans and results. If I didn't have a job and a husband, I would move here just for the chance to work at the lab and keep abreast of your progress. Thank you all so very much for allowing me to sit in on this historic meeting."

Jessica and Heather looked at each other and laughed. Heather said, "Sure, Cheryl, we can just see you moving down here. Scott would arrive by jet and take you home before you could even unpack!"

Dr. Laird said, "It's nearly time for lunch; I'm starved! Let's go eat and it's on me. I want to hear more about the details of the procedures used in connecting the memories of the rats."

With that, the group left for Club 36 and a warm reception by Dan Roberts. Dan and Michael had been good friends for many years. Dan was an accomplished watercolor artist and had won many awards at art shows throughout the nation. Michael dabbled in watercolors and was a collector of Dan's paintings. They also shared a love for music, especially jazz and zydeco. Dan was glad to see Cheryl again, as she had become very close to Jessica's circle of friends.

Dr. Laird sat between Jessica and Heather, and was deeply involved in the details of the procedures that she and Heather had devised to achieve the transfer of memory. Cheryl was telling the others that Scott had been extremely busy on several urgent assignments in Europe and the Mideast, and that gave her ample time to visit her friends in Fayetteville. She explained she had become interested in Jessica's parents' craft and antique business, and had been doing some special shopping for Mavis and Steve in the Washington and Virginia area. She had shipped three boxes through, and they were at the airport.

Since the medical group wanted to return to the laboratory to further discuss the research program and its funding, Dan offered to take Cheryl to the airport to pick up the boxes, and then on to the home of Mavis and Steve where she would be staying. Cheryl was soon settled in for the week and was going through the boxes of antique items with Mavis.

At the laboratory, Dr. Judy Clark was on the telephone talking to Rebecca Coles, the Federal Administrator for Research Grants to American Universities. Dr. Judy had tracked Ms Coles to Purdue University in Lafayette, Indiana, where she was attending a seminar. Dr. Judy quickly reviewed with Rebecca the recent developments in the Fulbright Research Laboratory.

Then she posed the question, "Rebecca, this is indeed a monumental achievement, and we want to broaden the scope of this work as quickly as possible. However, we don't want to attract media attention until we run many more confirmation tests. Would it be possible for you to meet with us in the next few days?"

Rebecca responded, "Judy, that is great news. The seminar here is winding up this afternoon. I was flying back to Washington in the morning, but I can certainly revise my plans and be in Fayetteville by noon tomorrow. From what you have told me, we should have no problem in expanding the program and obtaining additional funding."

Dr. Judy said, "Thank you so very much for your support. Have your secretary advise me of your arrival time and I'll be at the airport to meet you. Incidentally, Cheryl Crockett, Jessica's friend from Washington, D.C., is here for a visit and Jessica's parents are having a barbecue tomorrow evening. They definitely will want you to join the party. I know you will enjoy it, so pack some casual clothes."

With the visit set, the research group went about making plans not only for the next day, but also for a little celebrating during the weekend.

Rebecca Coles arrived Friday morning. After having lunch with Jessica, Heather, and Dr. Judy, the research group met to lay out the formal plan for the additional funding that would be required to accelerate the memory transfer program. In addition to the group that met for lunch, the others in attendance were Dr. Michael Laird, and Drs. Robert and Sue Cantrell.

The Cantrells were husband and wife with individual private practices. Both participated in the research programs at the university. Dr. Bob Cantrell was a cardio-vascular surgeon and Dr. Sue Cantrell was an anesthesiologist specializing in neurosurgery. She often worked with Dr. Laird, and the two had collaborated on several medical textbooks.

The meeting lasted about four hours and much was achieved in terms of laying out the needs for additional staffing, increased computer support, and the promise of the doctors involved to allocate as much of their time to the project as was required. They all recognized the potential of this program.

Rebecca Coles had been on the phone to her superiors three times during the meeting, and when the gathering was concluded, all were in agreement on the accelerated research program plans. They had secured tentative approval of the Federal funding needed. Dr. Judy Clark had also secured approval for the university funds that would be required.

That evening the entire group met at the lakefront home of Mavis and Steve, an A-frame house with a huge front deck that overlooked Beaver Lake. The lake was large and located about fifteen miles north of Fayetteville. It provided good recreational boating, water skiing, and fishing.

As the group arrived, Steve served drinks and Dan Roberts and Dr. Bob Cantrell were doing the barbecuing. Mavis and Cheryl set up the buffet while all the rest were busily chatting.

After enjoying the barbecue and buffet, the group scattered in small groups on the deck and on the boat dock, watching the sunset across the lake.

Steve and Dr. Bob Cantrell fished for bass from the dock, their conversation carrying out across the water. Dan and Dr. Michael Laird sat on a bench watching the two fishermen and talking about music in New Orleans, possibly a trip to Mardi Gras. Heather, Rebecca Coles, Dr. Judy, Dr. Sue Cantrell, and Anita Roberts sat on the deck, drinking coffee and chatting. Rob and Jessica were at the far end watching the fading sunset. Jessica was on Rob's lap with her head on his shoulder. They were talking about how good their lives were, how lucky they were to have such fine friends, and the great careers they were experiencing.

Cheryl and Mavis sat on the deck steps and engaged in a rather serious conversation.

Cheryl was saying, "I'm used to Scott being gone for several days or a week at a time, but this time he's been gone for three weeks with very few phone calls to me. I talked with him two days ago, and he sounded tired and under stress. You know how it is, after you're married for so long, you can read your husband well. I just know that Scott is involved in a very serious situation, and I'm extremely worried! I know that I can trust you and confide in you, Mavis, and I just have to talk to someone about my concerns.

"Scott is an operations officer in the CIA. Max Thorn is also a CIA agent and works for Scott. The travel agency is a front for a CIA unit. Both Scott and Max have been in the Mideast for three weeks with very few calls to anyone that I know of with the exception of Rozann. All she will tell me is that both are busy and okay. The group in the travel agency has been working night and day. As you would expect, they are sworn to secrecy and can't tell me anything about what is going on.

"Frank Hughes, the Vice-President, visited in the office for a short meeting with the group. He stopped in my office very briefly, and said that Scott is fine and sends his love. He gave me a hug, a kiss on the cheek, and then he was gone. When he was about to leave, I overheard him tell someone to call and have Double-D ready to leave in three hours."

Cheryl continued, "Double-D refers to the plane and pilots that Scott uses for certain special assignments. The plane is a Gulfstream V which is an ultra long range business jet equipped for CIA business. The Double-D refers to pilots Darrel and David.

"I've known them both for a number of years. Both are good men and great pilots. From what I heard, Frank Hughes must be flying to join Scott and Max wherever they are. I know that they are all extremely capable men, but if they're involved with a radical group, you don't know what may happen!"

Mavis put her arm around Cheryl. "There is nothing you can do, Cheryl, except to keep your faith in Scott and all his associates. They are strong, capable individuals who are certainly doing something necessary on behalf of our country. Keep saying your prayers, and I know that God will bring them back safe and sound."

Mavis continued, "I must say, you did shock me when you told me that Scott works for the CIA. You two kept a good cover, I'm sure no one here has the faintest idea of what Scott really does. You have my word that I won't tell anyone of this discussion.

"Cheryl, since your office knows how to reach you, why don't you stay here with Steve and me for a while? We'd love to have you, and we'll keep you occupied so your mind is off your worries!"

Cheryl looked at Mavis and smiled, "Thank you so very much, Mavis. I would appreciate staying with you for a time as I feel at home here, and I can feel your love and support."

CHAPTER 6.

FAR AWAY IN THE UNITED Arab Emirates, a different kind of action was being taken. In the city of Abu Dhabi, Amahl and Lattah were driving to the international airport to meet Dr. Dimitri Ivankov, a Russian nuclear weapons expert who at one time was a very important part of the Russian nuclear arms program. With the collapse of the Russian military structure, the nuclear arms program was in shambles, leaving many scientists out of work with no income and no prospects for employment in Russia.

It took Amahl three weeks to locate Ivankov. To support his family, Ivankov had been selling his expertise to Iraq to help in their efforts to rebuild a nuclear weapons arsenal. Israeli air strikes had previously destroyed a nuclear reactor near Baghdad in June of 1981, claiming that the reactor could be used to produce nuclear weapons.

Iraq suffered further setbacks in their nuclear programs when the U.S.-led coalition soundly defeated the Iraq forces in four days after they had invaded Kuwait. A number of Russian nuclear scientists were recruited to get the Iraqi nuclear program going once more. With UN trade sanctions and UN inspection of all their weapons programs, the Iraqi nuclear programs had come to a virtual standstill except for a few clandestine efforts that were hidden from UN observers.

However, with the assassination attempts on President Saddam Hussein and his son, and the degree of unrest in Iraq, Saddam accelerated the development of nuclear weapons. Ivankov was anxious to take advantage of these opportunities. He was fifty-one years old, and with no prospects for a future in Russia, he was open to any offers and had little concern for the ethics of a particular cause.

Petr Karshev, Amahl's contact in the Russian mafia put Amahl in touch with Ivankov. Amahl explained that he had a definite need for a man with Ivankov's qualifications. They arranged a meeting and Ivankov was soon to arrive at the airport in Abu Dhabi. Ivankov, a tall slender man, slightly balding, with a barely perceptible limp, walked up the ramp to meet Amahl and Lattah. He wore a bright red tie and a wristwatch on his right wrist as additional identification for Amahl to pick him out of the arriving passengers.

As Amahl stood back and surveyed the situation, Lattah walked to the ramp and quickly recognized Ivankov.

"Dr. Ivankov! Over here!" Lattah called out. "My name is Lattah, and I am an associate of Amahl Jabel. Hope you had a comfortable flight."

Ivankov smiled and held out his hand. "Hello, Lattah. My pleasure to meet you, and, yes, I had a very good flight. Where is Amahl Jabel?"

Lattah responded, "Amahl is here; he had a phone call to make just as your plane arrived at the gate, and I'm sure he will appear quickly."

As soon as Lattah said that, Amahl approached with his hand outstretched. "Dr. Ivankov it's nice to meet you, and thank you for coming here to listen to our proposition."

For the next three hours over lunch, Amahl laid out what he wanted from Ivankov, and how much he was willing to pay.

Without revealing the details, he explained, "We want several one-megaton nuclear weapons loaded into containers and then intricate timing devices installed to explode each of them at appropriate times. I'll pay you 50,000 American dollars up front, 50,000 American dollars when you finish loading and arming the devices, and 50,000 American dollars after the devices are successfully exploded.

"You will tell no one of this proposition. I must tell you that Omar Habash, head of security for Col. Qaddafi of Libya is sponsoring this effort, and any violation of security regarding this project could result in your death. However, if you can keep your mouth shut, you can earn 150,000 American dollars for about two or three weeks of work."

Ivankov was clearly shocked by all elements of the radical proposition: first, by the fact that these people had somehow obtained major nuclear weapons; second, at the destruction that could be caused by an attack with multiple nuclear weapons. However, he was willing to subordinate any feelings of apprehension or guilt to the exciting thought of having the 150,000 American dollars.

After a pause to digest all he had heard, Ivankov spoke to Amahl, "How did you manage to get such nuclear weapons?"

Amahl looked at Ivankov sternly and said, "I've told you all you need to know. Do not ask any questions, as I will tell you nothing more. I've told you what is expected of you and what you will be paid. Now I need to know, are you interested?"

Ivankov quickly turned things over in his mind. He recognized that he was dealing with a radical terrorist, and that if he refused the deal, he well might be murdered before he left Abu Dhabi. Omar Habash sponsored Ivankov believed Amahl when he said the project since he had no way of knowing that Amahl was lying. Ivankov had heard of Omar Habash and knew that he was a man to be feared. He could reach into any

Mideastern, Asian, or European country to murder or torture an individual.

Ivankov was inclined to say yes for that reason alone, but also the money was a big factor. To walk away today with 50,000 American dollars, and then to get the additional 50,000 in a few weeks, with 50,000 more to come when the deed was done, was intoxicating to Dr. Dimitri Ivankov. In fact, he envisioned future work with Amahl with the prospects of making hundreds of thousands of dollars. He rationalized that somebody would do the work for Amahl even if he didn't, so he might as well be the one to make the money.

He stuck out his hand to signify agreement. "We have a deal. I can do all the things you want done with the assurance that everything will work exactly as you plan. I understand the security requirements as I have worked in a security-tight atmosphere my whole career. I have no further questions except to ask when you want me back. I assume you will pay the first $50,000 before I leave?"

Amahl shook hands with Ivankov and nodded agreement. "You will receive the $50,000 before you leave today. I'll expect you back here within five days. When you return, call the office number on this card, and tell my secretary that the merchandise from Iraq has arrived in Abu Dhabi. Give her your local number where I can reach you."

Then Lattah reached into her bag and retrieved four large envelopes, each containing 12,500 American dollars, and handed them to Ivankov who tucked them into his coat pockets.

Amahl said, "One last thing, Demitri. When you leave Baghdad, tell your Iraqi people that you are returning to Moscow for a short leave. As a precautionary measure, take a flight to St. Petersburg in case you are followed. Then re-ticket and fly from there to Abu Dhabi."

Ivankov indicated agreement and shook hands with Amahl and Lattah as he started down the ramp for his return flight to

Iraq. In four days, Ivankov was back in Abu Dhabi where he found an inexpensive apartment in which to live for the next several weeks. He contacted Amahl, and arrangements were made to start work the following day.

The next morning Amahl drove to pick up Ivankov at his apartment and proceeded to the secret warehouse where the nuclear weapons were stored. A chain-link fence that was eight feet high with razor barbed wire on its top surrounded the warehouse. Amahl waved to the security guard as he drove through the gate that was opened for him. He drove to the side entrance of the warehouse, and used a remote device to open the large sliding door that permitted him to entrance into the building.

Amahl parked the car and got out, motioning Ivankov to follow him. They walked through the building, which was full of new and used repair parts for ocean-going vessels, primarily tankers. In the far corner of the building was a small maintenance shop with metalworking tools and welding equipment.

Amahl turned to Ivankov and, smiling, said, "This will be your office for the next several weeks. Stacked over there are the eighteen propane tanks on which we will be working. In that darkened area across the aisle and under the tarps are the nuclear devices. Join me at that desk and I'll show you the plans I want you to follow."

Amahl continued, "When you examine the tanks, you will notice that eight of them are different. The ends of the tanks have interior hinges that can be unlatched and swung upward so that both ends of the tank are open. Three one-quarter inch thick steel straps extend from both ends of the tank at the sides and bottom positions. Three large set screws in the appropriate positions in the dish-shaped ends of the tank are attached into the steel straps and keep the ends of the tank securely fastened when closed."

Amahl had ordered the edges of the ends to be beveled to facilitate welding the ends closed, so that the tanks could be used to carry propane after the demonstration period was completed. He had done this in an effort to allay suspicion about the use of the eight tanks. He also had ordered the eight tanks to be built to special specifications, so they could be used in demonstrations of the interior construction and valve features.

He then opened a desk drawer, and pulled it all the way out to expose a locked compartment. He retrieved a key from his pocket and opened the compartment. He withdrew a pencil sketch of the placement of the nuclear weapons and timing devices in the tanks.

Amahl looked at Ivankov and told him, "Study these very carefully. Observe what I have designed and then make what changes you think are necessary to accommodate the end result I am after. Keep in mind that you are the only person who will have seen these sketches, so if any word is divulged, I'll know the source of the betrayal.

"Special attention must be given as to how to secure the weapons inside the tanks. The tanks will be moved by ship and will be subjected to rough handling, possibly being dropped several feet by a crane. The timing devices must have a time range of at least three months, preferably 120 days, and must be a dual system, so that if one fails, the backup system will take over.

"When you have answers to these design requirements, call me at my apartment. Time is of the essence, so please proceed as rapidly as you can. If you exceed my expectations as to the time required and the quality of the design, there will be a substantial bonus for you! Keep the sketches with you at all times and do not copy them."

With that, Amahl stood up and left the building.

CHAPTER 7.

IN THE FRANKFURT OFFICE OF the CIA, a meeting was underway. In attendance were Scott Crockett, Max Thorn, Colm O'Hara, Director of the CIA Frank Hughes, Vice President Sergei Andropov, personal representative of Russian President Nicolai Padrov, overseeing matters of Russian national security Dayle Sutton, CIA officer in charge of the CIA Frankfurt office, and a newcomer to the group by the name of Ali Hassan.

Ali was an Algerian born CIA agent who for several years had been working very closely with Scott and Max. Ali was an imposing figure with an athletic build, dark features, and a broad smile that flashed brilliant white teeth. He was a little over 200 pounds, 6'4" tall, with a small waist, broad shoulders, and bulging biceps that reflected his fitness discipline and his expertise in martial arts.

Frank Hughes, as the ranking official, presided and opened the meeting by stating that each individual would report his findings and then the group would decide the next course of action. He first requested Colm O'Hara review any pertinent new information that he and Davis Benson, National Security Advisor, had found in Washington through their massive review of all recent information fed into CIA and National Security Agency computers from around the world.

Colm leaned forward in his chair and started his summary of potential situations or terrorist activities that might relate to the problem they faced. "Since our last meeting, Davis and I have had a team of forty-six agents covering three shifts and working twenty-four hours a day, reviewing every bit of information from American agents around the world, as well as information brought in by intelligence operations of our western nation allies who have been alerted to the situation.

"In the Central Intelligence Agency, we have the Directorate of Operations and the Directorate of Science and Technology feeding information to the Directorate of Intelligence where it is reviewed by the particular office whose expertise is in that specific geographic location or to a specific issue or kind of analysis.

"It would seem obvious that we can assume that none of our western allies would be involved in the theft and nothing in the analysis indicated as much. Also, we have concluded that other major non-western nations such as Japan, China, and India would not be involved in a scheme to purchase eight nuclear weapons. Therefore, we have focused primarily on events in the Balkans, Eastern Europe, the Mideast, and certain countries in North Africa."

He continued, "We very carefully compiled all of our information from sources in Chechnya so that Sergei can compare our information with what he has from his Russian sources. Our concern in Chechnya stemmed from the recent terrorist attacks in southern Russia that were aimed at disrupting the peace process being carried on by Russia and Chechnya.

"With the election of Asian Maskhadov, the candidate that Russia preferred as President of Chechnya, and the five year peace treaty signed by both countries as an effort to define their relationships, it seemed that tensions had subsided. However, even though those recent terrorist attacks are of concern, we found nothing of any significance that may help us."

Colm swiveled in his chair and faced a large world map that covered one wall of the conference room and pointed to Turkey. "At this time, there is absolutely nothing reported that may implicate Turkey. The Turkish government is having its ongoing skirmishes and problems with the Kurds. They are heavily involved with Russia in negotiations to double the capacity of its natural gas pipeline from Russia.

"It is a $13.5 billion, twenty-five year deal and is of major importance to the Turks. At this point in their negotiations, there is no way they would condone any actions to steal eight nuclear weapons. We are well aware of Prime Minister Necmettin Erbakan's anti-western rhetoric and his Islamic tilt, but he is closely held in check by the Turkish military."

Colm turned around in his chair to face the group. "As you might expect, we looked very carefully at Iran and Iraq, particularly Iran since Iraq has been, and is being, closely monitored after the Gulf war. Information from not only our own sources, but from Saudi and Israeli intelligence authorities, focused on a group of Shiite Muslims, particularly the activities of Brig. Ahmad Sherifi, a senior Iranian intelligence officer and a top official in Iran's Revolutionary Guard.

"He had been closely associated with a Saudi Shiite arrested recently in Canada, Hani Abdel Rahim Hussein Sayegh. Canadian authorities identified Sayegh as a direct participant in the bombing of the American military compound in Saudi Arabia. He is a member of the Saudi Hezbollah, an Iranian backed group of Shiite Muslims.

"Brig. Sherifi's duties include organizing Hezbollah cells in Arab countries around the Persian Gulf. He is well known to Saudi officials due to his involvement in several restaurant and hotel bombings in Bahrain. Israeli and Saudi agents have closely watched him and nothing in his activities indicates involvement in the theft of the nuclear weapons. Sayegh was in jail in Canada with all his communications being monitored at the time of the theft, so we feel that he was not involved.

"Several days ago President Hartmann summoned Palestinian Authority President Yasser Arafat and Palestinian Security Chief Jibril Rajoub to a secret meeting at Camp David. They were transported by the Air Force and taken to Camp David by helicopter at night under the cover of darkness. There was a blackout of information about the meeting.

"Only Davis Benson, Jordan Henning, and I had knowledge of the meeting and only Davis and I were in the meeting. The President's personal staff, the Cabinet, Congressional leaders, and all agency directors were not informed of the meeting. World leaders, with the exception of Russian President Nicolai Padrov, also were not informed."

Colm continued, "Knowing Arafat's desperate need for American support in his struggle with Israel in the peace negotiations, President Hartmann gambled on Arafat's confidential support, cooperation, and pledge of honesty. Before the President related the situation to them, he requested that they swear the meeting would be held in complete secrecy without any part of it being divulged to anyone. He stated that any leaks of information would result in extremely serious repercussions in all relations between the Palestinians and the American and Russian governments.

"The President then laid out the complete problem and requested their help in preventing the possible deaths of tens of millions of innocent people, many of whom could be Palestinians. The resulting chaos and instability of societies and governments throughout the world would benefit no one. We would be returned to the dark ages with sickness, famine, and starvation rampant in every country.

"He explained that the focus of the investigation was becoming centered on the Middle East and that he needed any knowledge they might have of any such theft having been carried out by splinter groups of the Muslim extremists from Hamas and the Islamic Jihad.

"To briefly summarize the meeting, both Arafat and Rajoub pledged to the President that they had absolutely no knowledge of such theft, and that they shared the concern for the safety of our planet. Arafat directed Rajoub to immediately and discreetly investigate any possible lead. Arafat will keep the President informed. Arafat has requested the President to direct this group to keep Arafat's involvement confidential, and the President has given his word that this group will never reveal information about that meeting."

Colm continued, "We looked at Libya and found nothing of real importance. Since the retaliation bombing in 1986, that injured Muammar Qaddafi and killed his infant daughter, he has been relatively quiet. We know he has continued providing facilities for the training of terrorists, but there is no recent activity that would link Libya to the theft. In reviewing Algeria, we found nothing of any consequences.

"President Liamine Zeroual is heavily involved in repelling rebel attacks against his government. Islamic militants slit the throats of thirty-two civilians and beheaded many of them. The government and the rebels are too involved with civil warfare and would have no need for nuclear weapons."

Colm stood up, stretched, and then continued. "We have reviewed all activity reports of every known terrorist group in Bosnia, Siberia, Croatia, Slovenia, Romania, Montenegro, Albania, and Macedonia. "We have found absolutely nothing that would give us any lead to the group that has done this.

"I dislike coming to this meeting with no helpful information, but it certainly isn't because of lack of effort. Our agents worked hundreds of long hours sorting out all the information from around the world, and, of course, they will continue searching for information. Frank, I'll turn the meeting back to you."

Frank shook his head and took a sip of coffee. "It really is frustrating to have no leads in this matter. As you know, I was in Algeria a few weeks ago, and I can readily concur with your evaluation of the situation there. During the past week, with the authorization of President Hartmann, I have talked confidentially with the heads of state in Egypt, Saudi Arabia and Jordan.

"All have expressed extreme concern over this threat of tremendous potential damage and harm to the world's entire population, and they have all pledged their support in tracking down the group involved. However, there is not a single clue as to who is involved."

Frank looked at Scott, Max, and Ali, "I hope to God that you three or Sergei has something to help us. I feel that time is so important, and it appears that we are at a standstill."

Scott leaned forward in his chair, "During the past two weeks we have been talking with every one of our agents, spies, and plants in the Mideast. We have nothing concrete, but we did find a few things that could be leads as to whom we are looking for. Ali, tell the group what you found out under cover in Algeria and Libya."

The group turned their attention to Ali, a very unusual individual in every way. Aside from his great intellect and tremendous build, he had a most interesting personality and countenance. He was very positive and radiated confidence. His facial features appeared to have a perpetual smile. In fact, you could visualize him smiling as he stuck a large knife in your gut and twisted it!

Ali related a very interesting development. "While contacting all my informants in Algeria, I ran across an old friend I hadn't seen in quite a few years. He had just returned from Libya where he had been working on a security detail for Omar Habash. You are all acquainted with that name?"

All indicated they knew who Habash was and what he represented.

Ali smiled and continued, "My friend was very angry with Habash as he had been promised a higher rank in the organization and then didn't get the appointment. He consequently quit the job. Furthermore, he said he was cheated out of a month's wages. I told him I was doing some work for a Canadian oil company and perhaps could find him a position later on.

"We spent two evenings together, and I listened carefully to his experiences in Libya. It seems that he and the nephew of Habash went through a terrorist school or camp together and had become fairly well acquainted. In fact, it was through the nephew that he met Habash and got the job he had in Libyan security. The nephew had left Libya, and my friend hadn't seen him in seven or eight years.

"For some reason, he went on reminiscing about his experiences in Libya and the days he spent in the terrorist school in Sebha with Habash's nephew whose name was Amahl Jabel. He told of Amahl being a radical terrorist with a deep hatred of anything to do with Western culture or society. As he recalled, the hatred stemmed from something bad that had happened to his family when he was a young child in Sidi-bel-Abbe s.

"I asked him if he stayed in touch with his friend and he told me no, that they had not been that close. However, he did know Amahl had organized his own small terrorist group, but he hadn't heard of any of their activities, or if they even had a name for their group. He also recalled that Habash had communicated with his nephew several times someplace in the United Arab Emirates, it might have been Abu Dhabi.

"We talked for another hour or so about past experiences, and then I told him I had an appointment early the next day and that I would then be leaving town, but that I would be returning in several weeks. He gave me his address, and I assured him I would be seeing him again very soon. I then spent three days in Libya in contacting several of my best informants. I could learn nothing more about Amahl Jabel.

"There is much fear of Omar Habash and how he might retaliate if crossed. It strikes me that it is very strange that we have no information regarding Amahl Jabel or his group. Where are they based? What are they after and why are they so quiet?

"My friend said Amahl had been gone from Libya for seven or eight years. Why would a group of terrorists be organized and active for that many years and never be heard of? I don't like the smell of this at all. I would suggest we pursue this lead as quickly and as thoroughly as possible!"

Frank Hughes was excited. "Great work, Ali! This may be our big break! My God, what luck it was that you ran into your friend. Maybe more than luck; it was providence."

Colm O'Hara was on his feet. "Well done, Ali! Before we start making plans to pursue this, let's hear from Sergei as he may have more pieces that may fit into our puzzle."

Sergei smiled, "I do have some pieces that could very well fit. Four days ago, the military truck that was stolen and apparently had carried the nuclear weapons was found in the harbor at St. Petersburg. There were two Russian men lashed to the truck, both had been shot in the head, and both have been identified with mafia connections.

"The tarp covering the truck bed had torn loose, becoming entwined with two empty petrol cans, and it all was floating on the surface of the water, although still attached to the truck. Because of where the truck was found, it is our opinion that the weapons left St. Petersburg by boat.

"Of course, it is entirely possible that the truck was dumped into the harbor to mislead us. However, because the truck was well-hidden and we only found it because the tarp tore loose, it seems more logical that the weapons were taken first to a warehouse prior to leaving the country, assuming that they have indeed left the country."

He continued, "We are running checks on all vessels into St. Petersburg the week before the theft and all vessels leaving St. Petersburg the week after the theft. I am particularly interested in any vessel that arrived within seventy-eight hours of the theft and any vessel that departed within forty-eight hours of the theft. We should be able to reduce the number of possible carriers of the weapons to a very few within two days. We are also searching every warehouse in the St. Petersburg waterfront.

"The two mafia men who were executed and ditched with the truck were known to be associated with a mafia group run by an ex-military colonel with the name of Petr Karshev. He is ruthless and runs a very efficient and effective mafia operation with a great deal of political and military influence. He and his entire organization are under complete surveillance.

"We have one mafia defector, an informer, who initially told us he wanted to get back at Karshev for allowing his brother to be murdered in St. Petersburg. His brother was one of the two men found in the submerged truck. Now he will say nothing; no doubt Karshev has somehow gotten to him, threatening him or his family. He is being held in protective custody and my men are continuing to interrogate him.

"It appears to me that there is no doubt that the mafia is responsible for the theft of the weapons. And based on the information provided by Ali, there is a very good possibility that there is a link between Amahl Jabel and Petr Karshev."

Scott was nodding his head. "I agree fully, Sergei, and we must move fast. This person, Amahl, intrigues me. Max and I have talked to many contacts in Egypt, Israel, Jordan, Saudi Arabia, and Turkey, and we haven't heard one word about this Amahl or his organization.

"What worries me is that if Amahl and his group have these weapons and they have been quiet all these years, you can bet they have an extremely well-conceived plan that could be in the process of being implemented as we sit here. We must really get on this thing hot and heavy!"

After three hours of reviewing and planning, and several phone calls to Presidents Hartmann and Padrov, the group was ready to move. Sergei and Dayle Sutton would fly to St. Petersburg to push on the search of the warehouses and be in touch with the investigation of Petr Karshev in Moscow.

Dayle Sutton would be the coordinator of all information flowing between Sergei and him in Russia, and Scott, Max, and Ali in the Mideast. All information would be coded and flow through the CIA office in Frankfurt. Scott and Max would fly to Saudi Arabia to again talk with their contacts for information on Amahl Jabel and then work their way into the United Arab Emirates.

Ali would fly directly to Abu Dhabi and start the search for the location of Amahl Jabel and his group of terrorists. Frank Hughes and Colm O'Hara would fly back to Washington to meet with President Hartmann and Benson Davis. Colm was anxious to meet with Benson and get all the massive computers going in a search for any particles of information on Amahl Jabel, and, also, to review satellite photos of the shipping traffic out of St. Petersburg during the week after the theft and then to track the route of each of the vessels.

Chapter 8.

LATTAH HAD BEEN VERY BUSY on assignment for Oman Oil. She was leasing new strategically located facilities for parts storage, propane tank storage, tank demonstrations and repairs in eight major cities of the world. Lattah explained to the warehouse and retail store rental agents that since harbor front storage space was quite expensive, her company preferred lower cost satellite storage space for low usage repair items and for propane tank showings for special applications.

Such space could be away from the waterfront and in a low cost warehouse or storefront facility in the inner city. That was the story presented in all of the eight cities in which warehouse and demonstration facilities were leased. All of the leasing contracts were sent to Amahl Jabel, Director of Warehousing and Traffic for the Oman Oil Company. All of the leases were for six months with an option to renew for an additional six months.

These were to be considered trial periods. However, Lattah made the point that Oman Oil Company had every intention of eventually signing lucrative five-year leases that would make any rental agent very happy. Amahl signed all of the contracts and returned them with cashier's checks paid for out of the terrorist drug income. Oman Oil Company officials never knew of these worldwide transactions. Lattah carefully selected the location for each of the eight nuclear bombs as the epicenter for maximum destruction.

Lattah and Amahl picked Rome as the first city since they considered Rome one of the cornerstones of Western civilization. The city represented over 2,500 years of unparalleled cultural accomplishment, the Western culture that the two terrorists despised. Rome, the Eternal City, the capital of the Roman Empire, the world center of the Catholic Church. A strategic placement of the nuclear bomb would wipe out all vestiges of the Eternal City, the heart of the Catholic Church, and a great Western civilization city.

Lattah chose a small store on Portico d'Ottavia, a street near the Theater of Marcellus and the Capitoline Museum located in the heart of Rome. She smiled as she signed the lease after it was explained to her by the real estate broker during their lunch at Giggetto's restaurant, a short distance from the leased property. She was thinking how pleased Amahl would be with her choice of that location.

It was almost exactly in the center of the Raccordo Anulare, a major road that is a huge circle with a radius of six miles from the center of the city, tying together the roads that lead into the city like spokes in a wheel. With the one-megaton bomb placed at that location, the blast would effectively destroy most people and structures within the ring described by the Raccordo Anulare. A large segment of Rome's three million population would be incinerated or suffer slow painful deaths caused by radiation burns or flying debris.

The blast would wipe out the Vatican City and all the administrative offices of the Catholic Church. The Palazzo del Quirinale, the residence of the President of the Republic; the Palazzo Chigi on the Piazza Colonna, the official residence of the Premier who serves as President of the Council of Ministers.

Also, the two houses of Parliament, the Chamber of Deputies housed in the Palazzo di Montecitorio and the Senate housed in the Palazzo Madama; the Palazzo di Giustizia on the right bank of the Tiber, which houses most of the law courts; the Palazzo del Viminale on the left bank houses the Ministry of the Interior; and the Ministry of Foreign Affairs at the northern end of Monte Mario on the right bank would all be completely destroyed along with all the personnel within those structures.

In addition, the headquarters of the Region of Latium, which embraces five provinces is on the Via Della Pisani; the Province of Rome is administered from the Palazzo Valentini on the Via Quattro Novembre; the Mayor of Rome and other city officials meet in the Palazzo Senatorio on the Piazza del Campidoglio; all of the foreign embassies; the colleges and universities, the Opera House, the Colosseum, all of the historical landmarks and symbols of Roman and Italian culture would suffer complete destruction.

Lattah flew out of Rome feeling very satisfied with what she had achieved. On the flight from Rome to Paris, Lattah reviewed maps of Paris and the locations of properties she had arranged to visit. She arrived at Orly Airport and took the courtesy bus to her hotel, the Orly Hilton. After checking into the hotel, she unpacked and made several calls to the brokers with whom she had appointments.

She immediately canceled appointments with two brokers since the third had two very good possibilities in precisely the location she had picked out in her study of the maps of Paris. Lattah met the broker at exactly 1:30 p.m., and by 3:00 she had inspected the properties and completed the deal. She signed the contract for a six-month lease with a verbal promise that a five-year contract was virtually a certainty following that trial period.

The particular building was quite small, but it was in the right location on Boulevard Saint Michel about two short blocks south of the intersection of Boulevard Saint Germain. A five mile radius from that spot would include most of Paris located within the Boulevard Peripherique, the major ring road that encircles Paris.

The nuclear bomb would obliterate all of the essential French government buildings, the foreign embassies, the French Military Academy, the Arc de Triomphe, the Eiffel Tower, the Archives Nationales, the Louvre, many of the fine cathedrals including the Notre Dame, the Pantheon; all of the important landmarks of the history of Paris would be leveled and burned. The city of Paris and most of its inhabitants would be gone.

Amahl will have exacted revenge for the deaths of his parents, which he blamed on the French Foreign Legion. Western civilization will have suffered the loss of another of its great cities. Lattah was becoming somewhat intoxicated with her perceived power as she considered the impact that she was going to have on history. A little orphan girl with only one name was going to change the world forever.

The following day she landed in Berlin at the Berlin Tegel Airport and took a taxi to her hotel, the Alsterhof, located at 5 Ausburger Strasse, just off of Kurfurstendamm. The Kurfurstendamm is the most famous boulevard in Berlin and a magnet for all visitors with its elegant shops, restaurants and cafes and all the many cinemas and theaters. She had selected the hotel on Ausburger Strasse because it was in the exact location she had pinpointed for the location of the bomb. With the broker, she inspected the small storeroom that had previously housed a bathroom accessories retail store.

Again, within two hours, she had toured the building, signed the six-month lease, and headed back to the hotel. The site she leased was on Augsburger Strasse, near the intersection of Joachimstafer Strasse. The damage to be inflicted on this great western city by the nuclear bomb in that location would be extensive. In addition to killing or maiming its 3.1 million inhabitants, it would destroy a major part of the unified German government.

Although the Bundesrat and eight federal ministries remained in Bonn, the Reichstag building had been remodeled and now housed the Bundestag, the lower house of parliament. The Reichstag and the many federal government offices surrounding the Reichstag would all be destroyed.

Lattah and Amahl had discussed whether the bomb should be placed in Bonn or Berlin. Although Bonn was the location of the German Chancellor and much of the administrative function as well as the Bundesrat, the upper house of parliament, they chose to bomb Berlin since it was the true heart of Germany and the destruction would be more symbolic.

From Berlin, Lattah flew to Brussels landing at the Brussels National Airport at Zanventem in the outskirts of Brussels and about six miles from the center of the city. For convenience, the rental broker suggested that Lattah stay at the Hilton Hotel with its mid-city location. Following her routine, she unpacked and then placed a call to the broker.

It was almost lunchtime and Lattah assumed that they would very likely meet for lunch and then inspect the properties. However, the broker was very apologetic in explaining that he had run into a conflict in his appointments and that he could not meet with her until later in the afternoon.

Lattah was quite upset with this unexpected change in plans. She quickly thought it over and decided it would be much more convenient to wait until 3:00 p.m. as was suggested than to show her anger and have to go through all the explanations to a different broker. She smoothly accepted his apology and arranged to meet in the lobby. She also described her appearance so he would recognize her.

Brussels had been chosen as a bomb target for symbolic reasons as the population kill would only be about a million people. The main targets were the international headquarters for the North Atlantic Treaty Organization (NATO), which was located on the Bruxelles-Zaventem Road, just east of the Avenue Leopold III, and also the headquarters of the European Economic Community.

The EEC headquarters was located at 200 rue de la Loi in the cross-shaped Berlaymont Building. That huge office building housed the 10,000 employees of the EEC, all of whom were the representatives of the twelve different western European countries that met in Brussels to promote industry and trade in their respective countries. Their mission: to improve the well being of the Western world!

The NATO organization is a regional defense alliance among all the western powers to unite their efforts for collective defense against the eastern block of the Soviet Union, the Eastern European nations, as well as certain Middle Eastern countries.

These two headquarters represented the economic and military alliances among all the western countries against the eastern bloc and third world countries. As such, they were prime targets for the hate-filled terrorists. The secondary targets were located in the eastern upper town, which houses the principal government buildings, including the Royal Palace and the Palace of the Nation.

Also, near the center of the blast would be the commercial quarter located in the western half of inner Brussels, referred to as the lower town. That area houses the domestic and foreign banking institutions and insurance firms, as well as an important European stock exchange.

Amahl had told Lattah of the hatred of the people of the Belgian Congo toward the Belgian government during the period that the Congo was a part of the Belgian Empire. There were stories of cruelty that the French/Flemish speaking Belgian military forces inflicted on the peoples of the Congo.

In his mind, Amahl equated this to the actions of the French Foreign Legion in Algiers, and he hated them intensely.

In 1960, uprisings in the Belgian Congo forced Belgium to withdraw from its African Empire. In June 1960, Belgian King Baudouin proclaimed the independence of the colony, which then became Zaire. Brussels would pay the price for being a focal point of western hostility towards the east!

In two hours, Lattah decided on the location of a small storeroom that had been a flower shop. It was several blocks north of the exact center of the area outlined by the Ring Road, but she felt it was just the location that was required. The shop was on the rue Nueve, just north of the rue du Fosse intersection.

The bomb blast would easily encompass the entire European Communities Headquarters and, with NATO Headquarters only three-and-a-half miles from the epicenter of the blast, it would be obliterated as well. At a table in the lobby of the Hilton, the six-month lease was signed, the two shook hands, and the broker left amidst the flurry of other business people in the lobby.

Suddenly a voice spoke out loudly, "Lattah! What are you doing here? Why didn't you tell us you were in town?"

Lattah froze in her tracks as she recognized the voice. It was the one thing that she feared could happen even though the odds against it were astronomical. The voice was that of Albert Mailian, the manager of the Brussels dock operations for Oman Oil Company. He was a frequent visitor to Oman Oil Headquarters and had a lot of contact with both Lattah and Amahl.

Lattah had never liked Albert. She felt he was untrustworthy, and she hated the way he was always looking her over, with his eyes fixed on her breasts, when he talked to her. Lattah knew she was very attractive to men, but some men bothered her when they looked at her, and he was one of them.

Her mind raced wildly for a plausible excuse for being in Brussels without notifying the local Oman Oil personnel. She smiled broadly at him. "Why, hello Albert. What a surprise! I can imagine that you're surprised to see me. I'm here on a very special political mission for Amahl.

"The Belgian government is considering raising certain dockage fees that would be a big problem for Oman Oil. He asked me to voice a strong protest if the report is true. However, he wanted to keep you and the local personnel on good terms with the government, so he directed me not to involve you or your people."

Albert was an inquisitive individual and was not going to accept that story without knowing more about the details of what was going on. Besides he would enjoy spending some time with her.

Albert said, "Let's have dinner together and you can fill me in on the details. I know a couple of very nice restaurants where we can talk confidentially."

Lattah replied with a rather firm statement, "Albert, I told you that Amahl directed me to carry out this assignment on a confidential basis, so I can't reveal the details to you!"

As Albert was again pursuing the issue, Lattah was thinking how this one incident could bring down the whole master plan that she and Amahl had worked on for so long. They had dedicated their lives to see that the plan was carried out. She knew Albert would take this as far as he could, later asking questions of people in the company's headquarters in Abu Dhabi.

Lattah made a quick and definite decision that Albert had to be killed, but how and where? She must do it before he had a chance to talk with any of his associates or friends.

Albert was saying, "My car is in the parking garage beneath the hotel. We can take it to the restaurant of your choice, and

I can suggest several that I know you will love! What do you say?"

Lattah looked at him and smiled. "Well, I guess it's alright as long as you keep it confidential. You wait here while I take my briefcase to my room, or even better, I'll meet you by the elevator in the parking garage. I'll be right back!"

With that, she left Albert, and took the elevator to her room. In her room, Lattah picked up her large travel purse with the two metal frames on the top that inter-locked and kept the purse closed. She took hold of the short side frame of the purse and flipped it upward. She then withdrew from the top frame a sturdy stiletto slightly over six inches in length that she placed into her small purse.

Then she looked quickly through her suitcase for a particular leather belt. The belt was very narrow with a ratchet-like buckle, so that when you pulled it tight it stayed tight until the ratchet was released. She made a large loop with the ratchet holding the loop in place. Lattah folded the belt and put it into the pocket of her jacket. She left the room and headed for the underground garage.

Albert was waiting for her as she stepped off of the elevator at the parking level and told her, "That didn't take too long; you look especially nice!" He assumed that she had been getting ready for their dinner date. He was right, in that she had been getting ready for him, but not for what he had in mind. They walked down two rows of cars and then toward a corner stall where he had parked his Mercedes 560 SL. He always parked in corners when possible to minimize door damage to his car.

Albert walked Lattah to her side of the car and helped her inside, closing the door for her. He then removed his suit coat, threw it into the rear seat, got into the driver's side, and fastened his seat belt.

Lattah pointed out of the driver's side window and asked Albert, "What does that sign mean? On the wall outside your window."

Albert turned his head to look, and as he did, Lattah plunged the stiletto into his neck. As Albert grabbed to reach the stiletto, Lattah dropped the belt noose over his head and pulled it as tight as she could around his neck. The ratchet kept the noose tightly in place. Albert's eyes were wide in terror, pain, and surprise.

He stopped trying to remove the stiletto and was clawing alternately at the noose and the seat belt. His eyes were bulging and his face was turning blue. He was strapped into his seat and struggling to get free. At the same time, he was fighting to grab the noose or the stiletto. His body movements slowed, and in a few minutes he was dead.

Lattah sat quietly, waiting to make sure that he was dead. She then reached into the rear seat for his coat. She used the coat to wipe her hands of any blood and then removed the stiletto and wiped it clean. The noose was so tight around his swollen neck that she decided not to remove it. Instead, she used the coat to wipe off the belt to remove any fingerprints.

To make it appear as though a robbery had taken place, she searched his coat and pants pockets for money, credit cards, and any identification documents. She removed whatever she found and, along with his watch, placed it all in her purse. She used the coat as a glove to unfasten the seat belt and pushed his upper body down into the passenger seat, so that it would not be obvious that there was a body in the car.

Lattah used the coat to wipe off any areas of the car that might have picked up her fingerprints. She then placed the coat over his body, set the door lock, and quietly pushed the car door shut. She walked back to the elevator area, got into the elevator, and went back to her floor without seeing one person.

Back in her room, she washed the stiletto with soap and water, dried it with the hair dryer, and replaced it into the sheath in the frame of her purse. Lattah carefully inspected her clothing and shoes for any blood spots. Although it was a black suit, there were visible flecks of blood on both the coat and the skirt. Her shoes were clear.

She carefully removed the labels from the clothing, rolled up the suit, and placed it in a plastic laundry bag. She would take the plastic bag to the airport in her small suitcase and dispose of the clothes in the ladies restroom trash can. All the credit cards and other items of identification were cut into small pieces that she would flush down the toilet at the airport.

Early the next morning, Lattah checked out of the Hilton and was in the Brussels Airport waiting for her flight to London. There had been no excitement or anything unusual going on in the lobby or outside the Hilton, so it seemed evident that Albert's body had not yet been found. She dumped the laundry bag in the trash can, flushed all the identification down the toilet, pushed his watch down between the cushions of the airport bus, and stood in line to check in for her flight. Her thoughts were about Amahl and how proud he would be of the job she had done on Albert to save their program.

Lattah boarded her flight and settled back in her seat, reviewing her map of the several potential store locations in London. It was a relatively short flight and the time passed swiftly. Lattah was soon retrieving her luggage and taking the escalator to board the Blue Line tube to Piccadilly Circus. The Holiday Inn Mayfair was only a short block from the Picadilly Station.

Again, it was the hotel suggested by the local rental broker with whom she had been dealing. Lattah unpacked and was soon on the phone talking with the broker. They made arrangements to meet for lunch in the hotel restaurant, the Louis XV, at 11:45

a.m. That gave Lattah time to first take a quick look at several newspapers for any word of the murder. There was nothing.

Then she called Amahl on his private line in his office. She quickly related what she had accomplished on her trip and then the details of her problem with Albert.

Amahl's initial reaction was of anger. "Lattah! What have you done! You've put us in a terrible position! The police will track you and uncover the program, how could you be so stupid!"

Lattah flushed with anger and humiliation, "You fool! I had no choice! I did what had to be done. You have no reason to be upset with me!"

Amahl quickly recovered and realized that Lattah was right. "Lattah, I am wrong and you are right. I love you, and I apologize. You did what had to be done, and I am very proud of you. Albert would have definitely caused a problem. There has been no word here in the office of any problems in Brussels. However, I am sure we'll have word of his death within a matter of hours. Give me your hotel number, and I will call you later this evening. I love you, and I am sorry for my reaction."

Lattah responded, "I understand, Amahl; I knew it would be a shock to you, but I did what had to be done for the good of our cause. Love you, and I'll be waiting for your call tonight!"

Lattah hung up the phone and headed for her appointment with the broker. The lunch was uneventful and expensive. Although the broker picked up the tab, she knew the cost of the lunch would somehow be worked into the cost of the lease. They reviewed the several prospective sites, and the lease rates and conditions for each. Lattah selected two sites to inspect first, as she said that one of them very likely would meet her company's needs. The first store they inspected was vacant and to her liking.

It was located in the Covent Garden area. Covent Garden was not the garden Lattah expected to see. Neither Covent nor

Garden aptly described the area. As the broker explained, the name is a corruption of convent garden, as produce was grown there over three hundred years ago for the monks of Westminster Abbey. Covent Garden is now a popular entertainment and shopping precinct. The address of the store was on Maiden Lane near Southampton Street just a few doors from the famous Rules restaurant that had been in that location for 200 years.

It was also only a block from the Jubilee Market and three blocks from the Royal Opera House. However, more importantly, a one-megaton nuclear blast from that spot would provide a one-and-one-half mile radius of complete destruction, maybe vaporization, of the heart of one of the world's most important financial, historical, and cultural centers.

Within that radius would be the Houses of Parliament; the Ministry of Defense; the Royal Courts of Justice; the majority of government offices, including the Cabinet War Rooms; Westminster Abbey; West Minister Hall, including Big Ben and the West Minister Bridge; Buckingham Palace; St. James Palace; the National Gallery; the Royal Academy; the Museum of Mankind; the British Museum; the British Library; the Bank of England; the Stock Exchange; St. Paul's Cathedral; and endless other landmarks of English history and culture.

The five-mile radius of destruction would very effectively erase the city of London. Another cornerstone of Western civilization would be removed! With a population of almost seven million people in Greater London, the death toll would be in the millions with other millions badly burned and injured. Again, Lattah was very pleased with her choice and very much relished her role in planning and achieving this devastating change in the balance of power and culture in the world.

Lattah and the broker returned to the hotel and completed the transaction for a six-month initial lease with promise of a five-year lease to follow. All papers and documents concerning the lease were to be sent confidential to Amahl Jabel, her superior at Oman Oil Company. Lattah requested that the locks to the store be changed and that the new keys be sent to Mr. Jabel. The broker assured Lattah that all would be taken care of and departed.

Lattah then walked through the lobby to the news stand where she purchased copies of the London Times, the popular International Herald Tribune, and a Belgian paper which she later noted was the previous day's edition and would have nothing about the killing.

She was tired after all the activities of the past twenty-four hours, so she went back to her room, kicked off her shoes, and laid down on the bed to look through the newspapers. Suddenly there was a sharp knock on the door that startled her, and she leaped out of the bed as she realized she had not fastened the chain lock on the door.

She quickly fastened the chain and looked through the peephole in the door. She breathed a sigh of relief as she recognized the bellman carrying the laundry and dry cleaning she had sent out that morning after checking in. She took the items and lay back down on the bed to continue reading the papers.

After reading a while, she decided to order an evening meal from room service so as to not miss the call from Amahl. Lattah finished her dinner and was looking through her airline tickets for the morning flight to New York City when the phone rang. It was Amahl, and she was happy to hear his voice as she missed him very much.

Amahl told her: "Lattah, this seems strange. There has been no word from Brussels. I called our dock office there on the pretext of needing information on the number of shipments they received in the previous month. I requested to talk with Albert, and his secretary, Valerie, said he'd gone to a meeting and hadn't returned as yet. She said she would ask him to call me as soon as he returned.

James Kerlin

"She then thought about the time difference, and said that he would probably call me back in the morning which I said would be fine. It was rather obvious she didn't know where he was and was trying to cover for him. If she had been aware of his death, I'm sure she would have told me. You would think that by now the hotel security would have found him!"

Lattah replied, "Maybe not. The corner of the garage in which the car was parked was quite dark and with him lying across the seat with his coat over him, he would be hard to detect. Since Albert was divorced, they may have had trouble finding the next of kin or locating his place of employment."

Amahl agreed, "Yes, that is probably the situation. We'll just continue with our plans until we see a need to change them. When you arrive in New York, call me, as I'll surely have some information by then. Love you!"

Lattah responded, "I will call you from my hotel in New York. Love you!"

CHAPTER 9.

THE NEXT MORNING LATTAH WAS on British Airways Flight 117 heading for New York. At 11:00 a.m., the Boeing 777 touched down at Kennedy Airport. An hour or so later, as Lattah was checking into the Marriott Eastside Hotel, the desk clerk handed her a message to call Mr. Amahl Jabel as soon as possible. Lattah completed the check-in and hurried to her room to call Amahl. He picked up the phone on the first ring.

Lattah spoke anxiously into the phone. "Amahl, what have you heard? I've read all the papers I could get my hands on, but couldn't find anything!"

Amahl relied, "I tried to reach you this morning before you left for the airport, but you'd already checked out. Valerie called me early this morning with the news that Albert had been murdered during a robbery in the parking garage of the Hilton Hotel in Brussels. The police finally identified him through the license plates on the car. Valerie tried to reach him all day yesterday and called his apartment until late last night when she ultimately notified the police that she thought he was missing.

"I think the two of them were involved because Valerie took his death very hard. In order to keep control of the situation from the company's standpoint, I called the police inspector, identified myself, and inquired about the situation asking if I could be of any help."

Amahl continued, "The inspector asked a number of questions about Albert, such as his position with the company, his personal life, was he involved in gambling or narcotics, and was he in any sort of love triangle. Of course, I wasn't much help to him. I asked him to keep me informed of developments, and that I was preparing to fly to Brussels to hire a replacement and to attend the funeral. I thought it best to go there to see if I could find out any details about the investigation."

Lattah commented, "I'm surprised it took them that long. You were smart to take the initiative in contacting the police on behalf of the company. I agree with your plan to go to Brussels. Do you think they have any clues as to what happened?"

Amahl replied, "I don't think they have the slightest idea. Why don't you call me at our Brussels dock office when you get to Los Angeles; you have the number. Love you!"

Lattah said, "I'll call you from Los Angeles as soon as I get there. Love you, Amahl, goodbye!"

She then called the broker, a young energetic lady in her thirties, who said she would be driving a red BMW convertible and would meet Lattah in front of the hotel. The broker said she had a new listing that she thought would be exactly what Lattah was looking for and in the right location.

At about 2:20 p.m., Lattah watched as the broker pulled up in front of the hotel. The convertible top was down and the broker's peroxide blonde hair was blowing in the wind. She waved to Lattah and motioned her to get into the car. Lattah stepped into the car, introduced herself, made some small talk, and then briefly reviewed the location and kind of place she was seeking to lease.

The broker said that was exactly how she had interpreted Lattah's letter, and she knew she had the exact place to meet her needs. She said how lucky Lattah was that she had chosen her to find the property that was desired. She didn't want to seem arrogant or immodest, but she knew the most about Manhattan commercial rental property.

The broker kept talking non-stop and Lattah was losing her patience. However, she made up her mind to put up with the woman and get the deal over with as quickly as possible. The broker seemed to personify all the things that Lattah disliked about Western culture. It crossed her mind once or twice how much she would like to send this woman to join Albert.

The location of the shop to be inspected was in the East Village area of Manhattan. The address was on Mercer Street near the intersection of Waverley Place. Lattah studied her map of Manhattan and the site was almost in the center of a circle she had drawn as the preferred location for the bomb. It was perfect.

The two locations that Amahl and Lattah had designated as the prime targets were the United Nations and the World Trade Center. The shop was located mid-point between the two landmarks. Each of the structures was within a two-and-a-half mile radius of the proposed lease site and would be completely destroyed by the bomb.

A five-mile radius of destruction would also include all the major historical and world famous landmarks such as the Financial District, including the New York Stock Exchange, and all the great financial institutions on and around Wall Street. The Civic Center with all its city, county, and federal buildings would be gone. The famous skyscrapers such as the Empire State Building and the Chrysler Building would all be taken down.

The churches and great cathedrals would be destroyed. Most of the universities, colleges, and schools reduced to rubble. Times Square, Radio City Music Hall, Rockefeller Center, Pennsylvania Station, Grand Central Station, the Brooklyn

Bridge, the Manhattan Bridge, and the Williamsburg Bridge would all be effectively annihilated.

The destruction would include hospitals like the NU Medical Center, the Beth Israel Medical Center, the Cornell Medical Center, Roosevelt, Memorial, Lennox, Medical Arts Center, Bellevue, Beckman Dow, and the Veterans Administration. All the many small medical centers and clinics would be destroyed and would be of no help to the millions of injured, burned, and maimed victims. The death toll would be horrendous.

The New York City proper population of about 7,500,000 people would all be directly affected by the blast, fire, and radioactivity. The population of New York's consolidated metropolitan area is 20,000,000. The death toll would be at least five or six million people with millions more suffering severe injuries and burns with no place to go for treatment, nor any doctors to treat them. The New York City bomb would strike a major blow against the hated western civilization.

By five-thirty the lease deal was done, all the papers were signed and would be sent to Mr. Jabel in Abu Dhabi along with the keys. They shook hands in the lobby of the hotel, and the broker was insisting that she buy drinks and dinner for Lattah to celebrate the closing of what she thought was a very lucrative deal. Lattah tactfully explained that she did not drink and that she had a previous appointment with a friend. The broker wished her a pleasant journey, thanked her for the business, and bid her goodbye.

Lattah was happy to get rid of her and headed back to her room where she deposited her briefcase, and checked for messages. There were none, so Lattah went to dinner at a small restaurant she had noticed a short ways from the hotel. She ate a quick meal and returned to the hotel with hopes that Amahl might call with more information on the murder. Finally, she gave up hearing from Amahl and went to bed.

The next morning, Lattah boarded TWA Flight 15 at Kennedy Airport and arrived in Los Angeles at 11:00 a.m. She had studied her maps of Los Angeles for several hours during her flight. Lattah and Amahl looked upon the Los Angeles area as a slightly different kind of target. They viewed Los Angeles and particularly Hollywood as a cradle or birthplace of most things they hated about Western culture and that were offensive to their Islamic religion. The films and all the events produced in this entertainment center represented and glorified greed, lust, infidelity, immorality, and a complete lack of ethics and morals.

They believed that all these things resulted in the worldwide disintegration of the family and the promotion of permissive sexual morality. Lattah and Amahl firmly believed, according to their Islamic religion, that the divine activities of creation, sustenance, and guidance end with the final act of judgment. The Day of Judgment.

On the Day of Judgment, all humanity will be gathered, and individuals will be judged solely according to their deeds. The successful ones will go to the Garden (heaven), and the losers, or the evil, will go to hell. Although God is merciful, and will forgive those who deserve forgiveness. Besides the Last Judgment, which will be on individuals, the Koran recognizes another kind of divine judgment, which is meted out in history to nations, peoples, and communities.

Nations, like individuals, may be corrupted by wealth, power, and pride, and, unless they reform, these nations are punished by being destroyed or subjugated by more virtuous nations. Amahl and Lattah were carrying out the punishment and destruction of the corrupted Western civilization for which they would be rewarded and be assured of going to the Garden.

Lattah collected her luggage from the baggage area and walked out to the terminal street to catch the courtesy shuttle bus to her hotel. She checked into the Crowne Plaza Hotel located about a half mile from the airport. As Lattah unpacked her suitcase, she noticed the red message light blinking on the telephone. She called the operator for the message that was to contact Mr. Jabel in Brussels as soon as she arrived. Lattah immediately placed the call to the Oman Oil Company dock office in Brussels.

Amahl had anticipated when she might call and quickly picked up the telephone before the secretary, Valerie, had a chance to hear who was calling. He told Valerie that his boss was calling and that it was a confidential call. She excused herself and went out to the atrium for coffee and a cigarette.

After Valerie left, Amahl continued his conversation with Lattah. "We may have a problem here with Valerie. The police have not made any progress at all in the search for clues or a motive for Albert's death, so I have nothing new to tell you about that. However, this morning after I interviewed a person to replace Albert, Valerie asked if she could talk to me about something very confidential. It surprised me, and I thought sure she was going to reveal that she and Albert were lovers. That was not what she wanted to tell me although I do think that they were lovers.

"What she wanted to talk about was the evening of the event when Albert called her at home. He called from the hotel while he was waiting when you went back to your room prior to leaving for dinner. She said he had called her to confirm what appointments he had the next morning. He then mentioned he had gotten tied up with company business that evening.

"She thought that it sounded like he was meeting somebody from Oman Oil, but she wasn't sure. She further said that she wanted to seek my advice before she told the police inspector about the incident since she didn't want to get the company involved unnecessarily. I feel certain that he was supposed to see her that evening, and that he called Valerie to either cancel the date or to say he would see her later.

"This makes a very difficult situation. I can appreciate the problem you faced with Albert. If she talks to the police inspector about the phone call, and possibly about a company representative in town that evening, then we'll have the police going through all the company travel records to determine who was where at what time and what were they doing there. We positively don't want that to happen.

"On the other hand, if I kill Valerie, it will only intensify the investigation and possibly bring in other company officials. There is no way to include her into our program, as she does not share our values and beliefs. She would probably divulge the entire plan."

Amahl continued, "What I've done temporarily is suggest to Valerie that she take a few days off to recover from the shock of Albert's death. There is no need for her to talk with the police as I'll handle everything and run the office for a few days. She has a sister in Dinant that is about a one-hour drive from here and is a popular resort spot on the Meuse River. She was very receptive and will leave in the morning for a week's holiday. If necessary, I'll explain to the police inspector about her nervous breakdown and her need to get away for a few days. What do you think?"

Lattah responded, "This is a bad development, but you've handled it well! I had no idea that he had made a phone call, nor did I think to ask him since it seemed the elapsed time was so short. I agree that we can't dispose of her at this point without raising a lot of other questions. What you've done will allow us a few more days to consider what to do with her."

Amahl responded, "I think I know how to do it, but I want to think it through before proceeding. Call me when you get to Washington; I will still be here. Love you!"

Lattah said, "Everything here is going fine; I will call you from Washington. Love you, Amahl!"

Lattah hung up the phone and unpacked her suitcase. She then called the broker with whom she had an appointment and made arrangements for him to meet her in the hotel lobby. As they left the parking lot in the broker's Mercedes, he reminded Lattah she had expressed an interest in the area just north of the intersection of Interstate 10 and La Brea Avenue. He had three properties to show her that fit the criteria she had sent him.

After looking at retail stores on Fairfax Avenue, Wilshire Boulevard, and 3rd Street, she chose the property on 3rd that was near the intersection of Highland Avenue. The location would be ideal in that it would easily ensure the vaporization of the heart of the decadent Western world entertainment industry, and along with it, all the so-called beautiful people involved in that industry who contribute to the moral decay of our planet.

A 4.5-mile radius from that location would represent the lethal area, the circle within which the entire population would be killed and virtually all buildings would be destroyed. People at an eight-mile radius from the center of the blast would suffer third degree burns. The blast would wipe out or permanently cripple a huge population representing the northwest quarter of greater Los Angeles: Hollywood, Beverly Hills, Century City, Studio City, Culver City, Universal City, Mar Vista, Westchester, Inglewood, Huntington Park, Downtown Los Angeles, Southgate, Monterey Park, Alhambra, Pasadena, Glendale, Burbank, and Van Nuys would be the cities suffering nearly complete devastation. The fatalities would be over two million with a like amount injured, for total casualties of about four-and-a-half million people.

Lattah and the broker returned to the hotel and completed the transaction. The broker gladly agreed to a six-month initial lease with a promise from Lattah of a future generous five-year lease. The papers and keys for the new locks were to be sent to Mr. Jabel at Oman Oil Company.

The broker did his best to interest Lattah in an additional location in south Los Angeles that was available and was by far the greatest bargain in commercial real estate in the area. Lattah was firm in her reply that the one location would permit her and her associates to take care of the Los Angeles area. She also turned down his repeated offers to take her to dinner. Lattah shook hands with the broker, thanked him for his help, and told him goodbye.

She bought that day's issue of the Los Angeles Times and a copy of the Washington Post that was a day old and returned to her room. Lattah kicked off her shoes, propped the pillows up against the headboard of the bed, and settled back to read the papers.

She had planned to go out to eat, but since there were no restaurants nearby, with the exception of those in the hotel, she picked up the phone and placed her dinner order with room service. She was in for the night and already thinking about her trip in the morning to Washington, D.C.

Early the next morning, Lattah was on the courtesy bus heading for the airport to catch U.S. Air Flight 6 scheduled to leave at 7:30 a.m.

Since it was quite early, she was sipping a cup of coffee that she had picked up in the lobby of the hotel and munching on some crackers that she had saved from the previous night's room service dinner. The bus carried her to the U.S. Air curbside check-in where her bags were screened; she proceeded to board her plane.

After an uneventful flight, she landed at Washington National Airport ten minutes ahead of time thanks to a favorable tailwind. Lattah took a taxi to her hotel, the Holiday Inn Capitol, at 550 C Street. Again, it was the suggestion of the broker that she stay in that particular hotel since it was very near the area in which Lattah had indicated an interest.

CHAPTER 10.

AFTER CHECKING IN, SHE UNPACKED and was on the phone tracking down the broker on his cellular phone. The appointment was made for 11:00 the next morning, which would give Lattah plenty of time to make her late afternoon flight to Abu Dhabi. Lattah then placed a call to Amahl at the Oman Oil Company office in Brussels.

He answered on the first ring. "Lattah! Is that you? Are you in Washington?"

Lattah answered, "Yes, just arrived. One more day of dealing with stupid western brokers and then I'll be on my way home. Everything is perfect. You will be pleased with all of the locations for the bombs. It is exciting to think how complete the destruction will be, and you and I will have done it!"

Amahl smiled as he told her, "My dear Lattah, you've done well, and I love your enthusiasm. However, we still have a major problem here to take care of. I've decided that we must get rid of Valerie. She could be of great danger to our program and us. She has left for Dinant and will be there for the next week. I think that we must arrange to have her killed while there, and have it appear as a suicide."

After a pause, Amahl continued, "I am convinced that she and Albert were having an affair, and I believe that she is very upset with his death. I feel sure that I could help convince the police that her suicide was due to grief over his death. I will send for el Ali to do the job for us. He is a smooth operator and very attractive to women. I am sure he can do it with a minimum of problems. What do you think?"

Lattah answered quickly, "I agree. If Valerie talks again to the police, it could be a disaster. The sooner she is killed, the better off we'll be."

Amahl said, "I thought you would agree. I will make the call to el Ali and start planning how the killing shall take place. Hurry home, Lattah, I am so anxious to be with you and to hold you!"

Lattah kissed him through the phone and said, "You are no more anxious than I am, my darling. I can't wait to be with you. Love you."

She hung up the phone, smiled with the thought of soon being in bed with Amahl, and continued smiling as she washed for dinner. She looked through a guide to restaurants in the area and decided that authentic Moroccan cuisine sounded good. Lattah was beginning to wear down as she neared the end of her exhausting trip, and she thought a relaxing evening with a good meal would do her good.

She called a taxi and took it to the Marrakesh Restaurant located on New York Avenue, about a mile-and–a-half from her hotel. She took with her the map of the city, which was marked with the prime targets for the blast, and the approximate location of the bomb. When she entered the restaurant, she requested a table with privacy as she told the maitre d that she was reviewing a presentation that she was planning.

As Lattah casually ate her meal and enjoyed the belly dancer entertainment, she carefully reviewed all the targets and their proximity to the bomb location. If the property to be leased was near the hotel as the broker had indicated, the three prime targets were the U.S. Capitol, the White House, and the Pentagon. All were well within range of complete destruction.

The U.S. Capitol, the Senate and House Office Buildings, the Supreme Court and the Library of Congress were all well within a one mile radius. The White House, the Blair House, the Executive Office Building, and the U. S. Treasury would all be within a one-and-a-quarter mile radius of the bomb. The Pentagon would be two-and-a-quarter miles from the center of the blast. The CIA, at eleven miles from the bomb, would be at the fringe of destruction and although perhaps not completely physically destroyed, the operation itself would be incapacitated. Also, most of the employees would be fatalities.

Along with those prime targets, there would be massive destruction of all the major Federal Government departments, agencies, and services. The Department of State, Department of Commerce, Department of Interior, Department of Labor, Justice Department, FBI, IRS, Customs Service, World Bank and National Archives would be just a few of the Federal operations totally destroyed causing a complete paralysis of the United States Government.

All the historical monuments and memorials, such as the Washington Monument, Lincoln Memorial and Thomas Jefferson Memorial would be destroyed. Most of the great cathedrals, churches, universities, and hospitals, would be gone. Lattah marveled at the fact that she and Amahl would be taking out the most powerful nation on the planet. She tried to imagine the terror and the despair that would grab the million victims that survived the initial blast.

Lattah finished her meal and reached down beside her chair to put her maps back into her bag. As she reached for the bag, her elbow knocked over a glass of water. She grabbed for the glass, and as she did, one map slid off the top of her bag and onto the floor under the table. Her airline ticket folder fell from the bag and dropped beside the chair. The waiter rushed to help her. He picked up the bag and the airline ticket, put them on top of the table, and proceeded to take his towel to dry off the bag and the sleeve of Lattah's jacket. Lattah quickly grabbed the bag and the towel and finished wiping her sleeve as she smiled and thanked the waiter for his help. She gave the waiter a generous tip and left to catch a taxi back to her hotel.

The next morning, the broker called her room to advise Lattah that he was in the hotel. He described his appearance so that she would recognize him, and told her that he would be waiting in the lobby. Lattah picked up her briefcase and headed for the lobby. She recognized him immediately and introduced herself.

Lattah smiled at the broker and said, "Good description! I recognized you right away. Did you park in the garage?"

The broker returned the smile and replied, "I've been looking forward to meeting you. Hope you've been enjoying our city! No, I didn't park in the garage as I think I have exactly what you are looking for just a short walk from here."

He escorted Lattah out the front door of the hotel and across C Street.

He motioned and said, "If you look toward the corner, you will see the CVS Pharmacy, and the property I have in mind is just two doors from there."

Lattah replied, "The location is fine, just so the store fits our needs."

The broker said, "The store has been a gift shop, and the proprietor died about a month ago. All the merchandise, showcases, and furniture were moved out to be placed in an estate sale. Let's see if this key works as it is supposed to."

The broker opened the door and escorted Lattah around the premises. She paid particular attention to the rear door in the storage area, making sure it was wide enough and tall enough to permit the stacked propane tanks to be moved inside.

Lattah said, "This will provide the display area and storage that we will need. As I told you before, we will need a six-month initial lease, and then at the end of the six months, we will need the option of a five-year lease renewable at the end of five years for an additional five years. The monthly lease rate that you quoted is acceptable and will prevail through the additional five years with an inflation factor not to exceed five percent per year."

The broker extended his hand and said, "We've got a deal! Let's go back to the hotel and complete the contract. I have one with me that is all made out except for the financial terms. The legal stenographer at the hotel can type it for us."

He was indeed happy as he hadn't had an inquiry on the property for the past three weeks, and this was shaping up to be a nice long-term lease.

They returned to the hotel, and in the lobby, they worked out all the details. While the stenographer typed the contract, they had a brief lunch at the hotel restaurant. After lunch, the contracts were signed and Lattah directed the broker to send all documents marked confidential to Mr. Amahl Jabel at Oman Oil Company in Abu Dhabi. She also requested that new locks be placed on all doors and that the keys be sent to Mr. Jabel. The broker invited Lattah to dinner, but she declined, saying she had a flight to catch. They shook hands and went their separate ways.

It was already 3:00 p.m., and Lattah was ticketed on British Airways Flight #216 which left Washington Dulles Airport at 6:10 p.m. She hurriedly went to her room, packed her suitcase, returned to the lobby, and checked out. Lattah took a taxi to Dulles Airport. She wasn't thrilled with the $45 taxi fare, but she was on her way to Abu Dhabi and Amahl, and she sure didn't want to miss that flight. At 6:25 p.m., the plane was in the air and Lattah was on her way home.

On the previous night, several hours after Lattah had left the Marrakesh Restaurant, the staff was cleaning the tables and floor and preparing the restaurant for the next day. A bus boy found a map under one of the tables, and he tossed it to a waiter named Alex, who had been serving that particular table.

The bus boy, grinning, said, "Hey, Alex, here's your tip! You can keep my part of it!"

Alex caught the map, wondering which party had left it. It was rather strange as the map was of the Washington area, but the writing was in a foreign language and the distances were in kilometers. And there was something even more intriguing: the major landmarks in Washington were all circled and then a larger series of concentric circles enclosed those landmarks.

He was thinking that perhaps the map had belonged to some kind of tour director and showed places that were to be visited. Maybe the tour director would return to the restaurant to pick up his or her map. Maybe it belonged to the attractive young lady who had lingered over her dinner and had been studying a document carefully.

On that basis, he gave the map to Lou Thoma, the manager of the restaurant. Lou also was intrigued by the map, not only as to its owner, but also the meaning of all the circles. On the top right hand corner of the map, there was a notation written in some kind of foreign language. He decided to show it his friend and customer, Troy Sheldon, who worked in the FBI building and usually had lunch and sometimes dinner at the restaurant with his friend, Rebecca Coles.

He thought that Troy was a special agent and had something to do with foreign espionage. Perhaps he could recognize the language of the notation and also the language used in the printing of the map. He placed the map in his desk drawer to show Troy the next time they were together.

CHAPTER 11.

A FTER AMAHL HAD TALKED TO Lattah in Washington, he called el Ali and arranged for him to go to Dinant, Belgium, immediately to dispose of Valerie. The next day, el Ali flew into Brussels, rented a car, drove to the city of Namur, and checked into a small hotel.

He then drove fourteen kilometers to the town of Dinant, and spent the day carefully investigating every part of the town in consideration of the best method of killing Valerie. He had a quick lunch in the small restaurant that was also the ticket office for cable car rides to the top of the cliffs that overlooked the town and the Meuse River.

El Ali purchased a ticket and rode the cable car to the top of the cliffs to visit the citadel that towered some 100 meters above the restaurant. The citadel was a fort-like foreboding structure that was built on the site of a historical fortress originally constructed in the 11th century. He took a quick walk around the grounds and then rode the cable car back down to the restaurant. El Ali carefully put the cable car ticket stub in his pocket for possible future use. He then returned to his car and twice drove by the home of Valerie's sister whose address was given to him by Amahl.

The next morning, el Ali again drove to Dinant and devoted the day to tracking Valerie and determining how and where she spent her time. Shortly after noon, she took a bus from her sister's home to the part of town where all the stores and restaurants were located along the riverfront. At about 4:00 p.m., she stopped at a small cafe that had a pleasant patio overlooking the Meuse River and had a glass of wine. Since she was alone, el Ali moved quickly to take advantage of the situation.

He parked the car and casually took a table facing the river but also partially facing Valerie's table. He ordered wine along with some cheese and bread. el Ali did not normally drink, but it seemed appropriate for this situation. After a short time, he caught Valerie's eye and nodded to her. She looked away but he pursued the visual contact.

He flashed his best smile and spoke to her, "Excuse me, I don't mean to be forward, but I do think we have met before. Are you from Brussels?"

The sudden approach and question surprised her, and she instinctively answered his question. "I, ah, yes, I am from Brussels, but I do not recognize you, nor do I think I know you."

el Ali smiled again and said, "Let me think. Yes, I think I recall where I met you. Do you work for Oman Oil in Brussels? My name is Ben Yosef, and I work for a maritime insurance company with headquarters in London. If I recall right, you are the secretary for my friend, Albert. Do you recall me now?"

Valerie's face clouded and tears welled up in her eyes as she answered, "Yes, I was Albert's secretary until last week when he was brutally robbed and murdered!"

el Ali feigned shock and surprise as he jumped to his feet spilling his wine and breaking the glass as he responded, "Albert dead? How can that be? He never hurt anyone! He was a gentle person! I can't believe it!"

Valerie was touched by his emotional reaction, "We have absolutely no clues or any obvious reasons why it happened. The police are baffled by the complete absence of clues or motivation for the murder, and they are inclined to believe that it was robbery. I was overcome by the tragedy, and Albert's superior suggested that I take some time off and come visit my sister for a week. I'm glad that you knew Albert and were a friend of his. And I apologize for not remembering you, but we have so many salesman calling on the office that I'm afraid I forgot you."

el Ali gave her a warm smile and said, "Don't apologize, no need to. I know how it is trying to keep so many faces and names at your fingertips. However, attractive women are not so easy to forget, and that is why I recognized you so quickly."

Valeric smiled and replied, "Thank you, and I appreciate your feelings for Albert. Sorry you spilled your wine; would you care to join me for a new glass of wine?"

El Ali picked up the plate of cheese and bread and moved to the other chair at Valerie's table. He nodded to the waiter who promptly served two fresh glasses of wine.

Valerie looked at Ben Yosef and asked, "What are you doing here in Dinant?"

Ben Yosef replied, "I am on a one week holiday, and I thought it would be interesting to explore this part of Belgium. I have often heard of the beautiful scenery in this part of the country, especially along the Meuse River. Then I plan to drive through the Ardennes before returning to Brussels on business and then back to London. I was getting a little burned out in my work and thought such a holiday would be beneficial."

Valerie smiled and said, "You have to take time out now and then to smell the roses and relax. You selected a beautiful part of Belgium to tour and enjoy. I often visit my sister here, and I always look forward to returning to this area. Are you just here for the day?"

Ben Yosef replied, "I have no set schedule. I had in mind just the one day here, but since meeting such an attractive young woman who can show me the area, I will definitely be back tomorrow. That is, if you can spare a few hours to show me the town."

Valerie laughed, "There isn't that much of a town to see here. The population is less than 15,000, so you can see most of it sitting right here. But I would be pleased to show you the landmarks of Dinant."

Ben Yosef said, "That would be wonderful, and I appreciate it very much. I especially would like to visit that beautiful church and also that fort-like building on top of the cliff."

As el Ali, he had visited both places the day before; he had spent an hour looking around the building at the top of the high cliffs and had very carefully planned the events that were about to unfold.

Valerie looked toward the church and told him, "That is the Church of Notre Dame, and it was built in the 13th Century. The old hotel you see there is the Hotel de Ville and contains many famous paintings done by Anton Joseph Wiertz who was born in Dinant and who painted during the early 1800s.

"The building at the top of the cliffs is the citadel. It is built on a site of a fortress originally constructed in 1040 and then destroyed in 1703. It was rebuilt as the citadel and it sits there on top of that sheer cliff over 100 meters above the town and river. There is a great view from up there of the town and the surrounding countryside."

"Very interesting," said Ben Yosef. "I'll look forward to our tour tomorrow. Suppose I meet you right here for lunch, and then we'll take the tour. I have some telephone calls to make in the morning, so how would 1:00 be for lunch?"

Valerie answered, "That would be fine, and I'll be looking forward to it. Thank you for lifting my spirits. I've been so depressed since the death of Albert."

Ben Yosef reached out and patted her hand, "It has been my pleasure. I do want to give you something that may be of some consolation to you. My sister gave it to me when our mother died."

Ben Yosef reached into his pocket and took out his billfold. From it he withdrew a crumpled piece of paper on which was written a poem about death and the peaceful transition from this life to the next.

He said, "I want to keep this copy from my sister, but I would like for you to copy it, and keep it in your purse to read from time to time."

"How very thoughtful of you," replied Valerie. "I would very much like to copy it. I have a pen and paper in my purse. Have another glass of wine and enjoy it while I copy the poem."

Ben Josef sipped the wine as he watched Valerie very carefully copy the poem in perfect handwriting. Ben Josef, or el Ali, did not have a sister. He had seen the poem in a magazine he was reading during his flight to Brussels and thought he may have use for it if this killing was to look like a suicide.

Valerie finished copying the poem and returned the poem to Ben Josef. "It is a beautiful poem. It was so thoughtful and kind of you to give to me. I will carry it and read it frequently."

Ben Josef took the poem and replaced it tenderly in his billfold. He then stood up and beckoned for the waiter and paid the bill. It was time for him to leave, and he shook hands with Valerie, reminding her of their meeting the next day. Then he drove off, waving to Valerie who was still seated at the table.

As Valerie walked to catch the bus, she was pondering whether or not to tell her sister of meeting this fascinating man since she had been in such grief over losing Albert. She was sure her sister would not approve of her showing a man around, so she decided to say nothing about the encounter with Ben Josef.

After leaving Valerie, el Ali drove up to the citadel and parked his car. He slowly walked around the grounds on the outside of the buildings looking down the steep cliffs that towered above the town and the Church of Notre Dame. He finally found a small area near the edge of the cliff that looked down on a desolate part of the town that lay well behind the church.

El Ali then looked through the loose stones until he found a rock about the size of a grapefruit that had the same appearance and coloring of the rock in the face of the cliff. He placed the rock beneath a bush near the wall of the citadel. He was ready for the tour the next day with Valerie. El Ali got into his car and drove back to his hotel in Namur.

The next day at shortly after 1:00 p.m., Ben Josef drove into the parking lot of the cafe and waved to Valerie who was sitting at their table on the patio. She was dressed in a light yellow dress and a beige sweater and looked very pretty. Her sister had questioned her as to why she had dressed up and why her spirits seemed up. Valerie told her sister that she was merely trying to cheer herself by dressing up a little bit. She never mentioned meeting Ben Josef, or their plans. She told her sister that she planned to spend the day in Namur. Valerie walked to the corner and caught the bus to town to meet Ben Josef at the cafe.

Ben Josef parked his car and walked across the patio to join Valerie. They shook hands, and Ben Josef patted the back of her hand, and told her how pretty she looked. He was thinking how attractive she was and what a waste it was to have to kill her, but business was business, and he had a reputation to protect.

Ben Josef was saying, "You look as though you are feeling somewhat better. I know what a shock Albert's death was to you, and I hope our brief encounter will help to ease your grief. Did your sister approve of our tour today?"

Valerie showed a faint smile and said, "I am feeling better and your visit really has helped to pick up my spirits. And no, I did not yet tell my sister of our meeting yesterday. I was afraid that she might have read something into it that would not be right. I will tell her at the appropriate time. Now, let's have lunch since I'm very hungry! The fish here is extremely good, as is their selection of cheeses and vegetables."

Ben Josef motioned for the waiter and they both ordered the fish special with vegetables and a dish of assorted cheeses. Both of them ordered mineral water to drink. As they ate their lunch, they chatted about Ben's travels throughout Europe and the Middle East selling maritime insurance and of the favorite places they both had visited. Ben explained that he had always been too busy with his work to get married and for a long time lived with his mother before she died.

Valerie talked of being a career woman who had never gotten married despite having several casual relationships. She didn't mention her close relationship with Albert, and Ben did not pursue it. She talked about her sister who was a widow with one young daughter; her sister worked as a secretary for a company that manufactured woolen textiles. The sister's daughter was quite close to Valerie and often walked with her, but today she was in school.

Ben asked, "Do you have to meet your niece after school since her mother is working?"

Valerie replied, "No, every day after school she goes home with a friend who is also a neighbor of my sister. I wasn't sure how long our lunch and tour would take. I told my sister that I had planned to take the train to Namur and that I may not be back until early evening. I know it's a white lie, but I didn't want her concerned about my meeting a strange man."

Ben smiled and said, "I fully understand. You did exactly the right thing as far as I am concerned. I would like to return someday and meet your sister so as to put her concerns at rest.

Do you know that we have been here talking for over an hour! I have really enjoyed it, and hope you will agree to do it again. However, we should probably get started on our tour."

Valerie glanced at her watch and commented, "I just can't believe how fast the time passed. I enjoyed it, too. You're right, if we are going to make the full tour, we better get started."

They left the small cafe and wandered through several shops selling wool, textiles, and the traditional copper and brassware. In one small bakery, they purchased two cacaos de Dinant decorated biscuits. The couple visited the Montford Tower and walked through the Church of Notre Dame. They headed back toward the cafe where Ben's car was parked.

Valerie looked at her watch and said, "The time has passed so quickly; if you still want to see the citadel, we must go now. To drive there, we will have to take the E 411 Motorway up the other side of the mountain."

Ben Josef was looking at his watch also and nodded in agreement. "Yes, we should probably leave now. We can watch the sunset from there; it should be very beautiful."

They got into Ben's car and drove to the citadel. It was late afternoon when they parked the car and walked through the parking lot. The walk through the citadel didn't take very long, and as they left the front entrance, Ben was looking out across the river below.

He said, "Let's take a walk around the outside terrace, so that we can get a better view of the river and the town and maybe look over the edge at the Church of Notre Dame."

"Good idea," Valerie replied, "it is spectacular, and you can get a good view of the church at some points along the fence."

They walked along the terrace and stopped at a small area where Ben thought he had a really good view of the church although it was mostly of the back of the church. Valerie walked to the fence, and was looking down at the church when Ben, looking around to make sure nobody was in sight on the terrace, reached under the bush and picked up the rock he had hidden. In a continuous motion, he swung the rock and hit Valerie on the back of her head. She never uttered a sound as she slumped to the ground.

Ben quickly took off her jacket, making sure there was no blood on it, placed the cable car ticket stub in the jacket pocket, neatly folded the jacket, and placed it on the ground. He took off her shoes and placed them beside the jacket. Then he opened her purse and took out the poem she had copied, laid the poem on top of the jacket, and placed her purse on top of the poem.

Ben picked up Valerie, walked to the edge of the cliff, and threw her body out as far as he could. He watched as it bounced off of the many protruding rocks on the way down. Ben very carefully covered over several small blood spots on the ground. The rock he used to hit her was tossed over the cliff. After a quick look for anything that might appear out of place, he walked around the terrace in the rear of the citadel to the far edge of the parking lot.

He got into his car and left for the drive to Brussels. No remorse, no sadness; mission accomplished! He had checked out of the small hotel in Namur that morning, so now he was heading back to Brussels to stay the night and then catch an early morning flight to Abu Dhabi. He would locate Amahl that night and advise him that the job had been taken care of very neatly!

Later that evening, a security guard found the jacket, shoes, and purse, along with the poem. A cable car stub was in her jacket pocket. Just after dark they found her body among the rocks at the base of the cliffs and notified her sister. Her sister was grief stricken, as was Valerie's niece. In talking with the police, her sister told them that Valerie had been upset over the death of a close friend, and that she had come to Dinant to spend time with her and her daughter.

She told police, "When Valerie first arrived, she had been very despondent. However, yesterday, the third day she had been here, it seemed that her spirits had picked up and she appeared happier. She even dressed up and told me she was taking the train to Namur for the day and would be home by late evening. After talking with her yesterday morning, I just can't believe that she committed suicide."

The police inspector offered his condolences and told the sister that very often a person bent on suicide will appear happier or more content once they have made the decision to commit the act. He said that based on his experience, he had no doubts this was a suicide.

The sister called the Oman Oil Company office in Brussels and talked with Mr. Amahl Jabel, the individual Valerie had mentioned who was kind enough to give her the time off to recover from the shock of Albert's death. Mr. Jabel was astounded to hear of Valerie's death. He could not believe what he was hearing! He said he knew that Albert and Valerie were quite close, and that she was upset with his death, but it would never have occurred to him that she would ever consider suicide.

Mr. Jabel asked if the police could have been wrong. Could it have been murder? The sister answered that the police were positive that it was suicide. Every clue pointed that way and what would the motivation have been for murder? Valerie had no enemies; her purse was intact with nothing at all missing. The police had already closed the case as a suicide.

Mr. Jabel informed the sister that Valerie had insurance with the company and that he personally would see that the proper financial benefits be sent to the sister to take care of the burial expenses. He requested the sister to notify him of the funeral arrangements, and he would make every effort to be there. Amahl knew that he would not be attending the funeral since he would be in Abu Dhabi at that time. He would make arrangements for a beautiful spray of flowers to be sent along with his sincere regrets for not being able to attend.

CHAPTER 12.

IN ABU DAHBI, DR. DIMITRI Ivankov was completing his work on the propane tanks that were to contain the nuclear weapons. He and Amahl had reached agreement on the design for the installation of the nuclear bomb, as well as the arming and fusing mechanisms. The complex timing devices to be used to activate the bombs were battery operated and would perform reliably and accurately for a minimum of 120 days. It was a tight squeeze, but Ivankov managed to provide the backup timing system that Amahl had insisted on. Ivankov was an extremely talented scientist and had constructed an efficient and effective nuclear bomb system.

He had all eight bomb/tanks lined up in a row and was waiting for Amahl to return from Brussels to inspect them. Amahl had promised him a bonus if the work was done promptly and effectively, and he was anxious to get the additional money. He was proud of his work, never giving a thought to the end result of his creation.

When Amahl returned, he was delighted with Ivankov's accomplishments. He was so enthused that he gave the scientist a bonus of 10,000 American dollars, not only to reward him, but to also keep him motivated to complete the process of setting the timing devices and preparing the tanks for shipping.

It was Amahl's plan to ship the tanks on board Oman Oil Company oil tankers. Since the Oman Oil Company had relatively busy dock facilities in each of the targeted cities, there would be a minimum of problems with custom officials in getting the tanks safely into the Oman warehouses. The tanks would be shipped on a schedule that was based on the distance and time required to reach their respective destinations.

The tanks to Los Angeles would be shipped first as the distance was 11,170 nautical miles from Abu Dhabi and would take thirty days to get there. New York and Washington, D.C., each a little over 7,500 nautical miles would take twenty-one days en route. The shipment to Rome was the closest at 3,420 nautical miles and would take nine days. The other shipments to target cities would fall between the parameters of nine to thirty days; all the nuclear devices would be in their respective warehouses by April 1.

Ivankov had done a masterful job loading and securing the nuclear warheads inside of the tanks. The arming and fusing mechanisms were all in place, carefully protected from abusive handling or dropping of the tank. At the other end of each tank was located the timing devices that would activate the chain of actions required to explode the bomb.

It was a very precise and sophisticated timing device that would ensure all the bombs would explode within seconds of each other so as to provide maximum chaos and despair throughout the western world. It would provide an excellent opportunity for any Third World nation to attack and take full advantage of any or all of the Western nations.

After the nuclear warheads and timing devices were installed, Amahl and Ivankov set the timing devices for October 19th, at 4:00 p.m. Greenwich time. That specific time would be 4:00 p.m. in London; 5:00 p.m. in Berlin, Brussels, Paris and Rome; 11:00 a.m. in New York and Washington; and 8:00 a.m. in Los Angeles. Amahl felt that simultaneous explosions with that timing would cause the maximum number of fatalities with extreme chaos.

This schedule provided thirty days to get all the bombs shipped to their respective destinations. Then there would be forty-five additional days to permit Amahl to fly to all eight cities and supervise the transfer of the tanks from the Oman Oil Company waterfront warehouses to the leased locations in the centers of the cities. Judgment Day for the Western world had been scheduled and would be fast approaching.

CHAPTER 13

I T WAS JUST AFTER 8 p.m., and Max and Scott were landing in Riyadh, Saudi Arabia, on Lufthansa Flight 624 when Max suddenly put down the newspaper he was reading and nudged Scott who had dozed off a few minutes earlier.

Scott sat up in his seat and looked at Max, "Just as I'm sleeping well, you get an idea! What is it? It better be good after waking me up!"

Max replied, "I think we've overlooked one good source of information that could provide some leads. Two years ago we worked with Joe Capela, the international arms dealer. He and his three sons, Joe Jr., Mike, and John, are legitimate dealers, and we established a good working relationship with them. In fact, they were extremely helpful to us in tracking down those Libyan terrorists. Joe and his sons cover the world in making arms deals, and it could be that the people involved in the theft of the nuclear weapons had approached one of them.

"Joe Sr. operates much of the time out of Lisbon, which serves as a headquarters for the operation, although his home is in Arroyo Grande, California. Mike has been working the Mideast. Joe Jr., works the European countries, and John has been covering the Far East. Could be a worthwhile contact."

"That's a great idea, Max. Since you worked closely with the Capela organization and are friends with all of them, why don't you fly back to Lisbon for a meeting. As soon as we land, we'll call Joe and arrange a meeting. What do you think?"

Max grinned at Scott and said, "You know what I think! Let's do it! Why is it that you're the boss, but I have to provide all the ideas?"

Scott elbowed Max in the ribs and replied, "I would think you'd have heard that a successful boss always hires people smarter than he is. Maybe it should say that a successful boss always makes his people think they're smarter than he is! Anyhow, it's a damn good idea, and I'll buy you a drink in the airport bar!"

Max was on the phone talking to Joe Capela, "It's good to talk to you, too, Joe, and I agree with you that it was an unforgettable experience. Sure we got shot at, but we all got back in one piece and had a great time putting the bad guys away. Right now, Joe, we need your help badly. A real emergency. Could you possibly meet with me tomorrow?"

Joe hesitated, but he recalled Max very clearly, and knew that when Max said it was an emergency, it was indeed that!

He then said, "Yes, I can arrange it. I was supposed to fly to Paris in the morning and meet with my son Joe on several prospects. I will either delay the meeting or have Joe go ahead without me. It should not be a problem. When will your flight arrive? I will meet you at the airport."

"Thank you, Joe," Max replied. "We appreciate your help. I'm leaving here tonight at 12:40 a.m. on Air France Flight 8253 connecting to Air France Flight 8600 at Charles De Gaulle. My aircraft is due to arrive at 9:30 a.m. in Lisbon. If Mike and John are available, they might be of help also."

"John is in Hong Kong, but I will try and have Mike here if at all possible. I'll meet your flight in the morning. Have a good trip!" replied Joe as he hung up and immediately got back on the phone in an effort to locate Mike.

Joe's thoughts were racing as he tried to think of what kind of trouble they might be getting into. Max was the kind of guy who played for keeps and Joe had seen that first hand. Joe located Mike in Cairo and made arrangements for him to arrive in Lisbon shortly after noon the next day.

He then called in his secretary and told her to cancel any appointments he had for the next day. He also asked her to pick up Mike at the airport and bring him to Joe's home. Joe, Mike, and Max would have lunch in privacy and discuss whatever it was that Max had in mind. Max could spend the night there, as Joe knew he would be tired from overnight traveling.

Max arrived on time, and Joe was there to meet him. The two men shook hands and were truly glad to see each other. Their previous harrowing experience with the Libyan terrorists had formed a firm bond between them.

Joe was smiling as he greeted Max, "It sure is good to see you, Max, I think! I'm dying to hear what we are about to be involved in this time!"

Max was laughing, "Hey, nothing like the last time, Joe. All I want is information that could possibly be important to us. I'll be up front; this is so important and so urgent that only a few people in the world know the story. I'm sworn to secrecy, Joe, so I hope you understand that I can't tell you many details about the situation even though I completely trust you and your sons. You can't imagine the immensity of the problem; it's terrifying."

Joe sensed that it was a nuclear situation as he looked Max in the eyes and said, "I know you well, Max, and I fully understand it if you request complete secrecy. There is a trace of desperation in your voice that I'm not accustomed to hearing from you. You can be sure we will do whatever it is you need to have done.

"Mike will be arriving later and will join us for lunch at my home where we can relax and have more privacy. We'll go ahead out there, so you can clean up and rest for a while before we meet. Marie will be glad to see you."

Max shook Joe's hand again, "Thank you so much, Joe, for both your help and your kindness. I'll certainly enjoy seeing Marie again!"

After retrieving Max's luggage, they drove to Joe's home in the country where Marie was waiting for them. Marie was Joe's wife and she was well acquainted with Max as he had spent several weeks at their California home, protecting them from a terrorist assassin. Max had become like one of the family and Marie and Joe treated him like a son. Marie was seated in a lawn chair and waved to them as they drove up the lane to the house. Marie and Max hugged and exchanged kisses, saying how nice it was to see each other.

They had always kidded each other, and Marie spoke, as she looked Max up and down, "I'm really surprised at the weight you've put on since we last saw you! I'll bet you've gotten married!"

Max feigned a hurt look, "You know very well I haven't gained a pound, and there isn't a woman alive who will marry me if she knows the job I have! Now girl friends are something else if you want to talk about that!"

Marie shook her head and laughed as she looked at Joe and Max. "You men are all alike! No, I don't necessarily want to hear about your various conquests! You and Mike can compare notes on that subject. Follow me, Max, and I'll take you to your suite."

Marie showed Max to a guest suite where he could shower, shave, and rest for a while before lunch. Marie assured Max that she would call him when Mike arrived for the meeting. As Marie was closing the door, Max called out, "Marie, do you still have some of our favorite wine? It sure would taste good this evening."

Marie was smiling as she recalled how she and Max had enjoyed a glass of wine every evening he had stayed with them. She enjoyed good wine, and since Joe seldom drank alcohol, she and Max had gotten into the habit of drinking a glass or two of wine every evening while Joe had a soft drink. Since the three boys were gone at that time, Marie, Joe, and Max had spent many enjoyable evenings just chatting and sipping their drinks.

Marie answered, "I'm ahead of you, Max. Your special wine is already being iced down. When you finish your business, you can have some wine, but not before!"

As Marie shut the door Max yelled out, "Yes, Mother!!"

When Max walked downstairs to Joe's office, he could hear Mike and Joe in serious conversation about an arms deal of some kind in Egypt. He cleared his throat to make sure they were aware of his presence. Max and Mike shook hands and spent several minutes exchanging pleasantries and reviewing fond memories. Both were capable men with a deep respect and friendship for each other.

Mike was saying, "Dad has told me you are here on a very serious mission, Max. How can we help you?"

"I'm not really sure that you can help, Mike, but any small bit of information could be extremely important in a rather desperate situation," Max replied.

Max reviewed the information for Joe and Mike, but revealed only that a nuclear weapon, or weapons, had been stolen from a certain base in Russia and presumably sold to a terrorist organization.

Mike responded with, "Does any intelligence group have a lead or any idea of what group is responsible? As you well know, Max, we deal in conventional weapons and certainly would not be involved in any kind of nuclear deal."

"I know that very well, Mike, and we certainly didn't think you had any kind of involvement," Max said with a smile. "We were hoping that maybe someone in your organization had been approached or had heard of a nuclear deal taking place."

Joe said, "I hate to think what a terrorist could do with a nuclear weapon in a major city; it would be horrible. I'll get in touch immediately with Joe Jr. and John to see if they've heard of anyone shopping for a nuclear device. You can bet your life that if a terrorist group has that bomb, they sure as hell plan to use it.

"We'll do our best, Max, but I'm not very optimistic about learning much from our organization since all the arms buyers in the world know that we deal only in conventional weaponry. Where can we get in touch with you if...."

"Hold it, Dad," Mike interrupted. "I just remembered something that happened over a year ago when I was in Abu Dhabi selling small arms to the security forces of the United Arab Emirates. A couple stopped by the hotel where I was staying and introduced themselves as agents for Omar Habash. They told me that Libya was looking for nuclear weapons for defense purposes and would pay liberally for any such weapons we could procure for them.

"The lady was very attractive and appeared to be an athlete. The man was medium height with a short black beard, and his name was Jabel, or something like that. She only used one name, but I can't recall the name. Of course, I told them that I could not help them with such weapons, and they had no interest in buying anything conventional."

Max jumped to his feet and shouted, "Beautiful! That ties right into our other information. Mike, I think you just hit a home run. We have other information that I didn't want to tell you about yet to avoid channeling your thinking. That man's name is Amahl Jabel, and the woman with him is known as Lattah."

Mike was shaking his head, "That's exactly right. It comes back to me now. Those were the names that they used. I would say they sure fit the profile. They were very intense, all business, and to be honest, I didn't particularly like either one of them. I recall that when I told them that I couldn't help, they left abruptly with no further conversation."

Joe looked at Max, "What do you suggest we do now?"

Max replied, "I think at this point it would be best if you didn't discuss this with anyone outside this room. It appears that we have the right terrorist group pinpointed, and we don't want to tip them off that we suspect them. Just be alert for any information that may be helpful."

Joe said, "I smell food; Marie must be cooking. Let's go eat lunch."

Max sniffed the air, "Sure smells good, and I hope Marie has that special wine for us. Can't wait to taste it."

Before they sat down to enjoy lunch, Max was on the telephone talking to Scott, briefly filling him in on the information that the Capelas had provided. He then called the airlines and made reservations for an early evening flight back to Riyadh that would arrive there at seven-thirty the next morning.

The four of them thoroughly enjoyed the lunch and the wine and lingered at the table recalling the good times they had enjoyed in California. Marie was disappointed when Max told them that he was leaving that evening. "Max, there is nothing so urgent that you can't take the time to spend the night here. We probably won't see you again for another two years!"

Mike interrupted, "Believe me, Mom, I would like to have Max spend some time here also, but he must leave. He's on a mission where every hour could be important."

Marie persisted, "You men and your secrets! I can't think of anything of such importance that Max can't spend the evening with us."

Joe smiled at Marie, "You have got to believe it, Marie. Max would like to spend some time here also, but he simply can't do it. We'll just enjoy the several hours we have yet before we take him to the airport."

Marie raised her arms, "Okay, okay I give up, even though I can't understand it. Let's take our wine out on the porch; it's so nice this afternoon."

They enjoyed conversation and the late afternoon weather. Just before dusk, Max gathered his things, and, after bidding Marie a tearful goodbye, and a handshake and hug from Mike, he and Joe were on their way to the airport and then his flight to Riyadh.

CHAPTER 14.

IN WASHINGTON, AT THE MARRAKESH Restaurant, Lou Thoma was seated at his desk talking with Troy Sheldon. Troy was a good friend and a frequent visitor to the restaurant. He was also Chief Investigator of foreign espionage in the United States.

Lou was explaining the map that Alex, the waiter, had given to him. "The bus boy found the map under one of Alex's tables. Alex thought it might belong to a foreign travel agent or escort and gave it to me to keep in case the owner of the map came back for it. I was curious about the map, not only because of the foreign language printing and notations, but also because of the landmarks that were pinpointed and the concentric circles around those landmarks."

Troy was frowning as he studied the map and then pointed to a notation in the center of all the circles. "Lou, this really concerns me. If that Arabic word means what I think it means, this could be extremely serious. I'll have to get help in translating the language, but I think that one word means epicenter. If that's what it means, then the concentric circles would indicate areas of damage that would be caused by the explosion of a bomb at the epicenter. Based on the large area covered, it would have to be a nuclear device."

Lou looked at Troy nervously. "Are you serious, Troy? Do you mean we could be in danger right now? What should we do?"

Troy said, "First of all, Lou, settle down. It worries me, too, but I've only given you my guess as to what it might be. Until I do get it analyzed, I want you to keep this strictly confidential. You must not discuss the map with anyone.

"You're my good friend, Lou, but you must take my words as an order from the FBI that you positively can't talk about this. I'm sure you can understand the mass hysteria if the story got out. It would only complicate our investigation. Furthermore, I could be completely wrong about my initial interpretation of what the map is showing."

"You have my word. I must admit it frightens the hell out of me, and I'm a little bit in shock, as I never expected the map to show what you think it shows," replied Lou.

Troy continued, "I would like to talk with Alex on the pretext that I am investigating tour scams and that this tour guide might be involved. Is he at work yet?"

"Yes, he came in about a half hour ago and is probably helping prepare salads," said Lou, as he got up to walk to the kitchen.

When Alex walked into the office, he smiled broadly at Troy who was one of his favorite customers. "Hello, Troy, I suppose you want to order from this messy office. I've offered to teach Lou how to file and clean up the stacks of papers, but he'll never take me up on it. He's afraid I'll take over his job, but I wouldn't want the cut in pay!"

Lou looked at Troy and grimaced, "What do I do with this guy? He's a great waiter, but a helluva smart ass! Bring a chair over and sit down, Alex. Troy has some questions about this map that you gave me."

Troy pulled off his suit coat, threw it on the end of the desk, and sat down across from Alex.

Alex grinned and said, "Hey, just like the movies. Am I gonna get the third degree?"

Troy looked at Lou, "You're right. Alex is a genuine smart ass! How do you put up with it?"

He then looked back at Alex, "Seriously, Alex, I do need your help on something as we're trying to bring down an organization of foreign tour operators who are scamming our senior citizens. What can you tell me about the person who apparently dropped this map?"

Alex described the woman as he recalled her, "She was of medium height, well built, and looked as though she was from one of the Mideast countries. She was very attractive. She took her time eating dinner and was completely absorbed in studying some papers and documents she had with her."

He continued, "I recall her quite vividly, not only because she was very attractive and by herself, but also because she spilled a glass of water on the table and on her bag or purse which was on the floor beside the table. Apparently, when I picked up the purse to dry it for her, the map slipped out beneath the table. Spilling the water didn't seem to bother her at all, but she left shortly after it happened. She gave me a very generous tip even though she wasn't very friendly."

Troy asked, "Would you recognize her if you saw her from a photograph?"

Alex replied, "Yes, I'm certain I would. I remember thinking how I'd like to take her out!"

Lou said, "I don't recall Troy asking you anything about taking her out. I should go back and check how you billed her for the dinner. Probably charged her half of what you should have."

Troy stood up, put on his coat, and shook hands with both men, "Thank you both for bringing the map to us and for all the information you provided. It could be a great deal of help. Again, please keep this confidential until I get back with you."

Troy then headed back to his office, knowing exactly what he had to do next. At the office, he got on the phone to his superior and requested an urgent meeting with the CIA/FBI liaison team working on the stolen nuclear bombs threat. He asked that an Arabic language specialist attend the meeting. He also requested a fast search be made of photographs of known female terrorists who could possibly fit the description that he provided.

In two hours, the meeting was taking place, with Troy laying out all the information he had obtained along with the map and its Arabic notes. His initial hunch was correct. The Arabic word in the center of the concentric circles did, in fact, mean epicenter. The handwritten notes within some of the circles described the degrees of damage that would occur in those specific areas. Gerry Chadwick, assistant to the Director of the FBI, immediately called the Director of the FBI, Gordon Brown, who in turn called Colm OHara, Director of the CIA.

Within an hour, all were in attendance and going through a review of the new information. They listened intently as Troy related in detail every aspect of his conversation with Lou and Alex.

Gordon asked the first question, "Troy, do you think that Alex would be able to positively identify the woman if we were lucky enough to find a picture of her?"

Troy was shaking his head yes, "I have no doubt. Alex was taken by her good looks and talked about how he'd like to have taken her out. Also, he was very perceptive in noticing that she was flying British Airways.

"We have agents right now working with British Airways getting the travel itineraries for all single females with Arabic names flying that night or the next three days following her meal at the Marrakesh Restaurant. Also, a team of FBI and CIA agents are working together to retrieve all pictures of known female Arabic terrorists. Alex, the waiter from the Marrakesh, will be here in two hours to start going through the pictures."

Colm OHara reached out and shook Troy's hand. "Great job, Troy, this could be a tremendous break for us. You know, the FBI and CIA are often accused of too much rivalry and jealousy, but this is a perfect example of what can be accomplished working together. It looks like you have all the bases covered, so I'll return to my office and brief my group on what has transpired. If you have any breakthroughs with Alex identifying this person, please contact me immediately."

Colm left the meeting and returned to his office where he started tracking down Scott, finally finding him in his hotel room in Riyadh.

Scott smiled as he recognized Colm's voice and motioned for Max to get on the extension. "Max is on the line, too, Boss, and we got news for you! Good news, even if it's only a lead. But first, it's your call, what's up?"

Colm related all the information he had received at the FBI meeting and answered their questions. He finished by saying he would be back to them just as soon as he had any more information on the ID of the suspected terrorist. Scott then filled Colm in on what Max had learned from the Capela family.

Max said, "All the pieces are beginning to fit, and they all point to the Middle East."

Scott was shaking his head yes as he was looking at Max, and into the phone he said, "Colm, I would suggest that you arrange an immediate meeting at our Frankfurt office involving you, the three of us, Frank Hughes, Ali, and Sergei. We must further involve our contacts in Saudi Arabia, the United Arab Emirates, and Iran.

"Also, we should consider to what extent we should discuss our problem with the heads of those countries. I'm concerned with how far we can trust their security forces. From here on it's going to be a power play, and we'll need a hundred percent backing of Presidents Hartmann and Padrov. We may need to force the cooperation and confidentiality of some of the heads of state."

Colm responded, "Agree fully. I'll notify Frank and Sergei and you find Ali. We'll meet in Frankfurt tomorrow afternoon as close to two as possible. If any complications arise, let Rozann know, and she will find me. Any questions?"

"Sounds good; see you tomorrow afternoon," Scott replied.

Scott was pleased they were making progress, but he recognized that the tough work lay ahead, such as diplomatic head knocking and some real life head bashing. His thoughts turned to Cheryl and how much he missed her. He felt guilty that he hadn't talked to her in four days. Even though he knew that she understood his job and expected such things, it was still rough on both of them when he was gone on assignments. The last time he had talked to Cheryl she had been in Fayetteville, staying with Jessica's parents, Mavis and Steve.

CHAPTER 15

IN THE FULBRIGHT LABORATORY IN Fayetteville, research work on the memory-sharing project was moving ahead at full speed. The experiments were more sophisticated, with dogs being involved as well as the laboratory rats. Doctors Michael Laird and Sue Cantrell were spending over fifty percent of their time working with the laboratory staff perfecting the process and technology of sharing memories.

Heather was working full time on the program, and Jessica was devoting as much time as possible while supervising the continuance of other research programs in the laboratory. The lab staff was doubled and great progress had been made, with success after success in the experiments.

Rebecca Coles arrived from Washington for a meeting with the group in response to a request for an increase in program funding. The meeting took place at the laboratory with all the major participants in attendance: Dr. Judy Clark, Dr. Laird, Dr. Sue Cantrell, Dr. Bob Cantrell, Heather Shelby, who had been appointed laboratory group leader for this project, and Jessica. Because of the far-reaching implications of successful transfer of memory, security had become of paramount importance.

The University hired Captain Sterling McPherson as Chief Security Officer for the Laboratory. Captain McPherson retired from the Army after thirty-five years of service in Army Intelligence that included tours of duty in Vietnam and the Persian Gulf conflict with Iraq. Working with the Fayetteville Police Department, he had the laboratory well protected with high tech security and surveillance systems. With all the sophisticated protection, the research group was unprepared for the situation that developed with the visit of Rebecca Coles.

Jessica was herding the group into the conference room as Lisa was serving soft drinks and coffee when Heather motioned to Jessica that she wanted to talk with her.

Heather spoke with a puzzled look on her face, "Jessica, do you have the logbook with the detailed notes on all experiments, the thick one with the black hard back cover?"

Jessica replied, "No, I haven't seen it for several days, but I wasn't looking for it. I'm not sure where I saw it last."

"I need it for the meeting, and I left it on my desk yesterday afternoon when I finished preparing for my presentation. I locked my office door when I left last night, and I know it was there when I left," Heather said, concerned. "I thought that you had probably taken it to look at before our meeting. Where in the world would it be?"

Jessica was also perplexed, and although she hated to think so, the thought crossed her mind that the notes might be stolen.

"Heather, call Captain McPherson and ask him to come to the conference room immediately. Then take the backup disk with the notes to Lisa and have her transcribe the notes covering your last two experiments with the dogs. While she is doing that, we can talk with the group about the missing logbook. I'll go right now and check my office to make sure it's not there."

Heather located Captain McPherson, briefed him on the situation, and requested that he meet her and Jessica outside of the conference room. She returned to her office to pick up

James Kerlin

the backup disk to give to Lisa. Heather opened the door to the cabinet beside her desk and pulled out the disk file. She looked in shock at the empty file. Not only was the backup disk gone, all the disks were gone - even those that pertained to other research programs. She looked closely and could see marks from a screwdriver or knife that had been used to force open the cabinet door.

In a panic, she brought up the computer to see if the original information had been deleted. She held her breath as she raced through all the information she had stored in the computer. Thank god! All the information appeared to be intact.

The phone rang and it was Jessica, "Heather, what happened to you? Captain McPherson and I have been waiting for you. The others are wondering what we are doing."

"Wait right there, we've got to talk. Something is going on!" Heather said, as she hung up the phone and hurried down the steps to the conference room.

She lowered her voice as she spoke to Jessica and Captain McPherson, "All my note logs and backup disks are gone, even the ones that do not relate to this project. It has to be an inside job as whoever did it knew exactly what to take and when to take it! The cabinet door was forced open."

Captain McPherson said, "Slow down, Heather, is there any chance of these items being elsewhere in the lab? Who else had access to them?"

Heather replied, "The note logs would not be any place else in the lab, nor would the backup disks. During the experiments, I took all the notes in longhand, and at the end of each day, I would transfer them into the computer and then immediately make a backup disk. I guess that anyone working here in the lab would have access to my office if they chose to sneak into it."

"As you know, all the offices have six foot high partitions or walls, and although I always lock my office door, a person could easily climb over the partition and get to my desk and storage cabinet."

Heather was visibly shaken and Jessica told her, "It's not your fault, Heather. We protected our work against outsiders, but failed to fully protect against a thief in our midst. We carefully checked all our employees before hiring them, but we obviously failed to detect this person, assuming it is an employee. Let's go back into the conference room and explain the situation to the group. It's best to lay the whole thing out as opposed to having them guess what's going on."

Captain McPherson stopped them from proceeding into the conference room and posed a question to them. "Before we go, let me ask you both a question. I have met all the people in the conference room, but I really don't know them. Would either of you have any reason whatsoever to suspect any person in there of taking the notes?"

Jessica looked at the captain in disbelief, "How could you possibly ask such a question?"

The captain smiled at her, "I can understand your reaction, Jessica, but I have learned from years of experience that you've got to consider all possibilities, no matter how remote. I know what I'm doing, so just go along with me."

Jessica nodded in agreement, "I know you're right; I was just shocked initially at the suggestion. But to answer your question, I can't think of any reason, however remote, that would make me suspect a person in that room of wanting to steal the notes."

Heather responded, "I think all the people in there are above reproach. They are a part of this research team, and they would have no reason to steal the notes. I would trust any of them with my life."

The captain said, "Thank you for understanding the reason for the question and for your candor in answering my question. You both gave a very strong endorsement for each of those persons. That is very important for several reasons."

The three of them walked into the conference room, and the group at the table showed their surprise at seeing Captain McPherson accompanying the two women.

Dr. Judy Clark looked at Jessica, "Where in the world have you three been? I thought for sure that you forgot us!"

"I do apologize for the delay in getting started," Jessica replied, "but we've just discovered a very serious situation. All the notes and backup disks for this project have been stolen."

There was a gasp from those at the table as Jessica continued. "Heather has checked the computer and all the original information is still in the computer. Lisa is in the process of making new backup disks. We have no idea, at this point, who the culprit is, or why it was done. Captain, any comments?"

"Yes, I have several things that I want to talk about. First, Heather, would you please ask Lisa if anyone is missing or absent. Following your conference, please stay away from Heather's office, as I will have the police dust the desk, cabinet, and partitions for fingerprints.

"Also, please think of any conversations you may have had with anybody, medical professionals or not, about this project. Who would you think would want this information? Please consider any possibilities, and if you have anything that might be helpful, please write it down. Because this is so confidential, I plan to only involve the police chief and two of his most trusted detectives."

At that point, Heather burst into the room, "We may have a suspect. Lisa said that Don Barrister is absent and did not call in this morning. At about 9 a.m., Lisa called him, thinking he may have overslept. The operator told her the phone had been disconnected this morning."

Captain McPherson asked, "Who is Don Barrister and exactly what did he do? I do know him to say hello to, but when I say who is he, I mean where did he come from and what all do we know about him?"

Dr. Judy Clark spoke up, "I referred him to Heather when she told me they were looking for a computer specialist who was experienced in medical research. He was working for Richardson Pharmaceutical in Tulsa. I had received a blind letter from a Dr. Blaine Johnson in their research group who explained that the young man was moving to the Northwest Arkansas area and would be looking for a position that fit his impressive experience. I believe that Heather called and talked to Dr. Johnson."

"Yes, that is correct," said Heather. "Dr. Johnson provided his home phone number since he preferred not to discuss references or qualifications on his business phone. I called and talked with Dr. Johnson, and he was enthusiastic in his support of Don's experience and qualifications.

"I told Dr. Johnson that Don's salary request was on the high side, but he said that Barrister was worth every cent of what he was asking. I discussed Barrister's resume and Dr. Johnson's endorsement with Jessica, and we felt that he was exactly what we needed in that position. On that basis, we hired Barrister and he's done an outstanding job. I'd be very surprised if he is the person who did this."

The captain asked, "Was Don Barrister aware of the importance and scope of this project?"

Jessica replied, "Yes, I am sure that he fully understood all aspects of the project. He seemed intelligent and was outgoing. Very friendly with all of the lab personnel."

Captain McPherson looked at Heather, "Do you still have Dr. Johnson's phone number?"

Heather winced as she replied, "Yes, it's in my desk. I know what you're thinking and you're probably right!"

Dr. Sue Cantrell, thinking along the same line said, "If you would like, Captain McPherson, I could call Sandy Richardson who is married to Dr. Frank Richardson, the CEO of Richardson Pharmaceutical, and inquire whether or not there is a Dr. Johnson and also whether or not Don Barrister ever worked at the company. I met her some years ago, and we see each other quite often at medical conventions and seminars. I know she would be happy to do this for us with no questions asked."

"That would be extremely helpful, Dr. Cantrell." Captain McPherson continued, "And, as you said, let's try to keep this whole thing as confidential as possible. I know how important today's conference is, but it would be helpful if Dr. Cantrell could find out that information immediately.

"While Dr. Cantrell is doing that, I'd like to hear from each of you regarding ideas or suggestions as to whom you think may have done this and what the motivation may be. Let's just sit here in a group and do this, as one idea may spark another. Dr. Laird, let's start with you."

Dr. Bob Cantrell interrupted, "Captain McPherson, before we proceed, I've got a question on involvement of the police agencies. It seems to me that if we involve several members of the local police force, and then have to involve other police agencies such as the county sheriff and police in other counties, there will be all sorts of questions about what was stolen and its significance. Then without a doubt the press will become involved and the confidentiality of our project will be gone."

He continued, "Because of the enormous importance and worldwide social impact of this work, we'd become deluged with all kinds of unwanted curiosity. Intelligence agencies of all nations would be interested in obtaining information on these experiments.

"My question is whether or not it would be better to perhaps involve the FBI. I think that a few agents could move from county to county and if necessary, from state to state, to track this person with a minimum of attention being drawn to them. It probably would involve fewer city, county, and state officials."

Captain McPherson nodded in agreement, "I agree with you that we could probably keep the investigation more confidential taking that route. I feel that I do have to involve the Fayetteville police chief, and that will not present any problem as I know him well, and have full confidence in him. However, I don't have a close relationship with any FBI agents, and we'd be shooting blind as to who might get involved."

Rebecca Coles spoke up, "Maybe not. I may have a solution. I have a good friend in Washington, Troy Sheldon, who is in charge of investigating espionage throughout the country. We often have lunch together and I've helped him do a lot of recruiting work for the FBI with graduates of many universities, including the University of Arkansas. He owes me a favor. I'm quite sure he'd be willing to help, and I'm equally sure that the FBI would be extremely interested in keeping this investigation as confidential as possible."

Jessica noted Captain McPherson's nod of approval and said, "I think that's a great idea. Bob's analysis of the situation is exactly on target regarding the need to involve as few officials as possible. Captain McPherson is right on the need to involve the police chief and brief him on what is happening. Rebecca, can you get in touch with your FBI friend immediately to see if he'll be available?"

"Yes, I'll phone him right now. Okay to use your office to make the call while Captain McPherson talks with you all?" Rebecca asked, as she retrieved her address and phone number book from her purse.

"Go right ahead, and dial direct as this is laboratory business," said Jessica.

Captain McPherson continued interviewing the group for all the information they could collectively provide about Don Barrister. Heather rooted through her files and came up with a picture of Barrister that appeared in an article about the use of the university computer in doing research for Alzheimer's.

It was a good likeness, and coupled with the description he obtained from the group, it provided McPherson with excellent information to put out in an APB. Furthermore, they gave a detailed description of his car and license plate number.

Rebecca located Troy Sheldon and explained the situation to him, asking him to keep the nature of the experiments strictly confidential.

"Rebecca, we've been close friends and worked together for many years, and I want you to know that I believe you, but I find it hard to accept that memory can be shared between individuals even if they're rats. How do you know that these research people are being honest with you?"

"I've been working with this group for a long time, Troy, and I know all the people involved. I have personally observed the experiments and I've seen memory shared!" Rebecca replied rather sternly. "You can readily understand the tremendous need to keep this thing confidential.

"We must find this individual and recover the experiment notes before he sells them or makes them public. It's imperative that it be done swiftly and as quietly as possible. You know how difficult it would be to try and keep it confidential while working through four or five public law enforcement agencies."

"Okay, Rebecca, if you say you saw this thing happen and you believe that it is the real thing, I agree with you entirely. Apprehension of this man should be given top priority and we'll cooperate completely. But you must agree, Rebecca, on the surface it certainly is hard to believe! This has been a helluva two weeks. I've been involved in another situation that is so terrifying that it's beyond my comprehension. I know you're going to ask, but as you well know, I can't tell you anything about it.

"Inform your group that we'll get involved immediately. I'll fly down there early tomorrow morning to personally make sure we're doing everything possible. I can only spend one day as the other situation requires me to be in Washington. When Captain McPherson finishes his interviews, have him call me and fax me all the information he has.

"I'll then alert certain agents in the major cities surrounding Fayetteville, such as Tulsa, Little Rock, St. Louis, Oklahoma City, Memphis, Dallas and Texarkana. They'll work with local law enforcement officials to achieve the apprehension. All that the local officials will be told is that the individual is wanted on a Federal charge, and he will be surrendered to our agents."

"Thank you, Troy. I appreciate your help on this, as it sounds as though you have your hands full. Next lunch at the Marrakesh is on me! Let me know when you'll arrive tomorrow morning, and I'll pick you up at the airport. Captain McPherson will call you later today and send the info you requested. Bye, Troy, see you in the morning!"

Rebecca returned to the conference room and briefed the group on her call. They were elated that the FBI would immediately take over the investigation. Captain McPherson said he would have the information ready for Troy just as soon as Dr. Sue Cantrell heard from Sandy Richardson in Tulsa. Lisa was already typing a copy of Captain McPherson's handwritten notes when the phone rang. Sandy Richardson was on the phone asking to talk to Dr. Sue Cantrell.

"Hi, Sandy! What a fast response. Thank you!" Sue said with a big smile.

"Sue, I've got a lot of interesting information for you. I'm sure it isn't what you want to hear, but it should help your investigation," Sandy replied.

Sue said, "Hold it a minute, Sandy, I want to put you on speaker phone, so the whole group can hear what you have to tell us."

Sue introduced each member of the group to Sandy and they exchanged greetings.

Sandy then continued, "As I told Sue, the news is not good, but it may be helpful in your investigation of this individual. Don Barrister is quite a character and a very accomplished con man. He did work in the Richardson research labs for almost eighteen months. He is an experienced computer specialist in the medical field and apparently a very good one.

"Our Director of Personnel is doing a confidential recap of Barrister's past working experience and places of his employment. He's sending it to you, Sue, with overnight delivery. You can give it to the person in charge of the investigation."

She continued, "I'm a little embarrassed to reveal some mistakes our personnel group made in keeping Barrister as long as we did. Twice it was discovered that he had lied about his past work experience and the reasons he had been discharged. He gave his boss a sob story about supporting his mother and invalid sister. At the time, we were overloaded with research work and badly needed his skills, so in both of those instances, right or wrong, he was not discharged as he should have been.

"However, he was fired just prior to the time that you received the letter from Dr. Blaine Johnson. Twice he was suspected of stealing drugs from the laboratory, but it was never proven. Then the CEO of Evergreen Drug Corporation called Frank and told him that Barrister had approached one of his sales representatives and offered to sell him information on a flu vaccine that Richardson is developing. Barrister was apparently unaware that Evergreen was not into research on such vaccines. I told Frank that if Evergreen had been in that business, they would have bought the information! He just frowned at me and shook his head saying that I am always too suspicious of people."

Sandy continued, "He wasn't prosecuted because the two companies didn't want adverse publicity, but he was fired immediately. After that, he wrote the letters that were supposedly written by Dr. Blaine Johnson. As you have probably surmised by now, there isn't a Dr. Johnson here at Richardson. Barrister lived in an apartment with two other individuals who I'm told are also shady characters.

"The name of one of them is Blaine Johnson. The phone number given by 'Dr. Blaine Johnson' as his residence was really the phone number of their apartment, and the person you talked to was Blaine Johnson, but not Dr. Blaine Johnson."

Heather and Jessica were looking at each other, and Heather said, "I really feel like a fool. He had me believing that he was the real thing! How could I have been so stupid?"

Jessica quickly replied, "Hey, don't blame yourself. You're not alone in this; the guy is a real pro and fooled all of us. I'm just as much to blame as you are."

"He tricked a great many people," Sandy added. "He's a very smooth operator. I just thought of one more thing our Director of Personnel told me. Somehow he knows that Barrister has stayed in touch with his buddies in that apartment, and also he has relatives in the Tulsa area."

"Sandy, this is Captain McPherson. I just want to thank you for the assistance. This information is tremendously important, and I'm sure it will help us find Barrister."

Sue also said, "Thank you so very much, Sandy. Please tell Frank how much we appreciate his cooperation."

"We are happy to help," Sandy replied. "As I said before, you should receive the other information the first thing tomorrow morning. If you need anything else, please feel free to call me. Bye, bye!"

Captain McPherson said, "She did a terrific job. Thank god you knew her, Sue, and could make the contact so easily. Many corporations would be reluctant to provide such sensitive personnel information. Since Troy Sheldon will be here in the morning, I would suggest that we put everything on hold until he arrives.

"I plan to go through Barrister's personnel file with a fine tooth comb. Why don't you all try to complete the meeting that you came here for, so that we have that out of the way. I know it's important and it may be difficult to do tomorrow."

"Good idea, Captain," Jessica responded. "Lisa can help with the personnel files and Heather's right here if you need her. Let's take a short break, and then we'll start the meeting."

The next morning Rebecca was at the Fayetteville airport sipping a cup of coffee and waiting for the arrival of Troy on the TWA commuter flight from St. Louis. The flight was already ten minutes late, and Rebecca was hoping the low ceiling above the airfield wouldn't cause the plane to be detoured to another city.

However, when she asked the agent at the TWA counter about the low ceiling, she was assured that the plane would positively be arriving. In about five minutes, the plane broke through the overcast and landed. Troy strode into the terminal and spotted Rebecca waiting for him. He greeted her warmly.

He was laughing when he said, "Hey, kid, got yourself in big trouble and had to call the feds, eh?"

Rebecca was laughing too, "Yep, this is out of my league, and I'm sure glad you came down here. Now I'll get a chance to see if you can do something besides recruit new agents. Did you have breakfast? Do you want to stop for a quick bite on the way to the lab?"

"No thanks, Rebecca, I had some of that good airline food on the flight from Washington to St. Louis, and per usual, even though I didn't like it, I ate it. I guess it's because I was brought up to always eat whatever's on my plate. Now give me a run down on the individuals I'll be working with."

As they drove to the laboratory, Rebecca gave Troy a brief summary of each of the participant's involvement in the laboratory's brain research and their individual backgrounds.

She again told Troy that she felt that each could be fully trusted and would cooperate in his investigation.

Troy responded, "I understand your feelings about them, Rebecca, but I must make sure of each individual. Using the information from Captain McPherson, I already have the Bureau running checks on each of them, including Don Barrister. I don't mean to imply that any of your friends are involved, but to solve the puzzle, you've got to have all the pieces."

"Troy, can we tell them that they are being checked out?" Rebecca asked. "I would feel better if they were aware of it."

Troy looked at Rebecca and replied, "No, Rebecca, I told you that in confidence, and it will have to stay that way. I will tell your colleagues at the appropriate time."

Rebecca nodded her agreement as she slowed down to turn into the laboratory parking lot. "I'll do as you say, Troy."

Rebecca and Troy entered the conference room and met Captain McPherson, Heather, Jessica, and Dr. Judy Clark. The doctors were all attending to their duties, having told Jessica that they would be available as needed.

Troy said, "First, I'd like to spend about fifteen minutes with Captain McPherson and then a half hour with the four of you. It's now almost ten after ten, so Jessica, could you arrange to have all the doctors involved meet here at eleven o'clock?

"I apologize for being so abrupt, but I have to return to Washington this evening on a very serious matter of national security. Jessica, would you please have Lisa arrange my flight back to Washington as late as possible this evening."

Captain McPherson quickly reviewed all the information he had sent to Troy, and also went through Barrister's personnel file, as well as the information provided by Sandy Richardson.

"A slick operator, a good con man, but apparently a lousy thief! I need to use your phone, Sterling. I discussed this last night with one of our agents, and I want to see what information he has," Troy said, dialing the Tulsa office.

"Hello, Carl, this is Troy. What have you found so far?"

Carl replied, "No apprehension yet, but we have found some interesting background on Barrister. He came to Tulsa about four years ago from Bartlesville, Oklahoma. His record there shows three arrests. Two for petty theft of computer parts and software and one for car theft, although the charges were later dropped.

"Then while he worked for Richardson Pharmaceutical, the police were involved twice with suspected theft of drugs from one of their laboratories. However, again the charges were dropped. This guy leads a charmed life!"

He continued, "His buddies still reside in the same apartment, and they both have records with rather minor infractions. As you requested, we have the apartment under surveillance, as well as the home of his relatives. So far he's a no show, but we'll keep it going until you tell us to stop. All the local authorities understand it's a Federal charge and warrant with no questions asked."

"Great job, Carl," Troy responded. "Sounds like you have everything covered. If you turn up anything at all, call me at this number, 501-555-1212. I'll be here all day, and then back in my office tomorrow morning. This is a critical situation, so do whatever it takes to get the job done. Thanks again."

Troy turned back to Captain McPherson, "Sterling, let's talk with the ladies and see what we can learn."

For thirty minutes, Troy asked questions about the project and the involvement and responsibilities of each person in the laboratory, as well as all the doctors.

At eleven o'clock, the doctors arrived, with the exception of Dr. Sue Cantrell, who was still administering to a patient. After introductions to Dr. Laird and Dr. Bob Cantrell, Troy questioned them for information they might have that may be helpful. He was particularly interested in how well they knew

Barrister, and how much they thought he knew about the research.

He was talking to Dr. Cantrell when the phone rang with a call for Troy that Lisa had transferred to the conference room.

Troy picked up the phone, "Hello, this is Troy. Okay, hold while I have this transferred to another phone. Jessica, would you please have this call transferred to Captain McPherson's office, I'll take it there."

He walked out of the conference room with no further explanation.

Heather looked at the silent group, shrugged her shoulders, and raised her arms up, "Hey, so I guess it's a very confidential call. Anybody want a coke or something to eat? I'm starved, and he might be on the phone for a while."

Heather took their orders and went to get the refreshments. It was a good thing she did as Troy was on the call for over twenty minutes. The group was busily chatting as he returned to the room just ahead of the arrival of Dr. Sue Cantrell. Troy and Sue were introduced, and Troy then pulled his chair up to the conference table facing the group.

He smiled as he unbuttoned his collar and loosened his tie. "This is what I enjoy most about my job. Every day is so very different. Two days ago I would never have dreamed that today I would be in a research lab in Fayetteville, Arkansas, talking with a group of medical people about a project that I find almost unfathomable.

"However, when Rebecca tells me that memory transfer is possible and, in fact, has been achieved, then I believe it. When I consider the outstanding group of professionals involved in this research, it just strengthens my belief.

"To be perfectly frank with you, yesterday, after Captain McPherson faxed me a list of all the individuals involved in this research, I had the Bureau run very thorough checks on each person working in the lab as well as all of you. Captain McPherson was included. I want you to...."

Dr. Judy Clark interrupted him, "I find that offensive, Troy. Why would you be investigating this medical group? Why would you be investigating Captain McPherson with his outstanding service record? Don Barrister is who you should be looking at!"

Troy smiled again and replied, "Dr. Clark, I fully expected that reaction from one or more of you. First of all, we're not completely sure that Barrister was the thief. It certainly appears that he is, but we don't know for sure yet. Until we do know, we must consider all possibilities. This is an extremely serious and urgent situation.

"To be effective, we've got to look at every possible angle as quickly as we can. You may consider that the bad news. The good news is that each of you came through the Bureau's investigations with flying colors. Mr. Barrister is something else. He has a history of minor criminal activity."

Troy continued, "As you are all aware, there are many parties who, if they knew about this research, would take any action necessary to steal the laboratory notes and any pertinent information. Such parties could well include foreign countries and their agents. That was my initial concern. However, from what I've learned about Barrister, I am pretty much convinced that he is a petty thief that recognized something of tremendous value and stole it without much thinking about how and who to sell it to.

"He probably has no idea that we have a six state alert for his apprehension on Federal charges. My guess is that he'll be caught in Tulsa trying to contact his former roommates. Our objective is to get him before he has a chance to talk to anyone about the research that is going on in this laboratory. As soon as he is apprehended, he'll immediately be put in Federal protective custody. In isolation at a Federal prison.

"Right now we have every place he has ever lived or frequented in Tulsa and Bartlesville under surveillance. State patrols and municipal police in all surrounding states are on alert with his description and that of his car. We have a big advantage in finding him since we acted so quickly. He is a relatively inexperienced thief, so he won't expect this dragnet being set so rapidly. I fully expect him to be picked up within the next few hours."

Troy looked at Rebecca and Jessica and continued, "Now, I must return to Washington as I am needed there for a situation that is of top priority. Lisa has found good flight connections to Washington if I leave Fayetteville on the 4:35 flight. The Tulsa FBI office knows exactly how to handle your case, and I will stay in touch with them.

"As I said before, as soon as he is apprehended, he'll be spirited away by FBI agents to a Federal prison where he will be held incommunicado on Federal charges. I will stay in touch with Captain McPherson, and he will keep you all informed. In the meantime, continue on with your business as though nothing has happened. I've really enjoyed meeting you all, and it was a pleasure to help you. Rebecca has offered to take me to the airport after I spend some time with Captain McPherson."

Jessica stood up and walked over to shake Troy's hand. "Thank you so very much, Troy, for all your help. I am both impressed and amazed at how efficiently you and the FBI have handled this problem. Thank you again, have a good trip home, and we wish you good luck on your other problem back in Washington."

As Troy and Captain McPherson were leaving the room, the others gathered around Troy and expressed their appreciation and good wishes. At 4:15, Rebecca and Troy were at the gate in the Drake Field Terminal.

Rebecca gave Troy a big hug and a kiss. "Thank you, Troy. I know it was an imposition to talk you into coming down here at a time when you're so busy, but I was concerned about the theft. I'm proud of how you handled the whole thing."

Troy had a big smile, "Hey, I always told you I was good! Don't forget that you owe me lunch at the Marrakesh. I'll be sure and tell Lou Thoma when I see him tomorrow. Seriously, Rebecca, you did right in calling me. If this research procedure does what you all tell me it does, and I still find it hard to believe, then this is a security matter of national concern, and the FBI should be involved. It was fun working with you and really a welcome break."

Troy walked through security and out to the waiting plane. As the plane took off, he was reviewing the events of the past two days, contemplating whether or not he had done the right thing in taking the time away from the problem of the nuclear bomb threat.

He had no way of knowing that his brief experience in Fayetteville, with his involvement in the shared memory research program, would be a key factor in a decision made by the President of the United States that would save the lives of millions of American citizens.

Rebecca returned to the laboratory and to the conference room where the group was in the process of finishing the meeting that had started two days before. By six-thirty, the meeting was completed. Rebecca had all the information she needed to increase the Federal funding, and Lisa had arranged for her morning flight back to Washington. The group adjourned, and decided to have dinner and drinks at Club 36.

Jessica told the group, "Hey, it's been a rough two days, and for all your help and the time you spent here, the drinks and dinner are on the laboratory expense account!"

She called down the hallway to Captain McPherson, "Captain, we're all going to the Club 36 for dinner, why don't you join us?"

The Captain responded, "I think I'd better stay in case we hear from the Tulsa FBI office."

"Lisa will be here for a couple more hours, as she wants to try and finish all the backups on the research notes. We'd love to have you along, and Lisa can always reach you at the restaurant," Jessica responded.

The Captain replied, "You got a deal! Sounds good to me. I'll meet you down there."

Just before eight o'clock, the group finished dinner and was having coffee or a drink, when Dan Roberts motioned to Captain McPherson that he had a call. Lisa had forwarded the call from the Tulsa FBI office to the restaurant.

The Captain took the phone, "Hello, yes, Carl, this is Captain McPherson. How's the search going?"

"The search is over," Carl responded. "We followed Barrister's previous roommates to a bar where they met him. We picked them all up before any conversation took place. Barrister is in Federal custody. We've confiscated all the materials that he had stolen. I left word for Troy to call me, and I'll fill him in, and await his direction as to what he wants done next."

"That's great news, Carl. You guys did an excellent job locating him so quickly. I'm sure the others want me to express their thanks for all you've done. If I can be of any help, let me know," Captain McPherson responded

The officer returned to the dinner table, sat down, and sipped his coffee. The entire group was looking at him and he feigned surprise as he asked, "What are you all looking at?"

Jessica said, "You know damned well why we're looking at you! Come on. Tell us what the phone call was about."

Captain McPherson laughed and said, "Oh, that! Seriously, very good news from the FBI. They have apprehended Barrister who was attempting to meet his ex-roommates in a bar in Tulsa. All the materials that were stolen were found in the trunk of his car. He is in the custody of the FBI and will be held temporarily in solitary confinement in a Federal prison."

A small cheer went up from the group at the table, which startled the other customers in the restaurant.

Jessica was laughing and shaking Captain McPherson's hand, "Great job, Captain, and what a tremendous job by Troy and the FBI. I want to thank each of you here for your help in this terrible situation. Especially you, Rebecca, for getting Troy involved so quickly. He knew exactly what to do and did it.

"And to you, Sue, for your contacts with Sandy Richardson. That information really helped us get a good line on Barrister. Now we can all get back to work. Rebecca has the information she needs to provide us with the funding to expand and speed up the program. Rebecca, when you see Troy, will you please thank him again for the great job he did. It's really appreciated."

"I'd be happy to tell him, Jessica," said Rebecca. "He's been extremely busy with a national security problem, but I'm sure I'll be seeing him. I owe him a lunch, and there's no way he'll let me forget it."

The next morning Rebecca was on her way back to Washington. The doctors were back working with their patients, and all the lab personnel were busy again with the research programs. Captain McPherson was working on new security procedures for the laboratory, especially hiring practices.

CHAPTER 16

AMERICAN AIRLINES FLIGHT 1883 WAS landing at Long Beach airport as Amahl Jabel noted that the time on his watch showed twenty minutes after one in the afternoon. The flight from Dallas was about twenty minutes late due to flying against a strong jet stream. The flight from Washington, D. C. through Dallas was late but uneventful, and today Amahl was in no hurry. He was quite satisfied with all he had accomplished on this particular trip and Long Beach was his last stop prior to completing his work and returning to Abu Dahbi.

Amahl had successfully transferred all the demonstration propane tanks from the waterfront Oman warehouses to the mid-town commercial properties that Lattah had leased. Rome, Berlin, Brussels, Paris, London, New York City, and Washington, D.C., were all completed. He was pleasantly surprised by the ease with which all the transfers had taken place. Los Angeles would be the last one.

After each of the transfers, Amahl removed the end plates from those tanks that contained the nuclear weapons and proceeded to inspect and put into motion the parallel timing devices that would eventually activate the nuclear weapons in all eight cities at the same time. October 19th would be a day of jubilation in the Mideast and one of indescribable horror for the Western nations of the world.

Los Angeles was the last city on Amahl's agenda. The tanks were in the Oman Oil warehouse at the Port of Long Beach, Pier B, near Berth 76. The ship and the cargo, including the propane tanks, had already passed customs. All that needed to be done was the transfer of the tanks to the store location in Los Angeles. It was no accident that all had gone so smoothly in getting the tanks through customs in the various countries.

Amahl had invested many years in promoting and maintaining a reputation for Oman Oil Company. It was a squeaky clean and efficient operation in working with the Customs and Port Authority agencies throughout the world. He had established close personal ties with the key individuals in all the ports of interest to him, and he was widely recognized as a hard-working, honest, and very efficient executive whose efforts and discipline made all of their jobs easier.

For several years, under Amahl's direction, Oman participated in the Automated Manifest System (AMS). The system is a cargo inventory control and release notification for sea, air, and rail carriers. Sea AMS is available to carriers and port authorities/service centers. Using a unique bill of lading number, manifest data can be transmitted electronically for all cargo headed to the United States prior to vessel arrival.

This allows Customs an opportunity to review the submitted documentation and determine, in advance, whether the merchandise merits examination or whether to release it immediately upon arrival. The carrier, upon receiving a release from Customs, is able to make decisions on staging cargo and further distribution of the merchandise. All of this can be done before the cargo actually arrives.

To continue processing through the AMS, participants must maintain a very high level of quality with a low error rate. Participants who do not maintain the specified standards are placed on a probationary status or removed from the program. Amahl had recognized very early that his success in getting the propane tanks through American Customs depended very much on Oman's successful participation in this program.

And Amahl made sure that the record of the Oman Oil Company was spotless. Customs and Port Authority officials often spoke of that record as a model of virtually error-free, high quality transmission of manifest data covering the cargoes of Oman carriers. They were high in their praise of Amahl and Oman Oil.

Amahl gathered his luggage and boarded the courtesy bus to the Long Beach Marriott that was a half-mile from the airport and a ten-minute taxi ride to the port area. After checking in and getting settled in his room, Amahl first called his warehouse manager, Abdul, to make an appointment for the following morning. Abdul was expecting him, and made the usual preparations for his visit.

Amahl then called an old friend, Matt Jenkins, Assistant Executive Director of the Port of Long Beach. Years before, when Amahl was new in his job and looking for a warehouse site, Matt was the Director of the Properties Division, Port of Long Beach. Matt not only was of tremendous help to Amahl, but also had befriended him.

That friendship had grown through the years, and, although Amahl had learned to control and freeze his emotions, he did feel a tinge of remorse for the future safety of his friend. However, the cause took priority and was more important than his friend's welfare.

Amahl was smiling as he spoke on the phone, "Hello, Matt! This is Amahl. I'm in town for a few days and would enjoy seeing you."

"Amahl! What a surprise. Haven't seen you in ages. How about having dinner tonight, or are you tied up?"

"I would enjoy it very much. I kept this evening open on the chance that we might get together. Why don't we go to that same restaurant that we went to last time, if you recall which one?" asked Amahl.

With his head nodding yes, Matt responded, "Sure I do. It was the Simon & Seaforts Steak and Oyster House. Why don't I pick you up around four-thirty, and we'll come back to my place and talk a while before we go to dinner. Where are you staying?"

"Sounds great, I'm staying at the Marriott by the airport. I'll be in front waiting for you," replied Amahl.

Amahl always enjoyed visiting with Matt and especially enjoyed his apartment. His twelfth floor apartment, located in the Long Beach Ocean Towers, Ocean Boulevard at Shoreline Drive, had an outstanding view of the harbor and the ocean. Matt was fifty-seven years old, a former star athlete, still lean, black, and a bachelor.

He was a great sports fan, associated with a number of professional athletes, and his apartment was filled with sports memorabilia and trophies. Although Amahl did not really understand American sports, he respected Matt's interest and sports collection.

At four-thirty, Amahl got into Matt's Lincoln Navigator, and after shaking hands, they were on the way back to Matt's apartment. Amahl walked out to his favorite chair on the balcony while Matt fixed the drinks. He was well aware that Amahl didn't drink because of his religion, so he poured a coke for Amahl and a scotch and water for himself.

Matt joined Amahl on the balcony and set the drinks on the small table between them. He related to Amahl all the recent developments at the port, including the politics involved. He then asked Amahl a question that caught him a little off guard.

"Several weeks ago, I noticed on the manifest of one of your vessels a listing of two propane tanks. Is Oman Oil getting into the business of selling propane tanks?"

Amahl was shocked that in his current position, Matt was still involved in examining the manifests of incoming vessels, and further that he had zeroed in on the propane tanks. He glanced sharply at Matt but recovered quickly, played it cool, and answered in a rather matter-of-fact way. "Yes, Oman has been selling such tanks in the Mid-East for a number of years. We recently developed tanks of a superior design in terms of both construction and controls operation that we think will sell well in your country. In fact, we are opening demonstration centers in many cities throughout Europe and the United States. That's one of the purposes of my visit, to try and finalize arrangements for the center in Los Angeles. But enough about Oman Oil and me. Are you still active in the game of golf?"

"Every chance I get. It's a challenging game, Amahl, and you should try it. You need the relaxation as you're probably the most work-oriented and hard-driving person I have ever known. However, I must admit that your hard work has made Oman Oil the most respected operation at this port."

Amahl had used their friendship through the years as a means of spreading such opinions through the layers of Port of Long Beach and Customs management. From the moment they had met, Amahl recognized that Matt was a respected and influential member of port management. Matt's vocal support of Amahl and Oman Oil was extremely important to Amahl's plans. Matt was sincerely fond of Amahl. Amahl liked Matt, but more important, Matt was very useful to him, and he used him to the fullest extent.

"Thank you, Matt. I appreciate your comments. I'm getting hungry! The airline food wasn't that good on the last flight. What do you say we head on down to the restaurant?" Amahl asked, turning the conversation away from the propane tanks.

The two men proceeded to the Simon & Seaforts Steak and Oyster House where they were greeted by the hostess and seated at Matt's regular table. The conversation centered primarily on business and port developments. Amahl told Matt about the continuing growth of Oman Oil and the need to add new and larger ships. Matt told how the Port of Long Beach was building rapidly to accommodate larger ships that require deeper waters and larger terminals.

Matt continued, "At the present time, one-forth of all the trade moving between China and the United States moves through the Port of Long Beach. The U.S.-Sino trade is experiencing tremendous growth. Last month I flew to Qingdao, China, to take part in a ceremony that celebrated a Sister-Port agreement between the Port of Long Beach and Qingdao.

"The agreement calls for the exchange of information and cooperation in the fields of cargo handling, port administration, personnel training, and technology expertise. Although the ports are 8,000 miles apart, they share the distinction of serving as gateways for trade between the two nations.

"I don't envy you, Amahl, in your flights around the world. That flight to China was enough to last me a lifetime. I probably walked twenty miles up and down the aisles. Qingdao paid for the trip, and thankfully they put us in first class. Keep your eyes on China; they're moving fast."

Amahl was in agreement, "Yes, our marketing group is following the progress of the Chinese very closely. It makes me laugh to think of you caged up for a flight to China. You pace in the office, you pace on the golf course, and you paced in your apartment. I would hate to have been the stewardess."

"You got me pegged right," Matt laughed. "Although I was very nice to the stewardess; she was a cute little gal!"

After dinner, Matt paid the bill, and they walked out to the car. Amahl thanked Matt for dinner, and said that he had better head back to the hotel as he some work to do prior to his meeting with the warehouse personnel in the morning.

Matt asked if there was any chance they could get together again before he left.

Amahl replied, "No, I'm afraid not, Matt. I've got a very full day tomorrow, and then I leave early the following morning. I really enjoyed this evening. I'll have to try and get back here more often."

"I enjoyed it, too," Matt said. "Stay in touch and let me know when you're due back here. Incidentally, I was curious when you mentioned the display facilities for the propane tanks; where is it located in Long Beach?"

Amahl had gotten out of the car and was leaning into the window on the passenger side of the car when Matt asked that question. Amahl stood up and cleared his throat and coughed. He was thinking fast. He was almost certain he had told Matt that the tanks were heading for Los Angeles. Why would Matt twist what he had said? Why was Matt pursuing questions about the tanks?

Amahl smiled at Matt and said, "Excuse me, Matt, I had something in my throat. What did you say?"

Matt responded, "Nothing important. I couldn't recall if you were sending the tanks to Long Beach or Los Angeles. Now I remember that you did say Los Angeles. Just curious about Oman's new sideline. I wish you good luck in that endeavor, but I don't think there's much of a market in either city for that product. Anyhow, good luck to you, and if you need anything, or find time to get together, give me a call."

The two men shook hands, and Matt pulled away from the motel.

Amahl was thinking many thoughts. He was upset with himself for possibly over-reacting to Matt's questions about the tanks. Certainly Matt had no reason to be suspicious, and possibly Amahl himself was causing the problem. He truly liked Matt, and he had some remorse in knowing that he would probably never see his friend again.

Early the next morning, Amahl had finished breakfast and was in the lobby waiting for a taxi. After a fifteen-minute ride, Amahl was at the Oman warehouse. He paid the driver and proceeded into the warehouse where he was greeted by a few warehouse personnel and the manager, Abdul.

Abdul shook hands with Amahl and gave him a hug. "Welcome, Amahl! It is good to see you again. It's always a joy having you here. Would you like to tour the warehouse and see how we're doing? I have one new employee I want you to meet."

Amahl responded, "Thank you Abdul. It is my pleasure to be here, if only for a short time. I do want to meet the new employee, but I'll have to skip the tour, as my time is too short. My main purpose in being here is to get those demonstration propane tanks out of your way. I'm going to move them to a showroom in Los Angeles."

He continued, "After I arrived here yesterday, I arranged with US Equipment Rentals to have a flat bed hoist truck and small lift truck here at nine o'clock to move the tanks. I had planned on using our equipment, but the big bosses want the tank sales group to be entirely independent of our dock and warehouse operations. Thanks to you all, we have been very successful in our operations, and they don't want any interference with that success. Let's go meet that new employee before the truck gets here."

Abdul and Amahl walked through the warehouse in search of the new employee. Amahl was pleased when he met him since the newcomer was a Muslim from Saudi Arabia. He did not want any strange westerners in the work group at this particular time. Amahl had spent a great deal of time and effort in staffing all of his operations with people he was sure of, people he could trust. At that moment, Abdul's secretary motioned to Amahl and indicated the truck had arrived.

Amahl spoke to Abdul, "I'll go supervise the loading and movement of the tanks. When the move is completed, I'll return here."

Abdul watched as the tanks were loaded and the truck with the two truckers and Amahl pulled away from the warehouse. He was mildly curious about this rather strange and somewhat secretive event. He had learned a long time ago that Amahl was a boss that you didn't question or cross. Anyhow, if they wanted a separate tank sales operation, it didn't matter. It was of no concern to him.

The rental truck hauling the tanks headed up I-710, north on I-405, east on I-10, and then exited at the La Brea interchange. Amahl was deep in thought. He was sitting in the rear seat of the super cab holding his brief case on his lap. The two rental truck employees were in the front seat, engrossed in baseball conversation.

Amahl kept thinking about Matt's interest in the propane tanks; he couldn't get it out of his mind. Matt's interest had to be just casual curiosity, but Amahl trusted his deeper instincts that had raised a warning flag. His gut feelings were usually right. He decided to make it a point to either see Matt or call him before he left Long Beach to see if he displayed any further interest in the tanks.

The truck finally turned off Highland Avenue into a service alley behind the 3rd Street store location. Amahl walked around to the front of the store, used his keys to enter, and walked through to open the doors at the rear of the building. The two workmen quickly unloaded the tanks and placed them inside the building in the rear storage area. Amahl confirmed with them the price he had been quoted for the move and paid them in cash. He put the receipt in his pocket, thanked the men, and gave each a ten dollar tip.

Amahl then opened his briefcase, took out his tools, and got busy removing the end plates of the special tank. He had been well trained by Dr. Ivankov as to how to set the intricate timing devices. There were two separate timing devices just in case one of them would malfunction. He very carefully set each device to start the detonation of the nuclear bomb at the precise same time as the bombs in the other seven western world cities.

After thoroughly examining everything he had done, he replaced the end plates of the tank. With a miniature spray can of white enamel he covered the scratches on the tank. It was a job well done. There was no indication of the work that had been done. Amahl replaced the tools in his briefcase, locked the doors of the building, and walked down the street to get a sandwich and a soft drink. By one o'clock he was in a taxi heading back to the Oman warehouse.

Back at the warehouse, he met Abdul and was soon going through a number of reports and situations that needed to be discussed. He again toured the new section of the warehouse, with Abdul proudly pointing areas of possible interest to Amahl. Finally at four-thirty, Amahl suggested they call it a day and have an early dinner, as he had an early flight the next morning. Before they left the building, Amahl placed a call to Matt. Matt answered the phone, which surprised Amahl.

"Hello, Matt. Are you playing secretary now?"

Matt replied, "Hey, what a pleasant surprise! No, I'm not playing secretary. She left about two o'clock for a dental appointment. What are you up to?"

"Abdul and I were just finishing up some business and heading out for an early dinner," Amahl said. "I have a very early flight in the morning, so I wanted to give you a quick call to tell you goodbye and that I enjoyed our dinner together. Next time, it's on me."

"I enjoyed it, too, Amahl. I'll be looking forward to your next visit. Take care of yourself, and have a good flight home!" Matt responded.

With that the two friends said goodbye and Amahl and Abdul left for dinner. Amahl was relieved that Matt had shown no further interest in the tanks. Very likely his imagination had taken over in his suspicions of Matt's probing. He found dinner rather boring, having to listen to all the minor problems of the warehouse operations when he had much more exciting plans to think about.

When their meal was finished, Amahl suggested that they head for his hotel, so he could pack and get ready for his early flight. In front of the hotel, he shook hands with Abdul, told him again what a great job he was doing, and bid him goodbye. The next morning he was on American Airlines Flight 1372 heading for Dallas, then to New York City, and on home to Abu Dahbi and Lattah.

CHAPTER 17.

A MAHL SAT BACK IN HIS seat, relaxed and extremely pleased with what he had accomplished. All the tanks had successfully passed through customs and were safely in their final locations. The bombs were in good shape, and all the timing devices were set to detonate at the same time on October 19th. He and Lattah and his small group of terrorists would be honored and recognized throughout the Mideast for this spectacular conquest of western powers.

He was very anxious to talk to Lattah and tell her how well things had gone. However, to leave as few tracks as possible, he avoided any long distance phone calls or car rentals and paid cash for every expense. Knowing that Lattah would want to share in the joy of their success, he decided to call her before he left New York.

At the same time that Amahl was in the air and well on his way to Dallas, Matt Jenkins was leaning back in his office chair, sipping a cup of coffee. His thoughts were about Amahl and their conversation regarding the Oman propane tanks. Matt had good instincts derived from years of experience interacting with people of all walks of life and from many countries. He was perplexed by Amahl's story about Oman Oil's plan to demonstrate and market propane tanks in the Los Angeles area.

Why would they ship such tanks all that distance for such a limited market? Why only two tanks for such a large market area? Matt had spent a great deal of time in central L.A., and he couldn't recall seeing very many such tanks. Also, he had noticed Amahl's reaction when he questioned whether the tanks were going to be located in Los Angeles or Long Beach. It was an innocent question, but for some reason it flustered Amahl. Something was amiss with Amahl's story, and Matt decided to find out what it was.

Matt motioned for his secretary to come into his office, "Sandy, would you please get me copies of the manifest for a recent arriving Oman Oil tanker that included the shipment of two propane tanks. The shipment probably arrived during the past month. Also, get me the name of the customs inspectors who checked the ship. Let me know as soon as you have the information. In the meantime, I'm going to visit the Oman Oil warehouse. Be back in about an hour."

Matt entered the office area of the Oman Oil warehouse and was greeted by several office workers. After so many years as an active port official, he was readily known by most of the port work force.

"Hi, Liz!" Matt said to Abdul's secretary. "Is your boss around?"

"Sure, Matt. He's in his office doing paper work. Walk right in," responded Liz.

Matt entered Abdul's office and spoke, "That's a mighty messy desk. I'll bet it wasn't that way when Amahl was here!"

"Hello, Matt," Abdul said smiling at Matt. "No, it wasn't. I had the mess stuffed in a drawer, and now I've gotta catch up. It's good to see you. How can we help you?"

"Just making the rounds and trying to keep up with all the changes going on in this port. I can't believe how fast we're expanding in all directions. It was good to see Amahl again, although he sure didn't stay very long. Usually we have a couple of dinners together and walk around the docks. I can't believe what he's into now. How in the hell is Oman going to compete in the propane tank market in Los Angeles? Some marketing guy sure sold them a bill of goods."

Abdul said, "I agree, but don't tell Abdul I said that. I can't figure out what they're doing. We're busy enough with all the tanker traffic. Of course, the tank sales will be a separate operation, so it won't bother me any. I don't know why Amahl got involved with such a venture."

"Yeah, it surprised me," Matt responded. "I bet you hated to waste your time moving those tanks for him, but on the other hand, it got them out of your way."

"I didn't like them setting around here, and it's good they're gone," said Abdul. "But we didn't have to move them. Amahl hired US Rental Equipment to move them, as he wanted to keep all the costs of the tank operation separate from the warehouse expenses. In fact, it's being kept so separate that he wouldn't tell me the location of the tank store. In a way, it offended me. Since we work for the same company, why shouldn't I be informed of what's going on?"

"I agree with you, Abdul. There's no good reason why you shouldn't know. I'm glad it's not my investment or responsibility," responded Matt. "Anyhow, the warehouse looks great. You run a good operation, Abdul. I've got to get back to work; nice chatting with you."

Matt headed back to his office deep in thought. His visit with Abdul had produced more questions than answers. Why would the tank operation be kept secret from Abdul? Oman Oil was a very efficient company and Amahl was a shrewd manager. Why would he spend money for professional movers to transfer equipment that could easily be moved with Oman equipment? It seemed very obvious that he didn't want Oman warehouse personnel to know the location of the tank display store. But why?

Matt poured himself a cup of coffee, and settled back in his chair. Shortly, Sandy brought him the information he had requested. He quickly read through the manifest and found the two tanks listed. No special notations.

He called one of the custom agents who had inspected that particular cargo.

"Hello, Al. This is Matt Jenkins. Need some help." Al responded, "Hey, Matt! How you doing? We haven't seen you for a while. Nose to the grindstone, eh?"

"Yeah, it's been a while, and I've been working my butt off," Matt replied. "How's your memory, Al? About three and a half weeks ago an Oman Oil vessel cleared customs with a routine cargo except for two small propane gas tanks. I couldn't remember them ever transporting such tanks before. Do you recall seeing them?"

Al said, "I sure do. We were kidding the crew about getting a grill and having a barbecue on the deck."

"Did you inspect the tanks?" Matt asked.

Al replied, "Sure did. Went over both tanks and even opened the relief valves on each one. Both were fully pressurized and contained propane. We recognized the odor of the gas immediately. Is there a problem, Matt?"

"No problem, Al, I was just curious, and wondered if we should expect to start receiving any volume of shipments of such tanks."

Al replied, "Nah, we haven't seen any since then, and there was no conversation about it at the time; probably won't see any more of them."

"I suppose you're right, Al. Thanks for your help," responded Matt, as he hung up the phone.

Matt was initially relieved with the information from Al. The tanks were just what they were supposed to be. He was obviously wrong in suspecting that something was not right in the situation. However, his intuition wouldn't let him let go. He instinctively knew that something was not right.

Could it be that Amahl was smuggling drugs? No way could he believe that. But on the other hand, if not that, then what the hell is going on? He did not want to stir things up and cause problems for Amahl and Oman Oil just on a hunch. But on the other hand, he felt compelled to do something.

Matt fingered through his Rolodex until he found the name of Frank Coffman, FBI special agent in Long Beach, with whom Matt and customs agents had worked for many years on matters involving port operations. He dialed Frank's private line and got him immediately.

"Frank, this is Matt Jenkins. How are you?"

"Hello, Matt. I'm doing fine except for my golf game. It's really gone to hell, but I'm ready to play any time you say. What's up?" replied Frank.

Matt responded, "Frank, I need to discuss a situation with you that may or may not be a problem. I've only got a few facts and a gut feel that something is wrong. I don't want to cause any unnecessary problems, so I'd sure like to talk this over with you and get your sense of the situation. Could you meet with me within a day or two?"

"How about now?" Frank asked. "I've got a meeting later this afternoon, so it would be better if I drove out right now. I'll pick up some Chinese food on the way, and we'll have lunch in your office."

Matt agreed, "Thanks, Frank, you know how much I enjoy Chinese. I sure appreciate your help on this."

After Frank arrived, the two men sat at Matt's desk eating their lunch with the hot tea that Matt had prepared. Matt reviewed the details of the past several days, and then laid out all the questions that led to his suspicions. Frank listened intently, and then sat quietly while he thought over everything that Matt had told him.

Finally Frank spoke, "Matt, that's a tough one. From what you tell me, I share the same gut feel that something's not right. Several things just don't make sense. The problem is we could be completely wrong, and if we push it too fast, we could end up with egg on our faces and with two very unhappy bosses. Aren't you and Amahl pretty good friends? I recall meeting him about a year ago when we all had lunch together. He seemed rather low key and all business."

Matt responded, "You recall him very well. Amahl is quiet, confident, very intelligent, and strictly business. We're good friends, and it bothers me that I'm suspicious of his actions."

"I understand your feelings, Matt," said Frank, "but there is something about these circumstances that's not right. From past experience, I've learned to respect your judgment, and it's obvious you have strong feelings about this. I think we are compelled to check it out.

"First of all, we've got to get to those tanks and look inside of them. It's fortunate that Abdul mentioned the company that moved the tanks. I can run a confidential check through US Rentals and find the address where the tanks were taken. I suspect the building is unoccupied, so after a little surveillance, you and I will find a way into the building."

Matt responded, "I thought you said we shouldn't move fast because we might be wrong. And just how are we going to look inside the tanks without tearing them up? I'm all for doing this, but like you said before, I don't want to see us lose our jobs over it!"

Frank replied, "I changed my mind. When I said look in the tanks, I didn't mean to take them apart. At least not yet. I'm going to get the L.A. FBI lab to help on this. They've got a device used to look inside drums of nuclear waste. The system uses gamma-ray spectrometry, computer aided tomography similar to a medical CAT scan, and something called SPECT, which is single photon emission computed tomography to peer into the drums.

"It can determine the presence and volume of various kinds of nuclear waste. The procedure can even pick out gloves or beakers that have been tossed into the drum along with the waste. It's quite a gadget; it even measures the thickness of the drum wall."

Matt replied, "You're way over my head, but it sounds like exactly what we need. I had visions of us getting arrested not only for breaking and entering, but also for destruction of property if we took the tanks apart."

Frank said, "Here's the plan. I've got to attend that meeting this afternoon, so we'll do the whole thing tomorrow morning. By that time, I'll have located the building address and arranged for the lab technicians to meet us with that device. One of the lab technicians is a locksmith, so we'll have no problem getting into the building.

"And just to cover our asses, I'll come by at eight in the morning, and we'll run by the Custom's Office and brief Dan Olson on what we're doing. He's close to both of us, and if something goes wrong, he'll back us in that we were checking a possible customs violation."

Frank left and Matt returned to his paperwork, but his mind was not on his work. Things were moving faster than he had anticipated. Suppose the whole investigation blew up and he lost his job. It was a good job, one that he really enjoyed, and it had a damn good retirement. On the other hand, he was convinced that something was not right, and he was determined to find out what it was. Matt leaned back in his chair thinking about Frank. He was glad that he had picked Frank to talk to as he was very intelligent, knew his way around, and was a man of action.

Just before eight the next morning, Frank walked into Matt's office, picked up Matt's doughnut, and dunked it in Matt's coffee.

Matt looked up and said, "Just what in the hell are you doing? That's my doughnut and my coffee! There's a plate of doughnuts and a pot of coffee on the credenza, so leave mine alone."

"Don't have time, Matt," Frank replied. "We're in a hurry. Besides it's probably your second or third doughnut, and you know they're not good for you. Let's take coffee with us. We can drink it on the way to see Dan Olson."

When they arrived at the Customs Office, Dan was there waiting, and waved them into his office where they all sat down; Dan closed the door.

Dan said, "I can probably guess why you're here, Frank, but I am surprised to see Matt with you. It's about the directive from your boss concerning tightening up on our inspections of cargo and shipments from the Mideast. To report anything unusual, or anything changing from past routines. Right?"

Matt was shocked at Dan's comments and shot a stern, questioning look at Frank and said, "Frank, what the hell is this? What's going on?"

Frank responded, "Hold it, Matt, I don't blame you for being pissed off. Let me explain. For some reason that we're not privy to yet, Washington is extremely concerned over shipments from the Mideast. I didn't realize that Dan had received that directive already since it originated out of FBI headquarters.

"I had just received mine a short time before we met yesterday. I was a quite surprised since I just read the directive and here I was already involved in that very kind of situation. I would have told you, but it was a confidential directive, and I wasn't really sure what to tell you."

Dan said, "Will one of you please tell me what's going on. You both asked to see me, and then you sit here discussing something between the two of you that I am totally unaware of. And, Frank, I got that stern look you gave me when you mentioned the directive being confidential. I just assumed that since Matt is a high ranking Port official, he had been informed about it."

Frank replied, "Okay, let me back up and start the meeting over. It appears, Dan, that although Matt was not involved in the directive, he's been doing the job for us, and a damn good one, too."

Frank, with Matt's help, related the whole story. Dan listened intently and was intrigued with the situation and their plan.

Dan said, "You know, Frank, you're kind of working in Custom's area of responsibility."

Frank responded, "I realize that, Dan, that's why we're here. I didn't want to get any more people involved than we have to. I told Matt that if we got into trouble, you'd cover our asses!"

"Man, you sure got balls, Frank. I'd like to see you out there flapping in the wind and begging for me to help you!" Dan said with a big grin. "You got a deal, but only on one condition."

Frank asked, "And what's that?"

"The deal is that I go with you and Matt to check out those tanks," responded Dan. "It'll still be all your show; I just want to go along."

"You got it!" Frank replied. "I'll call the FBI lab guys and tell them where we're going. US Rentals came through with the address yesterday afternoon."

Following Frank's call, they walked out and got into his car heading for the inspection of the tanks. When they arrived at the address, the FBI van was already parked in the drive behind the store. Frank got out and walked over to where the four men were standing and shook hands with them. He motioned to Matt and Dan to join them for introductions.

Roger Clark was the lab agent in charge of the group and he told them, "We made an inspection of all the doors and it appears that the front door offers the best chance to gain entry. This large steel rear door is locked and bolted from the inside. Once we get inside, we can open this rear door and back the van inside the storage area. You all wait here and Stan and I will go open the front door. I don't see any evidence of a security alarm, so we should be okay."

Matt was amazed how quickly the men were inside the building and had opened the rear door. Stan got into the van and carefully backed it into the building. The group walked around the two tanks that were stacked one on top of the other. The gleaming white tanks were quite visible but were contained within a cage of 4" x 4" timbers built up from the heavy pallet on which the tanks rested. The ends of the tanks were accessible, but it would be difficult to scan the tops and sides of the tanks.

After discussing the situation with his crew, Roger said, "Frank, to do the job right, we have to tear this thing down so that both tanks are accessible and on ground level. I realize you would prefer not to disturb the wooden structure, but we have no choice."

Frank quickly responded, "Let's tear it down, but be careful because we want to reassemble it afterwards in good condition, so that we don't tip our hand that we've been here."

Roger said, "Good! That top tank probably weighs close to a thousand pounds, so we'll need help in getting it to floor level. Mark, call the lab and have them send us the tow truck service we always use. He can easily lower the tank. Stan, get the crow bars and sledgehammers out of the van, and then pull the van back out into the drive to make room for the tow truck."

Matt and Dan stood out of the way as the FBI crew disassembled the wooden structure. They quickly found that it had been fastened together with large lag screws with special threads for wood. Instead of crowbars that would have been used to pry the timbers apart if spikes had been used, they reverted to wrenches to remove the lag screws.

Roger said, "Well, at least that takes care of the problem of damaging the timbers by prying them apart. I'm surprised that such care was taken in the packaging of these tanks. It adds to the suspicion of it being a special situation."

All the timbers had been removed with the exception of the platforms on which the tanks were resting and Roger said, "Stan, check those relief valves and see if the tanks are charged with gas."

Stan complied, and when he opened the top tank valve, it hissed and he said, "Phew! I hate the smell of that gas! There's no doubt that one is charged."

He then checked the second tank with the same result. Both tanks were charged. Frank and Matt glanced at each other and Dan was frowning. With both tanks charged, were they wrong in their suspicions? No one spoke but their glances reflected doubts.

Finally, the tow truck was backing slowly into the building with the lifting boom on the rear of the truck barely clearing the top of the doorway. Each tank had two lifting eyehooks on top. The truck operator ran a heavy cable through the two hooks and fastened the cable to the large hook on the boom. He carefully applied the power and raised the top tank several inches off its platform.

He then pulled the truck forward and gently set the tank down about ten feet from the other tank. Frank spoke with the truck driver and explained that after they finished their work, they might want the tanks stacked again. The driver gave Frank his mobile phone number, indicating he would be on call for another six hours. Frank closed the sliding doors after the truck pulled out.

Roger and his crew were busy setting up the equipment to scan the two tanks. Matt and Dan watched with admiration as the crew quickly and professionally went about their business. They scanned the first tank on one side and then talked among themselves. The tank was scanned again on the other side.

Roger walked over to Dan and said, "This might be a wild goose chase. That tank is perfectly clean."

Dan replied, "One down and one to go. Let's get after it."

The group moved their equipment and started the second scan. They had just started the scan when there was a murmur among the technicians.

Roger called out to Matt, Dan, and Frank, "Come here and watch this! I think we've hit pay dirt. We're getting images of items that don't belong in that tank, but I'll be damned if I know what the hell they are."

He continued, "Stan, run that scan all the way across again. Now watch, Frank. When you start the scan, you first see two device-like things and some wires or cables. Then it shows what appears to be a baffle plate that seems to seal off the first third of the tank. The center third of the tank appears to be clear, and that's where the propane is stored.

"Then look at the remaining portion of the tank. It's some kind of device that's a little larger than a basketball, and I think it's wired to the two smaller devices at the opposite end of the tank."

The group watched as the tank was scanned again. No one in the group knew for sure what they were seeing.

Frank looked at Matt and said, "Matt, you sure as hell had the right hunch, but I have no idea of what we're dealing with here. I suspect it's a bomb of some kind, but beyond that I'm not sure what we have."

Roger warned them, "We've got to be very careful with this. It might be booby-trapped. We have no clue what will set it off or how much time we have if timing mechanisms were used. Any ideas, Stan?"

Stan replied, "We're going to have to get additional help on this, Roger. I hope to God that I'm wrong, but I think it's a nuclear device."

That statement got the group's attention. It created a few seconds of silence that reflected a degree of fear and apprehension among the men. They were clearly shaken by Stan's statement.

Frank spoke, "Here's what we've got to do. First I'll call FBI Headquarters in Washington and advise them of what we've found. Troy Sheldon put out the FBI directive on Mideast shipments, so I'll contact him. He heads up the FBI activity, monitoring any subversive action in this country. He'll advise us on what we should do next."

"Dan, I know that you feel obligated to notify your superiors at Customs, but I think this group should sit tight on this information until we know what's going on. We don't want this to get out and cause a panic throughout Los Angeles and the nation."

Roger nodded in agreement and Dan said, "I agree entirely, Frank. Let's find out first what the hell we're into. What do you think, Matt?"

Matt responded, "What I'm thinking right now is that I wish I wasn't here and that I hadn't opened my big mouth!"

The men all laughed, nervously, but it did help to break the tension.

Matt continued, "Seriously, I think we should do exactly what Frank has suggested. However, I think that whatever we do, we should move fast."

"Roger, can you get someone from your lab who can study these scans and tell us what we've got? Maybe someone who knows about nuclear devices as well as conventional bombs."

"Yeah, I know just the person we need," said Roger. "Rollie Weeks is retired now, but he is an expert on any kind of explosive you want to talk about. Rollie worked at both Los Alamos and the Livermore Laboratories for over forty years. He lives in Santa Monica and has consulting contracts with the FBI and other law enforcement agencies. I can get him here in two hours."

Roger first called his office to get Rollie's phone number and then called his residence. Rollie wasn't home, he was playing golf, but Mrs. Weeks gave Roger the number for his cell phone. In three rings, Rollie was on the line.

"Hello, Rollie, this is Roger Clark. How many holes have you played and are you winning money?"

"Hey, hello, Roger," replied Rollie. "We just finished the fifth, and yes I'm winning money. Wish you were here, I'd be taking yours, too! However, I know that when you call, there's trouble in the air. What's going on?"

"I hate to interrupt your golf game, Rollie, but we need your help on a very urgent issue," said Roger.

"Well, we should be finished in about three more hours. Suppose I give you a call back then?" replied Rollie.

"Sorry, Rollie, we need you here as soon as possible. This is a critical situation that involves national security. I don't want to discuss it on your cell phone. Would you please get to a pay phone as soon as you can, and call my office to get our location, and then get here as fast as you can," Roger insisted.

Rollie said, "Damn it, Roger, this is the best I've played in months, and I'm just getting back part of the money these robbers have taken from me. But, you do sound desperate, so I'll make the call and leave immediately."

Frank then called Troy Sheldon at FBI Headquarters. "Hello, Troy, this is Frank Coffman. We've got a problem here that relates to the directive that you just put out concerning shipments from the Middle East."

Frank told Troy all that had transpired during the past several days. He described the scanning and the opinion of Stan that there was probably a nuclear device inside the tank. He also told of Roger's call to Rollie Weeks for help in determining the contents of the tank.

Troy was excited, "Great work, Frank. Give the group our thanks for providing a very important piece to a horrible puzzle. I know you've probably already told the others not to talk about this, but remind them again to keep this confidential. This must not be discussed with anyone. I'll make arrangements to have a military jet fly me out there immediately, so I should arrive within four hours. When I arrive, I'll call you on your cell phone, and you can arrange to pick me up."

Frank related to the group his conversation with Troy, which further intensified the gravity and danger in the situation. Matt and Dan both called their offices to notify them that they would be out for the rest of the day. Frank asked Mark if he would go out and get some sandwiches and coffee while they waited for Rollie to arrive. It was going to be a long hard day, and they might as well have something to eat.

Roger was standing on the sidewalk in front of the store waiting for Rollie to arrive. He was munching on a ham and cheese sandwich and sipping his cup of coffee. Very shortly Rollie drove up, and Roger raised his hand with the sandwich to direct him to park in back of the building.

Rollie parked his Explorer beside the FBI van and then walked over to shake hands with Rollie. "I sure hope you saved one of those sandwiches for me. I wheeled that golf cart off the course, changed shoes, and here I am in golf clothes and hungry."

Roger replied, "Got plenty of sandwiches and coffee inside. While you eat I'll fill you in on what's going on."

After being introduced to the group, Rollie was sitting on one end of the tank eating his food while Roger and Frank explained the situation.

Suddenly, Rollie looked up and stopped eating. "Are you telling me that I've got my butt on top of a nuclear bomb?"

Roger smiled and said, "That's what Stan thinks it is and yes, you're sitting right on top of the damn thing."

Rollie stood up and stuck the last bite of sandwich into his mouth. "Let's get that scan going, and I hope to hell that Stan is wrong."

The crew again started to scan across the tank, and Rollie closely examined the image of the two devices in the first third of the tank. "These are definitely timing devices. They appear to be identical, so one is probably a backup to try and make sure that the detonation takes place as planned."

The middle third of the tank was scanned to show it was clear and only contained the propane. Then they scanned the final third of the tank and Rollie recognized the image immediately.

"Son-of-a-bitch! It is a nuclear device! I was sure hoping you were wrong, Stan. There is not the slightest question in my mind as to what it is. We must disarm it as soon as possible. Have you examined the tank for means of getting into it? I would doubt that the ends are welded in place."

Stan answered, "No, it's not welded. I noticed on the first scan that the ends are fastened in place with large setscrews that have been painted over. We should have no problem getting into the tank. My only concern is to whether or not it's been booby trapped."

Rollie said, "I would doubt it very much. First, the person or persons who built this bomb were meticulous in every thing they did. Even the wooden cage containing the tank was made carefully. These people were confident of success. I doubt they saw the need for a booby trap. Also, a booby trap of any consequences would have shown up in the scan."

Roger directed, "Mark, get the tools out of the van and we'll get those end plates off."

Frank suggested, "Perhaps we should wait for Troy to arrive so he can be here when we take it apart."

Rollie spoke up, "I don't think we want to take that chance, Frank. We have no way of knowing when that thing might be detonated. If it goes, it would take the lives of hundreds of thousands of people, and we simply can't take that risk."

Frank said, "You're right, Rollie. Let's get moving."

Mark took a screwdriver and chipped the paint off of the tops of the screws. Twenty minutes later Mark and Roger removed the end plate revealing the timing mechanisms. Rollie took a flashlight and carefully studied the mechanisms and how they were wired. He disconnected four of the wires and removed the first device.

He repeated the process and removed the second mechanism from the tank. A big sigh of relief was heard from the group that had been intently watching his work. The other plate was removed and the nuclear device was exposed.

Rollie said, "The nuclear device itself is extremely heavy. As soon as you people are through with it, it should be taken to the Livermore Lab for removal from the tank. Both the timing devices and the nuclear warhead are Russian made."

Roger asked, "Is that a small nuclear bomb?"

Rollie replied, "They have greatly decreased in size and tremendously increased in destructive power. That appears to be a one megaton thermonuclear warhead that, if exploded, would kill millions of people."

Matt said, "I would never have suspected that Amahl would be part of such a scheme. Why would he have such hate that would result in the killing of so many innocent people?"

Frank replied, "That's a question that only Amahl could answer. I doubt that we will ever know."

The phone rang and Frank's office advised him that the military jet carrying Troy Sheldon was approaching Van Nuys Airport. Frank immediately left in his car to meet Troy. When Frank arrived at the airport, Troy was already in the lounge of Petersen Aviation, one of the general aviation operations at Van Nuys Airport.

Frank approached Troy with a smile, "Sure glad to see you, Troy! Thanks for coming out right away, as we need help to figure this damn thing out. I'll fill you in during the ride."

Troy picked up his bag and fell into stride beside Frank, "The pieces are beginning to fall into place, Frank, but not fast enough. We have no idea what the terrorist timetable is. We're hoping that the timing device in the bomb you have may give us a clue."

Troy tossed his bag into the rear seat of Frank's car, and they were on their way to the bomb site. Frank related to Troy the entire story, especially the role Matt played in being so perceptive and pursuing his suspicions. When Frank got to the part that Rollie Weeks played in examining and taking the bomb apart, Troy expressed surprise.

"I though Rollie was retired! I was at his retirement party at least five years ago. We played golf and had a few too many drinks! How's he doing and how'd he get involved?"

Frank replied, "He's been consulting for various state and federal agencies. He just seemed the appropriate person to call in this situation."

"You couldn't have made a better choice. Thank goodness he was near by and available. I'm shocked that you got him off the golf course; he's a helluva golfer."

Frank parked the car behind the building housing the bomb, and they walked inside. Rollie was the first to greet Troy and gave him a handshake and a hug.

Troy said, "Rollie, you old fart, what're you doing here? I thought you would be in a rest home someplace!"

"Rest home my butt!" Rollie replied. You guys keep interrupting my golf games because you can't do without me. I don't know what you're gonna do when I really retire!"

Frank made the introductions all around and Troy expressed his thanks to Matt for the great job. The small group sat on the floor and leaned against the walls while Troy debriefed each individual and took detailed notes.

Troy made each man take an oath of confidentiality, and then explained the worldwide nuclear threat. The men were horrified at the scope and urgency of the situation.

Rollie confirmed that the bomb in front of them was of the same type and size of the stolen Russian bombs. He also looked at Troy and said that the timing device for the Los Angeles bomb had been set for October 19th.

Troy took some additional notes, and then stood up and said, "Thanks to each of you; you've helped to hopefully save our western civilization from a terrible fiery ending. Now, Frank, I've got to hurry to Washington. My plane is waiting for me, and I've got to get this information back to the President."

With that, Troy zipped up his briefcase and he and Frank headed for the airport.

CHAPTER 18.

Troy had just said goodbye to Frank, and as Frank's car pulled away, Troy's cell phone rang. It was his secretary, Ginny.

"Troy, you are so hard to track down! I've been trying to reach you for the past hour. You told me to avoid using the cell phone for security reasons, so I called Frank's office and nobody there knew how to find you or Frank. You sure you're out there on business! I've talked to your pilot twice and he...."

"Hold it Ginny, you got me, and believe me, it is business. What's up?" interrupted Troy, smiling at her irritation with him.

Ginny continued, "Good news! The waiter at the restaurant identified a photograph of the mystery woman. She is an employee of the Oman Oil Company based in Abu Dhabi, United Arab Emirates. Her name is apparently Lattah, and she works for a man named Amahl who is in charge of scheduling and controlling Oman tankers and freighters around the world. She and Amahl are frequent visitors to the U.S."

"Jackpot! Jackpot!" yelled Troy, jumping into the air. The receptionist in the terminal lobby gave him a quizzical look as though he had lost his mind.

"Ginny, if I was there, I'd give you a hug and a kiss! But first things first! I'll be leaving here immediately on the military jet, so I'll be back late this evening. Call Chadwick and have him set up a 7 a.m. meeting with the President, Frank Hughes, Colm O'Hara, Jordan Hennings, Glenna Quisenberry, Davis Benson, and anyone else the President thinks necessary for this extremely urgent situation.

"Tell Chadwick I'll pick him up for the meeting and brief him on the way. Also, make sure that Scott Crockett and Max Thorne are available for a conference call from the President."

Ginny replied, "Damn, Troy, I've never heard you so excited. Jackpot, jackpot, a kiss and a hug, flying back tonight with an early morning meeting! I knew you'd like the news, but I never dreamed it was that good. I'll make the calls, and get the meeting set up. Bye, Troy. See you in the morning."

At exactly seven the next morning, Troy walked into the Oval Office where the group was already assembled, having a breakfast of coffee, Danish, and orange juice, and deep in conversation. When President Hartmann spotted Troy, he jumped to his feet and strode across the room to shake hands and welcome him. Troy exchanged greetings all around, and President Hartmann called the meeting to order.

"Troy, you're the guy responsible for getting us all up early for this meeting, so you have the floor to tell us why we're here."

"Thanks, Mr. President. Sorry about the early gathering, but when you hear this information, you'll understand the urgency. I have two separate, but related, situations to tell you about. Let's first discuss them independently, and then later as to how they intertwine."

Referring intermittently to his pages of notes, Troy spoke for twenty-five minutes. He related Matt's experience with Amahl, his suspicions, tracking down the bombsite, and the examination of the bomb. He told how the bomb had been scanned, and how Rollie Weeks had been called in to examine and verify what the bomb was, and to disarm it.

He was high in his praise of the work done by Matt. Without his keen perception and perseverance, the bomb would not have been found. Next Troy took questions and led the discussion.

President Hartmann then summarized the situation, "This pretty well confirms that the stolen Russian nuclear devices are involved in this terrorist plot and that they have been deployed. I think we have to assume that all eight devices have been placed in strategic locations, probably throughout the Western world. Rollie Weeks has provided us with a timetable for one specific bomb. We don't know if that timeline is the same for all the bombs. We have one out of eight. How in the hell do we find the other seven? We know that Amahl is a terrorist, and we know where to find him. But are there other terrorists involved?"

Troy said, "That's where situation number two comes in. We were damn lucky to have Matt to come through in the first situation. Now we're damn lucky to have an observant waiter at, of all places, the Marrakesh Restaurant."

Troy looked around the room at the expressions on the faces of group. "I know, you're thinking Troy is really reaching now! How in the world does this tie into our situation? Well, I'll tell you."

Troy went through the whole story of the lady's visit to the restaurant, how she dropped her map, how the waiter found it, and gave it to his boss thinking that she might return to claim it. The restaurant owner subsequently involved him out of curiosity as to the language on the map.

Troy continued, "Again, luckily, the waiter was infatuated with her, and recognized her immediately when he was later shown her passport photo. The woman was identified as Lattah, an employee of Oman Oil whose superior is none other than Amahl! We've got to assume that, with the markings on the map and the presence of Lattah, there's a nuclear device here in Washington!"

President Hartmann was frowning, "My god! This is terrifying, Troy. Why such hatred of millions of innocent people? We've got to track these animals down, and find where the bombs are located!"

He took a deep breath and looked at Troy, "You've done a great job, Troy, and we're indebted to you."

Troy responded, "Hey, I'm just the messenger. We have a great many just plain citizens to thank for all this information. God bless them!"

President Hartmann said, "Let's discuss what we do next, what our plan of action should be, and which foreign associates should be involved."

Colm O'Hara spoke up, "Mr. President, several of my agents and Frank Hughes are presently in Saudi Arabia. We had planned to meet in Frankfurt today for a briefing and to plan our next moves. They also have determined through their own investigations that Amahl and Lattah are the terrorists we are looking for. I have canceled the Frankfurt meeting, and, at Troy's request, I have the agents standing by for a conference call for instructions on matters that may arise."

Colm then proceeded to tell the group about the information that the Middle East team had discovered.

Colm continued, "It would seem to me that we have to assume that Lattah and Amahl are the only ones who know exactly where the bombs are located. There may be others, but those two are the only ones that we know of. This means that they are the only known sources of information we have. We must capture them alive, bring them back here, and then somehow get the information from them.

"This presents the major problems that accompany a snatch of two individuals by our agents in a foreign country. I feel we must use our agents to assure that we get this pair alive. I don't think we can trust foreign agents to turn them over alive. Nor can we risk having a foreign government imprison these two for any length of time where we can't get to them. We have got to promptly grab them with our agents, and bring them out alive. They must be alive or all is lost."

He continued, "However, we must have the cooperation of the United Arab Emirates to facilitate flying into their country, grabbing the pair, and flying out. We have the agents and the equipment to do this. The question is, will that country provide the secrecy and cooperation required. I'd like your views and comments on this assessment of the problem, and then I'd like to propose a plan of action."

Glenna Quisenberry said, "Thank God it's the United Arab Emirates! President Sheikh Zayed is a very intelligent and reasonable leader. I had the good fortune to work closely with him at the United Nations, and I was greatly impressed. He has the full support and following of his people and is very influential in the Arab community. I am sure that he will cooperate fully."

President Hartmann responded, "Yes, I know he is highly respected. Glenna, did the two of you have a close working relationship? Were you well-acquainted?"

Glenna raised her eyebrows and smiled, "Just how well-acquainted do you mean, Mr. President?"

The group laughed, and the President responded, "Well, just how close were you two?" Then he smiled and said, "Seriously, the reason I asked is that once we have a plan of action, I think you and I should call Sheikh Zayed, explain the situation, and seek his confidential cooperation."

Glenna nodded her agreement, and rest of the group concurred.

"Now," said the President, "how do we grab those bastards?"

Colm O'Hara responded, "I've been thinking about this as we talked, and I would like to propose a plan. In my opinion, we need a rapid strike with as few personnel as possible, based on the premise that you and Glenna succeed in getting the full cooperation Of President Zayed."

He continued, "We already have two excellent agents in Riyadh, Scott Crockett and Max Thorn. In addition, Frank Hughes and Ali Hassan, one of our Algerian agents, are there as well. It would be impossible to find a more effective group to carry out such a mission, each individual an outstanding mixture of athleticism, brains, brawn, and experience.

"Scott, or Frank, would be group leader and direct the operation. Scott, Max, and Ali would grab the couple at night in their house or apartment. It will be up to President Zayed to arrange the cover, secrecy, and non-interference required."

Then he added, "Scott directs a special CIA trouble-shooting group that has at its disposal a Gulfstream V Executive jet that has been out-fitted for such missions. The pilots, David Keeler and Darrel Millard, are CIA agents and former military jet pilots. They are extremely capable and referred to as the Double-D unit. Those two would complete an outstanding strike team."

Colm looked at the President, "I would like to suggest that in addition to your proposal of you and Glenna calling President Zayed, that she accompany Double-D to Abu Dahbi, and that she pave the way in our planning by meeting with President Zayed and his associates. I think that would be of great assistance. What do you think, Glenna?"

Glenna didn't hesitate, "I think it's an excellent idea, and I would love to be a part of the team. I'm sure I can be of help."

President Hartmann was nodding in agreement, "I think it's a very workable plan. What do the rest of you think?"

A spirited discussion followed, considering the pros and cons of the plan. In the end, there was a consensus to proceed.

Consequently, President Hartmann directed Colm O'Hara to begin as quickly as possible, and to keep him fully informed.

President Hartmann then spoke to Glenna. "Would you please stay after this meeting, and we'll place the initial call to President Zayed. I plan to tell him that we have an extremely grave situation and that we badly need his cooperation. That it is so confidential that I am sending you as my personal emissary to relate to him in person all the details. Also, that I must have his word on keeping this confidential. Certainly, I don't think he would particularly want the Arab world to know that he helped the Americans kidnap two Arab terrorists."

Colm corralled the rest of the group, and asked them to join him in the War Room in the basement of the White House.

Colm told them, "I want to run through this plan a few times, as I envision it, and you all critique it. We can't afford to screw up. I'll brief Glenna later."

As the group started to leave the Oval Office, Gordon Brown, Director of the FBI spoke up, "Mr. President, one more detail before we adjourn. Chadwick, Sheldon, and I were just discussing the bomb that could possibly be here in Washington. It is our plan to take as many FBI agents as it requires, give them each a picture of Lattah, and contact commercial real estate agents in and around the city.

"It is our belief that Lattah followed the same procedure in each city in locating and renting small vacant store rooms or storage units. She probably used an agent or broker to facilitate the search. We'll use the markings on her map to focus our search. Of course, we'll not divulge the reason we are seeking a certain property. Only that it relates to a drug operation."

The President responded, "Very good! The sooner the better. In this crisis, forget any budget or organizational constraints. I've got complete faith in you, so do what you have to do, and let's get the job done. Our country and our civilization depend on our success. God speed to each of you!"

The President then shook each person's hand as they left the office. The door closed, and the President and Glenna walked back to his desk to call President Zayed.

CHAPTER 19.

SEVERAL HOURS AFTER THE MEETING in the Oval Office, Colm was in his office having lunch with the Double-D pilots, Darrel and David, and the Secretary of State, Glenna Quisenberry, who was now a member of the strike team. They were making plans for the flight to Abu Dhabi and the equipment that might be needed. As soon as these plans were completed, David and Darrel would call Scott and Max in Riyadh to arrange a meeting with the two of them, Frank Hughes, and Ali Hassan to plan the next step of the strike.

Glenna had related to the group the results of the discussion with President Zayed. He was very cordial and pleased to hear from the President and especially pleased to talk with Glenna and renew their friendship. The President outlined the problem in general terms, stressing the extreme gravity of the situation. He explained that it was necessary to send a small delegation, including Glenna, to inform His Highness of the details of how he could help.

President Zayed pledged his cooperation and suggested that they meet after dark on the chosen day aboard the Gulfstream V they were flying into Abu Dhabi. He would arrange that the plane be accommodated in the high security hanger used by the royal family. It was agreed that he would wait for a call from

Glenna to tell him the time of the meeting, and that he would arrange his affairs so that he would be immediately available.

The only other person he would bring to the meeting would be his Chief of Security. His bodyguards would escort him to the hanger and provide security. Glenna said that both she and the President were very pleased with his complete willingness to help.

Colm then turned to David and Darrel and said, "Now let's list the special equipment and arms that will be needed. I've talked with Scott. He, Ali, Max and Frank envision taking the pair at night. As quietly and quickly as possible. They want the handguns equipped with lasers and silencers. Also, they want each of the four men who will do the grabbing to carry a tranquilizer hypo in a sheath of some kind. This will be to quickly immobilize the two. Since the action will take place in the dark and in strange quarters, it will be a matter of chance as to who has the best opportunity to jam the needle into the individual."

Darrel replied that the Gulfstream was already well equipped with an assortment of handguns, shotguns, assault rifles, and grenades, with plenty of ammunition in the plane's armory.

Colm asked, "Since this will be a close up encounter, what kind of handguns do you have?"

David replied, "There are four Glock 22 Auto Pistols. They are .40 calibers with 15-shot magazines. Scott and Max both have their personal weapons on board which are Sig Sauer P226s; they are 9mms with either 16 or 21 rounds in the clips. There are two Heckler & Koch MP5 9mm submachine guns, with folding stocks, which can be used in close quarters. All are equipped with Alpec's Beam Shot Laser sights."

Glenna was smiling as Colm exclaimed, "My god, you're equipped to fight your own little war! Did I approve all that stuff?"

Darrel looked at David and they both grinned, "We really don't know; we think it all came with the plane! Even better, David and I, as well as Scott and Max, are all fully qualified as experts on the use of every piece of armament in that plane. We can put it to good use if need be."

Colm replied, "Seriously, that's great to hear, and I'm now more than ever convinced we've got the team to do the job. Now, an additional item that might be needed. I was talking with some of the FBI people, and they have been using an immobilization device developed for the Army, but certain law enforcement groups are already using it. It's called a Pulse Wave Myotron."

Colm reached over into his briefcase and pulled out four small polycarbonate plastic devices, each about the size of a pack of cigarettes and shaped like a small electric razor. Colm explained that it is similar to a stun gun only much smaller and a great deal more powerful.

"I have seen it demonstrated and believe me, it is effective. Push that little button, and it gives new meaning to the saying of reach out and touch someone! The device emits pulse waves to overpower the neuromuscular system using electrical levels that are safe, non-injurious, and non-lethal. It can penetrate through clothing and won't cause an electrical charge-back to you even if you're touching the person when the device is applied."

Colm continued, "The pulse waves generally affect the voluntary muscles from the point of contact downward on the body. If the target is standing upright, and the contact is made to a major muscle group, such as the stomach or back, the person cannot use his legs. Even with a brief contact of less than five seconds, the subject will collapse with nausea, loss of bladder control, and will be neutralized or impaired for up to half hour. Recovery will be complete within one hour with no remaining effects."

Darrel responded, "Man, that's the first I've even heard about these devices. David let's try one out and see if I can knock you on your ass!"

David said, "No way, buddy. But what I will do is have us each take one and have a little one-on-one to see who can touch the other first!"

Colm said, "Knock it off, guys, we've got work to do. You can have your duel when you get back, and I'll even referee it for you. As Scott's group requested, I have here the four leather sheaths each containing a hypodermic needle with an appropriate shot of Midazolam Hydrochloride, known commercially as Versed. It's a fast-acting sedation that is generally used by surgeons prior to short diagnostic or endoscopic procedures. It's about four times as potent as Valium."

He continued, "Versed acts to swiftly sedate the individual, relaxes skeletal muscles, and blocks memory of events taking place. It prevents feeling pain, but enables the individual to follow commands. This should be helpful in moving the terrorists from the place of seizure to the plane. With each sheath is a written explanation of the drug and how it should be used as well as a description of the after effects.

"As I mentioned before, we're planning a swift and silent mission under the cover of darkness. To answer the group's request for silencers on the handguns, our CIA arms people have recommended that we add four special handguns, silenced High Standard HD Military 22 caliber pistols. They have a little less hitting power, but are extremely quiet."

Then Colm picked up a legal pad from his desk, and reading from his notes, he said, "In talking with Scott and his group, and with Glenna, here is the schedule we have worked out. You'll take off tomorrow morning at 5:30 and fly to the Rheim-Main Air Base at Frankfurt, Germany, where you'll stay overnight at the 469th Air Base Group. With a six hour time difference and a seven-hour flight time for the 4100 miles, you'll arrive at about 7 p.m.

"There you'll stay overnight, refuel, get your rest, and meet with Dayle Sutton for a conference call to Scott and his group to discuss and plan your flight to the King Khaled International Airport at Riyadh, Saudia Arabia. There is a one hour time differential between Frankfurt and Riyadh and about a 4 1/2 hour flight time. So you all and Scott's group can arrange your arrival time in Riyadh, keeping in mind the urgency of the situation."

The group then had a brief discussion recapping their plans, and their determination to successfully accomplish their assignment. David and Darrel left immediately to stow the equipment Colm had given them and to ready the Gulfstream V for the mission. Glenna left to pack for the trip, and Colm left for the White House to brief the President on the pending agenda.

It was just before 5:00 a.m. when Glenna arrived at the secure hangar at Andrews Air Force Base. David and Darrel were busy with the pre-flight inspections of the Gulfstream V when Glenna arrived. Darrel grabbed her suitcase and briefcase to stow on board and David handed her a cup of coffee.

David smiled and said, "Since you have reservations, you may choose any seat in the cabin. The cabin attendant will serve you as soon as we reach the appropriate altitude. Of course, the attendant may be Darrel, you, or me! Depends on the activity. Come on, I'll give you a tour of the plane; it's a beauty."

It was 5:30 a.m., just before dawn, as the jet raced down the runway and raised smoothly into the faint light of the rising sun. The three aboard the plane were quiet during the takeoff period, contemplating the oncoming adventure and the dangers involved.

Darrel broke the silence using the intercom to talk to Glenna. "Glenna, we're going to be busy for a little while, so help yourself to the food and coffee that's in the galley. Or if you want to, just take a snooze. We'll be all squared away up here in about twenty minutes or so."

Darrel was looking back at her from the cockpit as he spoke. Glenna flashed him thumbs up that she understood and indicated that she was going to take a catnap. He smiled and returned the thumbs up. Their lonely mission was underway and the lives of millions of people depended on their success.

CHAPTER 20.

IT WAS 6:40 P.M. AS the jet was making its approach to Rheim-Main Air Base. David was at the controls and was receiving landing instructions from the tower. After landing, he was told to follow a white truck with the flashing lights to a special secure hanger. In front of the hanger, a tow truck took over and towed the jet into the hanger. The hanger door slammed shut and the jet steps were lowered.

Darrel was the first one to leave the plane, and he immediately spotted Dayle Sutton who was waiting to greet them. The two were shaking hands as David and Glenna joined them.

Dayle smiled as he spoke, "Man! You all wasted no time in getting here. You're about twenty minutes ahead of time. Of course, when you've got a couple of hotshot pilots like Double-D, you should expect it! I had to rush to get down here in time to meet you."

Darrel said, "You're just pissed because somebody woke you from your nap or took you away from Happy Hour!"

Glenna shook Dayle's hand and said, "Don't let him get to you, Dayle. He's just grouchy from the long flight. Seriously, we're grateful for your help in making all the arrangements for our brief stay here."

David was looking around at the facilities and asked Dayle, "Whom do we see about servicing the plane?"

Dayle pointed to a small office where a master sergeant was talking on the telephone. "That's Wally Netzle, who is probably the finest aircraft maintenance supervisor in the Air Force. You and Darrel can join him in his office and discuss what you want done. He is well aware of the extreme importance of this mission and will certainly do his part to ensure its success.

"When you finish, we'll go have dinner and make our plans. I've been in contact with Scott and Max, and we'll have a conference call with them later tonight."

In Riyadh, Scott, Ali, Max and Frank were meeting with an emissary of President Zayed. Scott introduced himself to the emissary and also introduced his three associates.

The emissary shook hands all around and said, "It is a pleasure to meet such men as you: selfless soldiers risking their lives to save the civilized world. You have my admiration and gratitude for what you are doing! I have not given you my name because it is of no consequence and could be of no help to you. I am merely an emissary for President Zayed."

With that, the group started their planning as to how the abduction would take place. After a few hours of discussion involving the pros and cons of several plans, they arrived at a consensus. The plan included the "requests" and "suggestions" submitted by President Zayed.

The Gulfstream would leave Riyadh at 11:30 p.m. and fly directly to the international airfield at Dubai where the plane would be housed in the personal and heavily guarded hanger of President Zayed. There would be seven persons aboard the jet including the pilots Darrel and David. The other five would be Glenna Quisenberry, Scott Crockett, Max Thorn, Frank Hughes, and Ali Hassan.

Glenna, Darrel, and David would remain with the Gulfstream while the kidnapping of the two terrorists was taking place. The pilots would oversee the servicing of the plane while Glenna met briefly with President Zayed in his heavily armored Chevy Suburban. The Suburban would be parked in a darkened corner of the hanger. Glenna would be the only person to see or talk with President Zayed. Assuming the abduction would be successful, the team and their captives would fly directly back to the Rheim-Main Air Base. There they would refuel and rest prior to the flight back to Andrews Air Base.

If anything unexpected or some kind of disaster happened, President Zayed and his emissary were never there and the Gulfstream would immediately fly out of United Arab Emirates territory. The UAE secret service and the Royal Family personal bodyguards heavily guarded the airfield.

For several days prior to the arrival of the abduction team, the Royal Family bodyguards had been carefully watching the movements and activities of the two terrorists. The terrorist pair was highly organized and followed a set routine, which would work to the advantage of the abduction team. Their apartment had been thoroughly "inspected" and pictures taken of the layout of the rooms and furniture placement.

Surprisingly, there were no secondary locks or security chains on the front door. Perhaps it was to avoid suspicion by their friends or landlord, but the agents were astounded at the ease of entry into the apartment. While the couple was at work, the agents and their locksmith lubricated the door hinges, lock tumblers, and latch. Two keys were made and Teflon coated to ensure a silent entry.

The work was done under the guise of a pest control company spraying the halls and stairways of the building. All tenants were required to vacate the premises for three hours because of the "toxic" fumes. In fact, the agents lightly sprayed the premises with a harmless liquid mixed with a bit of kerosene to create an odor to make the action more noticeable and believable.

CHAPTER 21.

AT 11:37 P.M., THE GULFSTREAM set down on the runway at the Abu Dhabi airport and, following the emissary's directions, taxied to the Royal hangar. The area was dimly lit, but David could see the hangar attendant directing him with his signal lights to the hangar entrance. The attendant signaled David to cut the engines as the hangar doors rolled open and a tow tractor pulled out of the hangar.

As the plane was being towed into the hangar, David and Darrel could see the silhouettes of several of the Royal jets as well as two black Chevrolet Suburban station wagons. The tow tractor positioned the Gulfstream with its nose facing the hangar doors. The four-man assault team quickly deplaned with their gear and followed the UAE emissary.

Each of the four was dressed in black with bullet proof Mylar vests and armed with a holstered automatic pistol with a silencer, a stun gun, a knife in the boot and nylon wrist restraints in their pockets. Black knit sock caps covered their heads, and night vision goggles were pulled up over their foreheads.

The UAE emissary led the team to a maintenance desk where he had laid out a diagram of the terrorists' apartment. He requested the team to study it while he met with Glenna Quisenberry. He then returned to the plane where Glenna was talking to Darrel and David as they were overseeing the refueling and maintenance of the Gulfstream.

The emissary took Glenna's arm and asked her to accompany him to the one of the black Suburbans parked in a darkened corner of the hanger. Glenna could see several figures with machine guns standing in the semi-darkness as she was helped into the rear seat of the Suburban. There, seated alone, was his highness, President Zayed. He greeted Glenna warmly as he shook her hand.

He smiled and said, "We meet again under strange and very perilous circumstances."

Glenna responded, "The situation we're into is unbelievable, a threat to the civilized world! Thank you so very much for your understanding and cooperation. Without your help, the world as we know it would be in terrible jeopardy. Certainly, if this mission is not successful, we will all face a global calamity."

President Zayed replied, "I have faith in the perception of this situation by your President and his advisors. It is a devious plot and could cause the deaths of millions of innocent people. And the possible retaliation by your government would account for additional millions of casualties. It is a problem that we must solve together!"

He continued, "Please understand that the participation of me and my country in this mission must be kept secret to maintain stability and avoid turmoil in this part of the world. Having said that, I do recognize that if the situation is as we think it is, prompt and preventive action must be taken, and I will fully support that action!

"My agents have done a thorough job in preparing for the abduction of the two terrorists. My emissary is now briefing your people on the preparations we have made to facilitate the abduction."

As Glenna and President Zayed continued discussing the abduction plans and other political issues, the emissary was busy briefing the four-man assault team. He reviewed all the details of the neighborhood, access to the apartment, and the layout of all the rooms and doors in the apartment. He also covered the locations and activities of the two terrorists based on three days of observations. Following his review, he invited questions from the four men.

Scott inquired, "Does the couple have any associates or allies in the building?"

The emissary replied, "No. We have very carefully checked to make sure that we will not face any other resistance."

Ali asked, "Have they been consistent in the times that they retire and the time they rise?"

The emissary replied, "Yes, very consistent. Based on our listening devices and observing when their lights go off and on, it appears that 10:30 to 11:00 p.m. is when they retire, and they arise promptly at 6:00 each morning. They have sex every night upon retiring."

He glanced at his watch, "By now they have finished and are sleeping soundly!"

Ali grinned and said, "Seems a shame to spoil the party!"

Scott explained to the emissary the plans the group devised for the abduction. "With our night vision goggles, dark clothing, and special socks over our shoes, we will quickly and silently enter the building and go up the stairs to their second floor apartment. Then we will silently open the door and move inside the apartment. Having memorized the layout you provided, we will move across the front room, down a hallway, past the bathroom on the right, and into their bedroom at the end of the hallway."

He continued, "Once inside the bedroom, Ali and Frank will grab and subdue Amahl with the stun gun, and Max and I will do the same with Lattah."

Ali grinned and said, "Why do you and Max grab the girl? How is it that you two have all the fun?"

Scott looked at Ali and said, "Hell, you probably couldn't handle her anyhow!"

Ali threw a seat cushion at Scott, but Scott ducked and the cushion sailed off into the darkness. The emissary was surprised by the horseplay and gave them both a disapproving glance.

Scott continued, "As soon as they are subdued with the stun guns, each will be injected with the Versed to keep them quiet and obedient while being carried or dragged to the Suburban and driven to the plane. We will not use our guns unless absolutely necessary, and then only to disable and not to kill. We must, at all costs, take them alive."

The emissary picked it up at this point, "The middle seat of the Suburban has been removed. In the front seat will be my driver, myself, and one of you. In the third, or rear seat, will be the other three of you. The two terrorists will be laid on the floor where the middle seat has been removed."

He continued, "At that point we will go directly to the hanger, transfer the prisoners to your plane, and you will depart immediately. Now this is important. If any thing unexpected happens, anyone is wounded or killed, you must take that person or body with you on the plane. No evidence of the abduction can remain in this country. Is that agreed?"

The team of four looked at each other and nodded their heads in agreement.

The emissary continued, "Good! We have two body bags in our Suburban in case they are needed."

The group again looked at each other at the mention of body bags.

Scott thought to himself, man, this guy came prepared. He's been through this kind of stuff before!

As though in answer to Scott's thought, the emissary said, "One final condition. If this action turns into a total failure with a shootout and dead bodies, the four of you will be arrested and placed in protective custody. Ms. Crockett and the pilots will be requested to fly out immediately, and there will be no trace of the abduction attempt or any American presence in the UAE."

Again the four men nodded their heads in agreement, and the operation was underway.

CHAPTER 22.

T HE GROUP CLIMBED INTO THE armored Suburban with the emissary, the driver, and Scott in the front seat, and Ali, Max and Frank in the rear seat. An overhead door at the back of the hanger was raised, and the Suburban pulled out into the darkness. The ride to the apartment building took about twenty minutes.

During the brief ride, the group reviewed the plans and made sure that each knew his role. As they turned onto the street where the apartment was located, the emissary pointed out two darkened cars, one at each end of the block. He explained that they were there for backup in case help was needed.

There were three armed agents in each car. As the Suburban approached the first car, it slowed to a stop and the emissary exchanged words with the occupants. He explained that he had been informed that everything was normal and that the lights in the apartment had been out for several hours.

With its lights out, the Suburban quietly coasted to a stop in front of the apartment. The four-man team quickly moved into the lobby of the building. With the heavy socks over their shoes, they silently crossed the lobby and went up the stairway to the second floor. The apartment was the second door from the stairway on that floor. Scott smoothly slid the key into the keyhole and silently turned the key to unlock the door. The lock tumblers and the door hinges had been well prepared as the door opened without a sound.

The four men moved into the room and closed the door behind them. They slipped their night vision goggles into place, and moved to the bedroom where the door was open. Scott peered around the edge of the doorway and saw that Amahl was on the left side of the bed. He signaled to Ali and Frank to take that side and he and Max would take the other side.

Scott gave a hand signal and the four men burst into the room. Ali leaped across the end of the bed and had Amahl pinned down. Ali immediately used the stun gun, which incapacitated Amahl. Frank followed with the Versed injection, which put Amahl completely under control.

Lattah had apparently been awake and sensed the presence of an intruder, although she had not awakened Amahl. As Max jumped over the end of the bed to pin her down, she rolled out of bed and onto the floor. As she fell, she pulled a machine pistol from under the bed, and quickly came up preparing to fire.

Scott realized immediately that to stop her, he had to shoot her. The laser beam from his pistol was showing on her right shoulder when he pulled the trigger. As he fired, she was raising up to fire her machine pistol, and it was a fatal move. Scott's bullet hit her in the chest and pierced her heart. She fell to the floor mortally wounded.

Scott said, "Son of a bitch! I didn't want to do that. We needed her alive!"

Max was kneeling beside her; he looked up at Scott and said "She's dead! Don't blame yourself. You had no choice! She would have killed all four of us. Go down and get a body bag and we'll clear out of here!"

Scott silently rushed down to the Suburban and found the emissary with the car door open and a body bag in hand.

He looked at the emissary with a quizzical glance and said, "How did you know? Did you hear the gun shot?"

The emissary answered, "No, we did not hear the gun shot, but when I saw you running down the stairway, I assumed that was the problem. What has happened?"

Scott responded, "The woman was awake and had a machine pistol, and I had no choice but to shoot her. She is dead and the man is a captive, stunned and sedated, but alive."

The emissary said, "Bring them down; it is imperative that we leave here as soon as possible!"

As Scott entered the building, Ali and Max were half carrying and half dragging Amahl through the lobby. The emissary jumped out and helped load the limp body onto the floor of the Suburban. In less than three minutes, Scott and Frank appeared carrying the body bag containing the lifeless body of Lattah. They placed the bag on the floor of the vehicle beside Amahl.

The doors were closed, and the Suburban quietly crept away from the building. In the morning, the emissary's agents would return to finish the "pest control" job as far as the tenants were concerned. However, in reality they were there to clean up any signs of the struggle or abduction.

The emissary inquired of the group if they had seen anyone or if anyone had seen them. Did they observe any lights or unusual activity? All the answers were negative, and it appeared that no one had observed or heard them. The Suburban picked up speed as it headed for the airport hanger.

As they approached the hanger, the overhead door was raised and the Suburban pulled inside. Glenna, David, and Darrel were standing by the aircraft stairway. The Suburban containing President Zayed and his bodyguards was already gone, as were most of the guards who had been stationed in the shadows around the hanger.

David signaled thumbs up that the plane was ready for takeoff. Ali and Max quickly carried the sedated Amahl up the stairway and into a seat at the rear of the plane. He was shackled to his seat and the seat belt was fastened. In the meantime, David and Darrel carried the body of Lattah to the cargo compartment and secured it in place.

Glenna was shaking the hand of the emissary and thanking him and his driver for all their help. The four-man abduction team, as well as Darrel and David, expressed their thanks to the emissary and requested that he thank President Zayed for his courageous cooperation.

Scott shook the emissary's hand and said that he would at least like to know his name.

The emissary grinned at them, "Gentlemen, you performed a superb operation, and you have my highest admiration for what you accomplished. And you have my best wishes for a successful completion of your journey. However, from this moment on, I will deny ever having met you or even having heard of you! And, of course, you may not have my name."

With that, he waved the group onto the plane, and the tow truck was ready to tow the plane out onto the tarmac. Within five minutes, the plane was airborne and heading back to the Rheim-Main Air Base. Amahl was well sedated and kept that way throughout the flight.

The group was relieved that the difficult part of the mission was over. However, they were disappointed that they had failed to capture the woman alive. All of them were exhausted due to the tension, stress, and exertion, and soon dozed off, with the exception of Darrel and David who were taking catnaps and taking turns flying the plane. The plane was at 40,000 feet and would not break radio silence until well out of UAE territory.

Two hours later, they were intercepted by two Saudi fighter planes and challenged to identify themselves. David gave them the code words provided by the Saudi high command. In about

45 seconds the code had been verified. The closest Saudi plane came very near to the Gulfstream as the pilot waved to Darrel and David, saluted, dipped the wing, and took off in a steep climb.

Darrel said, "I wonder if he knows what the hell we're doing over here?"

David replied, "Doubt it. We'll never know what he thought"

The stay at the air base was brief, just time for a shower, shave, clean clothes, and hot meal. Amahl was taken off the plane under heavy guard and, although quite groggy, he managed to change clothes, shower, and have a little warm food. He was bewildered by what was going on. He didn't know what had happened, where he was, or what had happened to Lattah.

In two hours, they were back in the air. The plane had been serviced and refueled and they were heading for home. Amahl was again shackled to his seat and given a shot of Versed. Scott was very quietly telling his group that he sure was glad that they had the Versed because when Amahl learns that Lattah had been killed, all hell is going to break out. Amahl will go berserk!

CHAPTER 23.

SCOTT HAD BEEN IN CONTACT with Colm O'Hara of the CIA and he was now relaying to Darrel, David, and the rest of the group, the instructions he had been given.

"The orders are to land at Andrews Air Force Base under the control of the Andrews Systems Control Facility. We are already showing on their radar. They will instruct us as to which runway to use and the hanger into which the plane must be taken."

"From there, our group will be transferred from the plane to the 89th Medical Group/Malcolm Grow Medical Center. We will all be housed there, including Amahl, in a special 'quarantined' ward. It has its own medical and kitchen facilities. The ward, as well as the exterior of the building, will be heavily guarded. There will be no contact between the guards and our group.

"There will be a small group of doctors, nurses, and professional military interrogators who will be housed in the ward with no contact to the outside. They all will be sworn to absolute secrecy. Amahl will be sequestered in his own windowless room in the center of the ward. Six guards working in two-man shifts around the clock will be stationed outside his door. The guards will also be housed in the ward with no outside contact of any kind."

Scott continued, "Our group, David, Darrel, Glenna, Max, Frank, Ali, and I, will be de-briefed on all details of the abduction, searching for anything in our subconscious that may be of help. We're under the same constraints as the others, no outside contacts and no leaving our ward. Our plane will be secured with no access to anyone but our group."

They all returned to their seats to think about their coming stay at Andrews. Amahl was still sleeping soundly with no idea of what to expect. Frank was on a secure radio channel talking with Colm O'Hara. Colm informed Frank that arrangements had been made for the interrogation of Amahl to start immediately after the Versed wears off.

The plane landed and events took place just as Scott had outlined. The group was transferred from the plane to the secured ward and assigned to their specific quarters.

Scott led the group into their quarters in the ward and asked, "Any questions?"

Darrel said, "Not a question, but I feel like I'm being punished, like being locked in my room for being bad! We need to have a little leeway."

David looked at Darrel with a big grin. "What bullshit! I know why you're upset. I saw you flirting with that good-looking blond gal on guard duty, and you're just pissed because you can't go see her!"

That brought a round of laughter from the group assembled in the hallway. Even Darrel had to chuckle at David's response. Scott led the group to the kitchen that was stocked with a variety of soft drinks, milk, tea, coffee and beer. In the refrigerators, were several loaves of various kinds of breads, as well as all kinds of cold meat and cheeses. Then they went to their respective rooms to relax and rest before each started their individual debriefing.

In several hours, Amahl was awakened, and he began his interrogation. The interrogators had been fully briefed on Amahl's background and temperament. The questioning of Amahl proceeded slowly, as he was completely non-cooperative. He refused to answer any questions, or even talk to the interrogators until he was told what happened to Lattah and where she was. After several hours of absolutely no progress, the interrogators met with the abduction team.

They weighed the pros and cons of telling Amahl that she was dead. They finally decided to tell him that she was being held in an unspecified town in Germany where she was also being interrogated. He was further told that her fate as well as his depended on their cooperation. If they did not cooperate, they would both be killed. That did not seem to faze Amahl, as he continued to refuse the slightest discussion or acknowledgement of their questions.

After twelve hours of questioning, humiliation, verbal abuse and threats, intimidation and sleep deprivation, no progress had been made. Another break in the proceedings was taken while the interrogators met with the resident psychiatrists. They discussed the use of hypnosis as well as the use of sodium amytal. The psychiatrists were not much in favor of using hypnosis, as the subject could possibly manipulate his answers, and there was no way to tell which were accurate and which were false. Since time was so critical, they could not afford to be following false information.

They finally agreed to use the sodium amytal as a last resort. As preparations were being made, there was a shrill scream of anguish and anger followed by a string of cursing in Arabic. Amahl had overheard the psychiatrists talking and heard that Lattah was dead. He was pulling at his wrist restraints, kicking the furniture, screaming, and trying to bang his head against a table. The psychiatrists were unsuccessful in trying to subdue him while avoiding his kicks.

Max, Ali, and Scott heard the commotion and came running to investigate. Although he continued struggling and screaming, he was quickly subdued by the three of them and dragged into his bedroom. There his arms and legs were tied to the bed with plastic restraints. One of the psychiatrists gave him a shot of Versed, and in a short time he was limp and quiet. Both the Versed and the exhaustion that followed his tirade had their effect.

Following that episode, the group met to decide what course of action should be taken now that the odds of getting any information from Amahl had diminished considerably. It was agreed that once the Versed had worn off, they would try the sodium amytal. However, most of them felt that with his current state of mind, the attempt would be futile. They also agreed that Scott and Frank should immediately set up a meeting in the White House with the appropriate individuals to discuss their options

Frank called President Hartmann and briefed him on all that had transpired. The President was pleased that they had captured Amahl, but was dismayed that they were stopped in their tracks on getting information as to the location of the bombs. Frank asked the President to arrange an emergency meeting that evening with the appropriate people to discuss the situation. Also, that Troy Sheldon be included in the group. The President agreed, and proceeded to arrange the meeting, which was set for 7 p.m. in the secure "Situation Room" in the basement of the White House. Hot soup and a cold food snack would be available in that room.

A number of reporters had picked up on the arrival of the several cabinet members and other VIPs. However, they were completely stonewalled by the President's press secretary who also had no idea what was going on. The individuals arrived within fifteen minutes of each other, and the fatigue of endless hours of investigation showed on all their faces. The President was already seated at the conference table munching on a ham and cheese sandwich and sipping on a cold soda. The others gathered their food and slumped down in their chairs, again showing their exhaustion.

Gordon Brown, Director of the FBI, spoke across the table to the President. "I located Troy Sheldon, and he will be here within the hour."

The President nodded and cleared his throat to speak to the group. "Why don't we go ahead and get started. We can fill Troy in when he arrives. Scott, or Frank, would you two bring us up to date with what has happened the past several days."

Frank motioned to Scott to start off. Scott told the story of the journey to the United Arab Emirates to abduct Lattah and Amahl. Frank interrupted briefly to tell of the cooperation from Saudi Arabia and especially the outstanding help from President Zayed and his personal staff in the United Arab Emirates. He said the operation could not have been successful without their help.

At that point, Troy Sheldon arrived. The President welcomed him as the others in the group nodded or waved. He grabbed two sandwiches and a cup of coffee and sat down. Scott continued telling of the secret meeting in the Royal Hanger, and the role that Glenna had played in negotiating with President Zayed and his "emissary". He had high praise for the skills and thoroughness of the emissary, not only for the detailed planning for the abduction, but for his smooth handling of the entire operation. Also, of the reluctance of the emissary to give his name or title.

Scott related all the activity at the apartment of Amahl and Lattah and the entire abduction operation. He explained the unavoidable killing of Lattah and that they probably lost valuable information with her death. He continued on, describing the trip back to Andrews Air Base, and finally, the dead end they experienced in the interrogation of Amahl. Especially his fury when he learned that Lattah had been killed.

Davis Benson was the first to speak, "My god! It sounds exactly like a Tom Clancy novel. You were all lucky to return in one piece. It is a loss that Lattah was killed, as she could have provided critical information. Of course, it is completely understandable why it happened, and we just have to accept it and go on from here. You two and your team did a remarkable job and we are grateful."

The President followed with, "I certainly second Davis's comments. You men were superb in what you accomplished! Our country owes you all a deep debt of gratitude. Now the question is where we go from here. We must somehow get the information from Amahl as to the location and the timing of the bombs."

Scott looked at Troy Sheldon and commented, "Troy, what's on your mind, you've been rocking back and forth in that chair, and I know that something is really bothering you; what is it?"

Troy replied, "Scott, you're very perceptive, and I hesitate to say what I'm thinking, as you will all think I have lost my mind!"

The President said, "Bring it out, Troy, we're desperate for ideas and time is critical. Any idea could be helpful."

Troy looked at Scott, "I'm thinking about Jessica West and her rats!"

There was a profound silence, and David Benson said, "Have you lost your mind? What in the world are you talking about?"

The others in the group were also looking at Troy as though he really had lost his mind; maybe all the pressure had gotten to him.

Scott stood up, startling the others, and said, "Troy, it's a hell of a long shot, but it's worth a try!"

The President looked at both of them, puzzled and exasperated, "Damn it, are you two trying to be funny at a time like this!"

He looked sternly at Troy and Scott, "No one here knows what the hell you two are talking about, and we sure don't have time for joking around!"

Scott raised his hands up, "Hold on Mr. President, we are being very serious with a perhaps unbelievable idea. But it is very much worth our consideration."

He continued, "Troy has been privileged to be involved in some very confidential research being done at the University of Arkansas regarding the transfer of memory. Troy, would you please tell us what you have observed, and what that small research group is accomplishing. It is fantastic, and may well be of help to us."

Troy related all his experiences with the group, and said he had been skeptical and ridiculed the idea until he saw for himself what they had accomplished. He related his observation of one rat using another rat's memory to navigate a maze.

The President asked the obvious next question: has this been tried on human beings, and was told it has not.

Scott excitedly said, "We don't know if it will work, but what other choice do we have at this moment? It is certainly worth a try, and as quickly as possible!"

There was a short silence and Scott continued, "Is it necessary to bring Jessica and her staff up here to convince you of this opportunity? I don't think we have the time to waste on that."

The President agreed, "If you and Troy are convinced this is feasible, then I think we should go for it. Does anyone disagree or have other thoughts?"

David Benson quickly agreed, "I find this a little like science fiction, but if Troy and Scott believe it's possible, then I'll support them all the way. Besides, what other options do we have at this time?"

The President directed Troy and Scott to take over the operation and make all the arrangements necessary to fly Amahl to Fayetteville as quickly as possible.

CHAPTER 24.

SCOTT WAS ON THE PHONE with Jessica within a few minutes. "Jessica, this is Scott. I need to talk with you, but I must make sure the line is secure."

Jessica was very surprised to hear Scott's voice,

"This line is secure, Scott, but are you? Where in the world have you been? Cheryl has been worried sick about you!"

Scott was shaking his head in acknowledgement, "I can well imagine. Please tell her I'm okay. Jessica, I'm deeply involved in a matter that is of great concern to our nation and really, all civilization. I need to meet with you and your most trusted people who are involved in the memory transfer project. It is critical that we meet tomorrow morning. I know that is short notice, but we must do it."

Jessica paused for a moment trying to arrange her thoughts as the mystery of his message and the urgency in his voice frightened her. "Scott, I'm just trying to understand what you're telling me and asking me to do.

First, you're scaring me so much I have to pause to think straight. Second, I'm not sure I can arrange the meeting that quickly; the doctors involved have surgery schedules and patients' welfare to consider. Some are probably seriously ill."

Scott said, "I understand that, Jessica. We'll have to work around that as best we can. But, please make them understand that our situation involves the lives or deaths of millions of people and time is extremely critical."

"Damn it, Scott! You're scaring the hell out of me. What are you talking about?" Jessica replied as she trembled slightly. "How are we involved with this situation? I don't see any connection."

"Jessica, I would tell you now if I could, but I can't do it over the telephone. Please believe me and have faith in me, and I'll lay it all out when we get there. Will you arrange it as best you can?" Scott asked.

He continued, "Troy will be calling Captain McPherson to arrange our aircraft landing at Drake Field in Fayetteville. We'll need a secure hangar and special transportation for the group, but Troy and McPherson can take care of all those arrangements."

Jessica was clearly apprehensive as she answered,

"I would usually say how nice it is talking with you, Scott. I don't know what to say to you now. And what should I tell the people involved in the meeting?"

"You can tell them exactly what I told you. They must arrange to attend the meeting as we are desperate for their help; we have no other options!" Scott said rather sternly. "Now I have to hang up, Jessica, as I need to prepare for the flight down there. I will never be able to thank you enough for your help! Don't forget to tell Cheryl I love her." Scott hung up the phone and hurried to meet Troy and make the call to Captain McPherson.

That call went smoothly, as Captain McPherson was a real professional. He would rent two Chevy Suburbans through the university. He and Dan Roberts would drive the vehicles to avoid the involvement of other officials. McPherson met the Fayetteville City Police Chief, Carl Couch, in the parking lot at the university football stadium to avoid any attention. He swore the chief to secrecy and proceeded to tell him as much as he needed to know.

One of the problems was where to safely secure Amahl, so that he was available to the group but to no one else. The location had to be very secure and soundproof, so Amahl's ranting could not be heard. Also, there was the problem of moving him between the place of his confinement and Jessica's laboratory. The location had to be secluded.

Chief Carl replied, "There is one place that is secluded, but you may not want to use it since it isn't quite finished yet. We've just added a small addition to the city jail. It's three stories high, unfinished as far as all the painting and finishing touches.

"However, it is habitable and has all the utilities ready and usable. It's very soundproof, as the cells on the second and third floors are off by themselves. All the cells have a bed and bathroom facilities. Another advantage is the back door, which opens out into a small parking lot just off the alley between the buildings. You can come and go as you please and very few, if any, people would notice."

Captain McPherson was enthused, "That would be perfect. We'll need six or seven cells set up to accommodate the prisoner and his handlers. Can you arrange that?"

Carl relied, "No problem, I'll have it done immediately. There's a small kitchen on the second floor, so we'll use that area and make sure the kitchen is fully stocked. We'll block off the entire addition for as long as you need it. You'll have the only keys for access to the building."

At 5 a.m., the Gulfstream took off from Andrews Air Force Base with Fayetteville, Arkansas, its destination. On board was the same crew, Darrel and David, along with Scott, Max, Ali, and Troy. Frank Hughes stayed in Washington to help coordinate the multitude of activities related to the situation. The flight was uneventful. With Amahl shackled and sedated, the members of the abduction team were discussing what might lie ahead. They were all fascinated with Troy's description of the laboratory's work.

Max was telling Scott, "I find this whole brain story mighty hard to believe. Don't be volunteering me for any brain work."

Ali was laughing, "Don't worry, Max, you never were requested for any brainwork! Brawn, yes, but brainwork, no."

Scott joined the laughter, "Max, you asked for that one. Walked right into it."

David announced that the plane was cleared for landing and was approaching Drake Field and, also, "Be ready for a hard landing and a possible abrupt stop at the end of the runway. The runway here is a little shorter than is authorized for this particular plane."

Max yelled up to David and Darrel, "What a pair of pilots! Why didn't you check this out before you try to land? Are there any parachutes on board?"

Darrel answered, "We've got two chutes and they're both up front, one for David and one for me. We're gonna put the plane on auto pilot, and you guys are on your own!"

Then he shut the door to the cockpit and turned on the fasten seatbelt sign.

The plane made a smooth landing and shuddered to a stop as the brakes were applied near the end of the runway. The plane taxied back to a hanger where two Chevy Suburbans were flashing their headlights. Darrel eased the plane up near the hanger where it was then towed backwards into the hanger and secured. The Suburbans also pulled into the back of the building. The hanger doors were closed as the group transferred their gear and their prisoner into the station wagons.

After David made arrangements for servicing the plane, the group climbed into the Suburbans and headed for the city jail. The transfer was made smoothly, as the new jail parking lot was completely empty and out of view from passersby. Amahl was like a zombie, barely able to move but following directions.

He was placed on the bed in his cell and given additional drugs. The rest of the group each settled into their individual cells and unpacked their gear.

David was laughing when he yelled to Darrel, "Hey, Darrel, I'll bet that cell brings back memories for you!"

"Yeah, that's where I first met the likes of you! I wish you'd shut up now; I want some peace and quiet. I'm gonna slam that cell door shut and then we'll be rid of you for a while," Darrel replied as he stretched out on his cot.

Troy and Scott were on the secure speakerphone in the second floor office of the prison addition.

Scott was talking to Jessica, "Hi! Jessica, this is Scott. We had a good flight down here, and now we're getting settled in our respective cells."

Jessica replied, "Like I told you before, Scott, nothing but the best for you guys in the service!"

Scott said, "Hey, it's better than some quarters we've had in the past couple of weeks. Now, about our meeting tonight, can we meet at seven at your laboratory? From what Troy has told me, Captain McPherson has provided you with tight security. Right?"

"Yes, he's done a fine job in securing the premises. We'll have no problem with that issue. I alerted the rest of the group to be available from 5 p.m. on this evening," Jessica said, and then continued, "but I'll tell you what is a problem: none of us know what the hell we're doing. Why all the secrecy and why are we meeting with you? No one here can figure out how we can possibly help you with an international problem. We're a small medical group in a small town in the Ozark Mountains; what's the connection?"

"Jessica, in about two hours you'll have all the answers. Right now you and your associates are the most important people in the world. When you hear the story, you'll understand the reason for all the secrecy and the need for security. We'll be there promptly at seven, and thank you so much for your help!" With that, Scott hung up the phone, and he and Troy returned to their quarters.

Upon returning to the cell area, Scott called a meeting with the group. He explained that he had been thinking about the meeting with the laboratory group and decided that he, Max, Ali, Troy, and Captain McPherson would attend the meeting, and David, Darrel and Police Chief Couch would remain in the cell area to guard the prisoner.

Scott said, "I may be overreacting to the number of us needed to guard the prisoner, but I don't think we should leave anything to chance. There is simply too much riding on the success of this operation. We'll sedate Amahl again prior to leaving for the meeting."

Chief Couch brought in a large pot of spaghetti, French rolls, and a bowl of tossed salad. They all were quite hungry and ate quickly. Then they had an hour to relax and watch television before it was time to leave.

CHAPTER 25

A T 6:45 P.M., SCOTT, MAX, Ali, and Troy climbed into the Chevy Suburban being driven by Dan Roberts. Dan was driving as he knew the area and would attract the least amount of attention in moving throughout the city. Dan knew Scott and Troy, but this was his first meeting with Max and Ali. Following introductions and small talk, Dan headed out to the laboratory with his carload of muscle and brains. When he arrived, he pulled behind the building to the back door where Heather was waiting.

Dan parked the car and led the group into the building following Heather. He introduced them as they walked down the corridor to the conference room. As Scott entered the room, he was a little surprised by the size of the group, but he trusted Jessica's judgment as to who should be involved. Captain McPherson had arrived before Scott and his group. Also in attendance was Jessica, Dr. Judy Clark, Dr. Sue Cantrell, Dr. Bob Cantrell, Dr. Michael Laird, and Heather.

Jessica introduced each of her associates with a brief summary of each one's background and specialty in surgery and medicine. Scott introduced each of his associates with an colorful summary of each individual's activity and service to his country. He related how proud he was to be a member of this strike group that included David and Darrel, their pilots.

Scott smiled at the group and said, "Now, if you will all sit back and relax, we are going to tell you of certain events that have occurred over the past several months. You'll find it interesting, terrifying, and almost beyond belief. If you like to read Tom Clancy novels, then you'll love this one."

He then related the entire story, starting with the initial meetings with the Russian representatives and all the activities that followed. When he got to the discovery of the nuclear device hidden in a propane tank in Los Angeles, he requested that Troy relate that segment of the story. Scott then told of all their activities in tracking down the terrorists responsible for the theft and planting of the nuclear warheads.

Dr. Bob Cantrell had been listening to every detail with rapt attention and couldn't help but interrupt Scott.

With a frown on his face and deadly serious, he said, "Scott, I know you're not finished yet, but that is terrifying story. It scares the hell out of me, and I can't imagine how we can possibly help. What can we do? Why are we involved?"

Scott replied, "Same questions Jessica had when I first called her to arrange this meeting. We're not sure you can help, Bob, but we're praying that somehow you'll find a way, as you all may be our last chance to save millions of people from horrible deaths. Now I'll finish the story, and you will understand how you can help."

Scott told of how they tracked the terrorists to Abu Dhabi and the ensuing kidnapping that resulted in the death of Lattah, which left Amahl as the only person in the world who knows where the bombs are located. Then he told of the failed interrogation attempts and the desperation that followed in meetings with the President.

That is when Troy told the group about your research and accomplishments in memory transfer. As soon as Scott said that, they all reacted to what was coming next.

Jessica was the first, "Scott, you can't be serious! We haven't done anything in the area of transferring memory in humans!"

She looked at Dr. Bob Cantrell for agreement, and he responded, "We haven't even discussed it yet. No one knows if it is even feasible."

The other medical professionals were shaking their heads in agreement.

Scott would not back down, "I fully understand that nothing has been done in that area. But you have to understand that we must try; we have no other alternatives! I can't believe that this group would not at least make the effort to transfer Amahl's memory. We are talking about tens of millions of lives!"

"We have done all we can do in bringing this terrorist to you, we are tired and desperate. We're looking at this group to help us!"

Dr. Laird replied, "Hold on, Scott, it isn't that we don't want to help. We don't know if we can do what you want. You took us by surprise. I have an overwhelming admiration for what you and your group have gone through and accomplished. The entire civilized world owes your group their eternal thanks. I know I speak for all my colleagues when I say we will do whatever needs to be done to help."

Dr. Bob Cantrell agreed, "I say, let's get on with it. Time is not our ally and this needs a quick resolution. Are we in agreement?"

The entire laboratory group indicated enthusiastic agreement.

Dr. Bob further said, "I would suggest that Michael lead this operation; any seconds?"

Jessica replied, "I don't think we need to get into parliamentary procedure at this point, but I fully agree with Michael heading up this endeavor. Michael, how about it?"

Michael looked around the group for affirmation and then stated, "Let's start tonight. We'll meet in this conference room, and Jessica and Heather will review in detail the procedures used on the rats and dogs. Lisa will take notes on comments we make as to possible changes in the procedure. Because of the success with the rats and dogs, I don't think it would be wise to vary much from what has been successful."

"It is now 7:45; let's try to finish the review by 11:00, and schedule the operation at 7:30 in the morning at Washington General Hospital. Dr. Judy would you and Scott go to the hospital and select an OR that is available and fills our needs, and reserve it for the entire morning. I want Scott to learn the layout of the hospital, so when he brings the prisoner to the hospital, he will know his way around. If you have to bump any prior commitments, don't hesitate to do so."

"We'll have both Jessica and Heather there to assist, so I don't think we'll need any additional nursing staff. And, of course, Sue will be doing the anesthesia."

Michael continued, "Scott, will you arrange to transfer the prisoner to the hospital at about 6 a.m.? Dan can drive, and Heather, if she will, can accompany you in finding your way around the hospital."

Heather and Dan both were shaking their heads in the affirmative.

Michael went on, "Dr. Judy, when you select the OR, make sure we have an adjacent room that we can use for preop. The prisoner might be noisy, so the more privacy, the better. Also, make sure that other equipment needed, such as the EEG, PET, and the MRI, is readily available. Any questions that may arise as to use, tell them Dr. Bob authorizes it, as he is Chief of Staff there.

"Troy, would you help Lisa gather all the computer hardware and software you might need in the OR, and make sure it is transferred to the hospital either tonight or early tomorrow morning. Maybe Max or Ali can help you with the heavy work. Let's get busy and meet back here at eleven tonight to see how we stand. Dan, could you get some food catered in here at about 10:30?"

Dan replied, "No problem, will do."

Dr. Bob expressed shock at Michael's barrage of instructions, "Michael, were you a first sergeant in some army before entering the medical profession? I can't believe the flow of orders we're hearing!"

Michael was laughing when he answered, "As a matter of fact, I was a master sergeant for three years in the National Guard. And just because you appointed me as group leader doesn't give you any authority to give me any lip, understood?"

Dr. Bob clicked his heels together and saluted, "Yes, sir! Any further commands?"

Michael replied, "Let's get busy with the review. I need to know every minute detail of the procedures used by Jessica and Heather. Especially the insertion of the probes and sensors into the brain."

He turned to Dr. Sue, "Sue, we need to keep the prisoner sedated enough to control him, but we also need him conscious enough to respond to instructions."

Dr. Sue replied, "It will be a fine line, but it can be done with very careful attention."

Michael said, "Fine, let's start the review from the very start."

Jessica and Heather started the laborious review through the logbooks. The three doctors were asking hundreds of questions, referring to textbooks, and taking reminder notes as they went along. They covered time and again the placement of the sensors and the functions of the limbic system, which included the thalamus, hypothalamus, the hippocampal formation, amygdale, caudate nucleus, septum and mesencephalon, the frontal areas of the cerebral cortex, and the corpus callosum.

After an hour and a half, they took a break to stretch and relax for a few minutes.

Michael walked over to get a cup of coffee and said, "This is like cramming for a medical exam; it's exhausting! Just to add one more thing to consider, how about this: we haven't talked about whose brain we're going to tap into to be the receiver. We are tapping into Amahl's brain, but who is going to provide the receiving brain? We can't use the rat!"

The members of the group looked at each other in astonishment; how could they have forgotten such a critical thing?

Heather was the first to offer to be the receiver.

Michael replied that it would be better to have her and Jessica as part of the operating team to answer any procedural questions that may arise.

Jessica interjected another thought; "Perhaps we need to use Ali since it is possible that any information transmission may be in Arabic."

Dr. Bob said, "I can't believe that we hadn't considered that possibility. Ali is our only alternative, and it's just by chance that he is here!"

Michael replied, "I think it is more than likely that the information will be in Arabic. I hope he is receptive to the idea; it's asking a lot to permit your brain to be tampered with. When he and Max return, we'll ask him. Let's continue, as we must proceed regardless."

Michael continued, "Sue, I've been thinking that the more I learn about this, the more I think we may need the help of one or two operating room nurses - those with experience in brain surgery. What do you think?"

Sue replied, "I agree fully, and I know exactly the two you have in mind: Katie and Daphne."

Michael answered, "Right on. Do you think they can be trusted to keep this whole thing confidential? If you do, let's get them down here right now. Tell them we know it's late, but that it's an emergency, and we'll explain when they get here"

Sue was shaking her head yes and said, "I'll call them both immediately. What do you think, Bob?"

Bob replied, "I agree completely. Both are outstanding nurses and entirely trustworthy. They would add valuable experience and knowledge to the team."

The group returned to the review, and continued in deep concentration until Dan arrived just after 10:30 with the "midnight snack". In just a few minutes more, Scott, Max, Ali, Lisa, Troy, and Dr. Judy had all returned. They were sitting at the conference table eating the late meal of sandwiches, hot soup, salads, coffee, milk, and apple pie.

The two operating room nurses, Katie and Daphne, arrived and had been briefed by Sue on the entire situation. They were initially stunned to hear of the successful lab experiments, and then both shocked and subdued to be told of the terrorists' plot. Both were eager to help and understood the need for the extreme security. They were introduced to the group. Ali's first question was if either one of them was single since both were very attractive. He smiled when told both were single.

Scott was smiling also when he told the nurses, "I hope you'll excuse Ali since he's had no female companionship for several weeks. We try to keep him on a short leash, but he gets out of hand every so often. Besides, he's married and has five children."

The group all laughed, and Ali just stared at Scott, shook his head and said, "Why would you do that to me, after all I've done for you!"

Michael broke into the conversation, "Ali, I'm glad you are in a good mood because there is something you can do to be the hero in this situation."

Ali was shaking his head, "I'm sure that no good will be forthcoming in this request from you! What is it that you want?"

Michael carefully and thoroughly explained the situation, the procedures to be used, and the minimum risk involved.

Ali said, "I don't mind doing this, as I recognize the need for the Arabic. However, tell me, suppose I have memories I don't want you delving into? I don't want to wake up and have you all laughing."

Michael responded, "Ali, none of us would want that either. Believe me the questioning will be very specific and will be directed at Amahl's brain, not yours."

Ali showed his big smile and said, "You got a deal. Just tell me what to do. Will one of you nurses be holding my hand?"

Daphne and Katie both assured him that they would be watching over him.

Just then the conference phone in the middle of the table rang, and Jessica picked it up saying, "Who in the world would be calling at this time of night! Hello, yes he is here. Troy, it's for you."

Troy took the phone, "This is Troy. Yes, I'll hold."

It was obvious from Troy's responses that it was good news and that he was excited. "I'll get hold of Rollie Weeks immediately! Have a military jet at Petersen Aviation in Van Nuys as soon as possible. I'll call you back after talking to Rollie!"

Troy turned to the group, "Great news! They have found the bomb in Washington! Apparently the FBI canvassed all the real estate agents active in the target area, and they found the right one. The broker said he leased the store to the Oman Oil

Company. The store had previously been a gift shop. That bomb would have been some gift!"

"The broker was told that the FBI is working on a large drug bust. That a very large cartel is shipping drugs from the Mideast using Oman Oil equipment, and Oman Oil is unaware of the shipments. The broker was told he could not talk to anyone about the situation. Not a single word about this find. To do so would result in jail time and fines for all concerned. This is a real break; now I have to find Rollie Weeks and get him to Washington."

Rollie was not hard to find, as it was nearly 1:00 a.m. Pacific Time, and he was home sound asleep. After three rings, Rollie picked up the phone and was wide-awake. Troy related to him all the details of the situation and that a military jet was being sent to Petersen Aviation at the Van Nuys Airport to pick him up.

They agreed that it would be beneficial for Rollie to do the job of disarming the bomb. There was an urgency to not only disarm the device, but to also compare the detonation date with the bomb in Los Angeles. This would make it two down and six to go!

The good news seemed to invigorate the whole group and made them more determined than ever to succeed in their operation.

Dr. Laird raised his fist in the air and said, "Now we must do our part. If it is at all possible, we are going to do it! Just think of the millions of people whose fate we hold in our hands. We must be successful; God will guide us!"

Then he finished giving instructions for the next morning. The plan he laid out was to have Amahl and Ali both in the operating rooms by 6 a.m. No food and limited liquid after midnight. To Ali's dismay, Katie and Daphne elected to stay at the hospital all night in order to get an early start in the OR preparations.

At 5:30 a.m., Dan, Heather, Scott, and Max were loading Amahl into the Suburban. He could barely walk and was placed in the middle seat between Scott and Max. It was only a short drive to the hospital, and they soon had Amahl up again and walking slowly to the operating suite. He was laid on a cot and was soon snoring in a light sleep. Ali had already arrived and was being prepped in an adjoining room.

All of the group's doctors and nurses were busy getting the equipment ready. That included all the surgical tools; sensory cables and probes; the video equipment that would show the positioning of the probes and sensors in the brain; and the anesthetizing equipment to keep both individuals at the exact required level of consciousness.

Jessica and Heather set up a projector and large screen to show their log notes that the doctors could refer to if necessary. Katie and Daphne, both experienced in neurosurgery, proved to be good additions to the team, as they quickly prepared each of the men for the operation. Ali's head was already shaved but Amahl had a thick head of hair which they quickly removed and then shaved his head.

The procedure was moving swiftly and smoothly thanks to the professionalism and experience of the two nurses and Dr. Laird. Three tiny holes were bored in each of their skulls and the sensors were inserted into the appropriate regions of their brains precisely following the large image on the projector screen that showed the placement of sensors in the brains of the rats.

As the procedure in Fayetteville went forward, the general population of the world was moving normally through another day of their lives, unaware of pending disaster. Troy and Rollie would soon be on their way to Washington to disarm the nuclear bomb in that location.

Chapter 26.

The FBI and CIA, in working with the airlines, had successfully traced the air routes and cities visited by the two Oman employees, Amahl and Lattah. Two groups were formed in the CIA to use the parameters established on Lattah's Washington map, and then independently review and determine the most likely epicenters for the bombs in the major cities on those specific air routes.

Again under the cover of searching for drugs and members of a drug cartel, the results of the studies of the two groups were sent to CIA agents in the target cities. Those agents worked with the local authorities and real estate agents to try and track down an Oman Oil Company lease in the epicenter areas.

The results were immediate, at least in New York. The agents working that city had, through sheer luck, contacted the very real estate agent who had leased the building to Lattah. It was the same flashy, blond bimbo driving the expensive convertible that had irritated Lattah so intensely. With the agents following her in their car, she first drove to her office to pick up the lease papers and the keys to the property.

When they arrived at the property, the real estate agent escorted the agents into the building. They entered the back room, and there it was! A gleaming white tank, holding the nuclear bomb that could kill millions of New Yorkers. The CIA agents look at it with awe and cold chills. When would it detonate?

The real estate agent was busy chewing her gum and asking questions. Would she get a reward for finding the tank with the drugs? Would the agents pick up the balance of the lease? How soon could they get the tank removed so she could lease the building out again? Would they at least pay her for the time she spent with them?

The answers were no, no, no, and no. And furthermore, they were going to confiscate the building, apply new locks, and install Federal guards around the clock. In addition, under penalty of Federal law, she could not discuss the situation with anybody. Any infraction would result in ten to fifteen years in a Federal penitentiary. She was asked if she understood?

By now she was trembling and rather pale. This was not what she expected. The two CIA agents thanked her for her help and sent her on her way. Rather abrupt, but they had work to do. Rollie and Troy were advised of the success in New York and told who to contact for help in finding the store and gaining access since the site was secured and heavily guarded.

After completing their work in New York, Troy and Rollie were to proceed to Pope Air Force Base in North Carolina. There they would meet a C-130J Globemaster with a CIA crew who would fly them to Europe to pick up the propane tanks as they were located. Their initial stop in Europe would be at the Royal Air Force Lakenheath, about seventy miles northeast of London. A little far out from London, but with good security and maintenance facilities.

Meanwhile, the procedure in Fayetteville was going well. Dr. Laird said he was astonished at what was transpiring! After Amahl had been sedated, and before the interrogation began, Dr. Laird produced a set of earphones that he had used during previous procedures. He gave Scott a microphone headset that he could use to interrogate Amahl; it would keep his hands free for taking notes. Dr. Laird explained that the headphones on Amahl would permit him to hear the questions from Scott, but would prohibit him from hearing Ali's translations of Amahl's responses.

The interrogation went smoothly, much better than Dr. Laird had anticipated. Amahl was lying down and the Versed had him relaxed. Scott started the questioning in English in a rather quiet and soothing voice. The initial questions related to Amahl's job and the various ports he had visited. To Ali's surprise, Amahl was answering Scott's questions, and in English!

They had anticipated that Amahl's memory would be in Arabic. Ali was most shocked the he "knew", and could give, the responses even though they did not originate in his brain. The responses originated in Amahl's brain and were transferred by sensor to Ali's. The interrogation continued at a casual pace while the two nurses kept the amount of Versed at a constant level.

When Ali started giving responses to the locations of the bombs, the whole group raised their fists in the air and gave thumbs up. Even Scott had a quiver in his voice as he continued the questioning. It was a moment of realization of not only what had been accomplished medically, but also what it meant to civilization. The group had witnessed one of the greatest moments in history.

At the completion of the questioning, Scott immediately called Troy who was still near London at the Royal Air Force Lakenheath. "Fantastic news, Troy! We have the locations of all the bombs! It's quite a story of how we got the information, but it will have to wait until I see you. First things first. Got a pen and paper?"

Troy responded, "Wonderful! I'm ready. Give me the locations."

Scott described all the European locations and then requested that Troy advise Frank Hughes of their planned itinerary to disarm and pick up the bombs.

Scott said, "Troy, give me a half hour to get in touch with Frank Hughes to fill him in so that he can advise the President of our plans. Also, the President will need to know the sequence of your 'visits' so that he can notify the appropriate heads of state prior to your arrival. When you get your agenda planned, let Frank know. Be careful, Troy, you and Rollie have a dangerous job."

Scott then called Frank Hughes and related all the information including the fact that Troy would be calling him within the hour to give him their planned route to collect the bombs. He further requested that once the President confirms the schedule of pickups, that Frank notify Troy to proceed. Frank agreed and told Scott that the President will be overjoyed to hear the great news. The President was indeed overjoyed, so much so that he hugged Frank, which was very much out of character.

However, he quickly recovered. "Frank, I must be honest with you. I had very little faith in the 'transfer of memory' experiments. I've been planning down other avenues of action."

Frank responded, "I can't blame you, sir, I pretty much felt the same way. Now we have a lot of work to do in a short time."

Frank reviewed his conversation with Scott and the action Troy and Rollie had requested of the President. Just then the phone rang. The President picked it up and it was Troy.

The President said, "Troy, I can't thank you enough for what you've done for all of us. Please give my thinks to Rollie as well. I know you're calling for Frank, and time is short, so I'll put him on."

The President handed the phone to Frank who started writing as fast as he could. He finally finished, and then quickly rewrote it all, so it was readable by the President. With a few more questions to Frank, the President was ready to make all the calls to the heads of state that were involved.

The President was at his desk looking at Frank who quickly realized that something was on the leader's mind.

"Mr. President, what are you thinking about? I know you're wondering about something that probably relates to me."

The President said, "You're very perceptive, Frank. It does involve you and all your associates. I want you to arrange a secret luncheon at Camp David with all those individuals who played an active role in this nightmare. Each contributed to saving millions of lives. They must be recognized for stepping forward and doing whatever needed to be done.

"Starting with Matt Jenkins, the Assistant Executive Director of the Port of Long Beach. His keen instincts and perseverance started this whole investigation. Following him is a string of individuals in various walks of life who each made a critical contribution. Lou Thoma, Manager of the Marrakesh Restaurant stepped forward with important information. I could go on and on, each a critical link in the chain."

He continued, "Frank, I want you to arrange this luncheon as quickly as possible. Each to be flown secretly to Camp David by helicopter. Also, invite our Russian friends, President Niolai Padrov and Sergei Andropov. They had the guts and integrity to tell us about the stolen nuclear weapons."

"Make a list of those who played key roles in this matter. I'm going to award each of them the Presidential Medal of Freedom, the highest award our country has that is just below the Medal of Honor. Of course, we can't publicize these awards, but at least their country, their President, and their peers in this operation will have recognized these heroes. I hope someday they'll be free to tell their grandkids how they won these coveted medals."

Frank responded, "I'd be honored to make such a list. I think it's a wonderful idea and well-deserved by all of them."

The President concluded by saying, "Frank, I better see your name on that list, too."

"Is that an order, Sir?"

President Hartmann responded, "That's a direct order, Frank."

CHAPTER 27.

TEN DAYS HAD PASSED AND things were getting back to normal for a small group of individuals who unselfishly did what had to be done to save their county and a major part of the world. All of the nuclear bombs in Europe had been located and disarmed by Rollie and Troy and were safely stowed in the belly of the Globemaster.

Rollie yelled at Troy over the noise of the plane's engines, "Hey, Troy, this is like the old west! A couple of cowboy marshals rounding up the bad guys, the bombs. Now we're gonna ride shotgun all the way back to California! Yahoo! What do you think about that?"

Troy looked at Rollie with a scowl. "I think you've lost your friggin mind! I've never been so tired in my life!"

Rollie smiled at Troy, "Poor Troy! I've got something to cheer up Mr. Troy. Look here!" Rollie reached in his coverall pocket and pulled out six miniature bottles of VO along with a handful of lemon twists.

Rollie said, "When you were back there at the officers' club socializing, I was busy doing my slight of hand confiscating. Pretty good job, eh? Now, you put your feet up on that bulkhead, and I'll go to the galley and get ice, glasses, and water."

Rollie was smiling when he glanced at Troy, but it was too late. Troy's chin was down on his chest and he was sound asleep.

Far away in Fayetteville, Arkansas, a group was having drinks before dinner at Club 36. It was the small group that had performed the procedure on Amahl with the addition of Frank Hughes. Frank had flown down from Washington to cover two items with the group.

He got their attention and proceeded to tell them of two very important events. "First, the President has planned a luncheon at Camp David to honor all the participants in this unbelievable event. If you are married, you may bring your spouse. However, you will all be sworn to strict secrecy."

"No one outside the participant group is to know of this event. Each of you will be awarded the Presidential Medal of Freedom, which as you probably know is the second highest medal awarded by our country. A well-deserved honor to a very special group of American citizens and a few foreign individuals whose integrity and fortitude helped save our Western civilization."

Frank continued, "You can thank President Hartmann as all this is his idea."

"Now, the second thing I want to talk about is what to do with Amahl. The Oman Oil Company in Abu Dhabi, for whom he worked, thinks that he is dead. The 'special representative' of the Sheik has told Scott that they positively do not want him back, as it may open a whole new situation."

"However, the Saudis have offered to pick him up at Andrews Air Force Base and fly him back to Saudi Arabia. No doubt at the request of Abu Dhabi officials. We have agreed to this solution, even though we doubt that he makes it across the Atlantic Ocean. An Air Force plane will be here tomorrow to pick him up. Scott, would you and Ali, escort him back to Andrews?"

Ali was already shaking his head yes when Scott answered in the affirmative, "It would be my pleasure as he is one bad dude! He never thought twice about the prospect of killing millions of innocent people."

Ali said, "It would save a lot of bother if you would let me at him for a little while. He deserves everything he's going to get!"

Frank said, "Hey! Dinner is being served. I guess I talked too long!"

There was much to talk about, and the group lingered over dinner for quite some time. Jessica stood up to give one final toast: "Here's to Doc Laird and his wonderful nurses. They did one helluva job! But, Michael, there is one thing I want to know. All during the operation, you kept humming one tune, and for the life of me I can't place it, and that bothers me!"

Dr. Laird raised his glass and said, "It's an old tune made popular by Bob Hope, but it seems so appropriate! I was humming it to Amahl, it's 'Thanks for the Memories.'"